I0564344

HIDDEN TRUTHS

BOOK ONE

LANIE WINDSOR

To my sister,

Thank you Tannis for being my biggest cheerleader.

Contents

Chapter One

The street hummed with the rhythm of the city. No one noticed the two men standing at opposite ends of the intersection, their stillness at odds with the flow around them. When the light changed, the crowd merged, strangers trading places. As the men drew close, a slim black envelope slipped from one hand to the other, the movement quick and unobserved. In the next breath, both men melted into the crowd, vanishing as if they had never been there.

After walking a few blocks, the man crossed through the park, ignoring the sound of children laughing. He slipped his phone from his inner jacket pocket. Picking the number to message took less than a second since it was the only one programmed.

Coded Message:

Foxglove: Orders delivered.

Nightengale: Complications?

Foxglove: None.

Nightengale: Wait for confirmation, then execute phase two.

Foxglove: Copy.

Things were falling into place now. All it took was a little planning and attention to detail. Now, everything that had been years in the making was falling into line. If everything came together, things would happen in quick succession. There would be no stopping the force that started—the time for second-guessing had passed. The plan was in motion, and all that was left was to sit back and witness the inevitable destruction.

Mina Turner sat in her window seat, her eyes following the water sliding down the glass. The beating rain hammered against the desolate silence. Her phone lay silent on the cushion beside her. She tried to ignore the crushing disappointment that weighed on her every time she glanced at the clock.

She should have learned her lesson by now. She was often left waiting in vain for her father's attention. The Sunday evening phone calls had been her father's idea. When she turned eighteen, her father agreed to pay her college tuition if she would talk with him every Sunday at seven o'clock. It was laughable that he thought she had to be forced to speak to him. All she wanted was to have a minute of her father's time. And for a period at least, she had finally gotten what the child within her had yearned for.

Each Sunday, she eagerly awaited the phone call. The conversations were never comfortable, often forced, and ended at the hour mark, but it didn't matter to her. Mina was happy to have the time with her father.

However, lately, things have changed. The calls have been shorter, often lasting fifteen minutes. Tonight was the first time he missed the call altogether. Mina tried not to let his neglect hurt, but it did—just as it always did.

The storm of emotions waging war within her matched the tremulant storm outside her window. The wind howled an eerie song of heartache. She pressed her face to the chilled window, cooling her flushed skin and fogging up the glass with the warmth of her breath. Her finger moved over the moisture, shaping a heart. A flash of color caught her eye.

Outside her window, a butterfly with vivid orange wings clung to the glass, its delicate frame battered by the relentless rain. Mina's breath caught at the sight. The wind must have torn it from its shelter, leaving it to fight a losing battle against the storm. Determined to save it, she slid the window open, rain lashing her arms as the storm invaded her space. Shielding the fragile creature, she felt its trembling wings against her palm. Relief washed over her as she gently brought it inside, cradling it away from the fury of the rain.

"You poor thing." Mina crooned. She closed the window and took the butterfly to the money tree in the corner of her living room. "Why don't you rest here where it's nice and dry?"

It took only a little nudge for the butterfly to cling to a branch buried behind some leaves. Mina could barely see the vibrant-colored wings nestled in the foliage. However, seeing such a fragile thing fight to stay alive in the heart of a storm renewed her spirits. For once, thoughts of her father's neglect didn't plague her mind.

"You and me, we are going to be fine. You'll see. No rain is going to keep us down. Tomorrow is bound to be brighter than today."

Chapter Two

M ina watched the butterfly flutter away, silent and resilient as the sun peeked over the horizon. She took a deep breath of the fresh, early morning air. She felt revitalized. Last night had been disappointing, but she had learned long ago not to let it get her down. Witnessing the butterfly's fight for survival inspired her. The quality of that day depended on how she shaped it. Regardless of the outcome, she was eager to discover what the day had in store.

With her signature bright and cheery smile, Mina headed to the elevator with a skip in her step. She waved in greeting to the few neighbors who milled around in the hallway of the apartment building she had called home for almost two years.

The music from the overhead speaker brought a wide smile to her face, her hips instinctively swaying to the catchy 80s ballad. She loved these songs—each one a time capsule of memories. As the familiar melody played, a wave of emotions swept over her. She could almost see her mother singing along with Bret Michaels in the kitchen. It was one of her rare, happy memories of her father before her parents split. He'd sweep into the kitchen, spinning her mother around in a playful dance. Back then, she didn't realize how true the lyrics were. Every rose did have its thorns, and now it was up to her to avoid getting pricked.

Mina strolled through the lobby, humming to the music, and paused to chat with Edgar and Abel. The two old men stationed near the door to the First Avenue exit seemed to have made it their unofficial duty to guard the entrance. From what Mina could tell, they spent their days doing little else but keeping watch, their sharp eyes missing nothing. No one came or went without enduring their quiet scrutiny.

Edgar's eyes warmed as he spotted her. "Off to work, are you?"

"Yep. Beautiful morning, don't you think?" Mina asked, her attention already shifted to the glass-pane doors to her left.

"That it is." Edgar agreed.

Abel grumbled, his face set in a perpetual frown. "Don't know how long it will last, though. That girl on the news said a storm is supposed to roll in by this afternoon." The notable complaint lingered in his voice, as usual.

Mina's smile widened further, a twinkle setting her caramel-colored eyes dancing. "How lovely! And just think of the beautiful rainbow that will be there afterward."

Edgar chuckled, slapping his knee. Too eager to let the opportunity pass, he poked at Abel with glee. "When are you going to give up? You'll never manage to dampen that girl's mood, no matter how hard you try." Abel snorted, feigning indifference. "I don't have any idea what you are rambling on about. I was only saying what I heard on the news."

Mina smiled as the deep cackle of Edgar's laugh followed her out of the building. It was the same routine every morning—a mix of grumbles from Abel and Edgar's amused jabs. They'd started this dance nearly six months after she moved in, once the two older men realized she wouldn't let anyone—or anything—pull her down.

She wasn't naïve. Life had its way of ripping your heart out if you let it. She'd learned that from her father, whose career and other priorities always overshadowed her. For years, she'd let it affect her, questioning her worth.

But not anymore. Over time, Mina realized she couldn't control what happened to her, only how she reacted. And she had decided: happiness was hers to claim, no matter what life threw her way.

As Mina turned onto Columbus Street, the sun's warm rays kissed her skin, making her golden complexion shimmer with a youthful healthiness. The cool breeze from the Pacific Ocean ruffled her long chestnut hair, whipping a few stray strands across her face. Mina walked toward Fifth Avenue, her eyes sweeping over the shop windows as she passed.

Almost five years ago, Columbus Street transformed into an artisan market. Store owners bought and converted the buildings from Ninth Avenue to Center Street. When all the available space had been claimed, other entrepreneurs spread down Fifth and Third Avenue. In time, more and more streets would convert to artisan style. It was how the tide was moving, at least for now.

Mina's face lit up as the familiar slice of lemon came into view. Her mouth watered at the tangy-sweet thought of the raspberry lemonade she adored from Squeeze. The little juice bar opened its doors around the same time Mina started her job at Blossoms, and since then, stopping by every morning had become her cherished ritual. It wasn't just the drinks—though they were incredible—it was the sense of connection, the friendly banter with the staff, and the comforting predictability of this one small joy that made her mornings brighter.

When one lacks a reliable family foundation, one learns that family can be formed in other ways.

Mina stepped inside, her heart lightening at the familiar and comforting sight. "Hi Jenny," she waved. Jenny was the owner of Squeeze. She and her sister opened the juice shop together after their youngest kids started high school. Their juice bar specialized in lemonade mixes, but they also offered a variety of sandwiches for breakfast and lunch.

Mina sighed and took in the savory scent of bacon cooking on the grill. "What's the special for today?"

"A poached egg over a slice of ciabatta bread with feta cheese, two slices of turkey bacon, and steamed asparagus. We're calling it Sunrise Plate." Jenny explained. Her green eyes shone brightly through the lens of her fashionable glasses.

"Mmmm. Give me one of those and my usual drink order, please." Mina reached for her purse but stopped short, a self-deprecating laugh escaping her lips when her hand met empty air. "Can I pay with my phone?"

Jenny's mouth twitched. "Sure. Forget your purse again?"

"No," Mina replied with a playful smile. "I left it at home on purpose. Didn't want the extra weight."

Of course, that wasn't true. Forgetting her purse had become a habit she couldn't seem to shake, no matter how many sticky notes, alarms, or tricks she tried. She sighed inwardly. Some things just never changed.

Mina adored the small-knit community she had built in San Francisco. When she first moved here, she wanted to disappear into the crowded city, and for a while, she succeeded. But as the months passed, the loneliness crept in, and she found herself craving connection again. Discovering the artisan community nestled in the bustling blocks of the city center was a blessing. She found friends and a sense of belonging that had eluded her most of her life.

Jenny chuckled as she retrieved a drink carrier and placed Mina's daily order of three drinks into the designated compartments. "I keep telling you to get an alarm or something to remind you to grab your phone and purse before you leave. Honestly, I don't know how someone your age forgets the basics so often. One of these days, you are going to land yourself in a world of trouble."

Mina snorted, lifting the drink carrier and to-go bag off the counter. "I have my phone. What's the big deal? Besides, I will never forget them both at the same time. As long as I have one of them, I'll be fine."

Jenny gave her a pained look. "Whatever you say."

The fifteen-minute walk to work had her swinging into Blossoms five minutes before her shift started. Kat and Brad stood behind the counter, stern expressions on their faces. "What's wrong?" Mina asked cheerfully, "I brought sustenance." She held up the drink carrier.

"You forgot your phone again." Kat accused.

"No, I didn't. That's how I paid for all of this. I know Jenny is laid back, but I doubt her flexible attitude would extend to giving me a free meal."

"Yes, you did. I called to see if you could pick me up a sandwich, but you didn't answer."

With a frown, Mina's gaze shifted to the front pocket of her jeans. "That's odd. I didn't hear it ring."

Kat's mouth twitched; her eyes sparkled with amusement. "I'm not surprised seeing how Jenny answered it."

After setting the drinks on the counter, Mina thumped a hand on her forehead. "Oh, no."

Kat and Brad's severe expressions melted away as they dissolved into fits of laughter. "Jenny said she'd plug it in for you, and you can pick it up tomorrow as usual."

"This isn't funny!" Mina pouted, tempted to stomp her foot. She knew she had a problem. It was evident in the way everyone adapted to her little quirks. In the back of her restaurant, Jenny had a plastic bin designated for the random items Mina left behind. Most of the time, they were insignificant, like a hair clip or a bracelet. Other times, she left her more important things, like her cell phone and even her wallet.

If not for the kindness of others, she would probably wind up living on the street with no money to her name and no possessions left in her care.

"I take it the writing on your hand didn't help?" Brad asked, laying a comforting hand on her shoulder.

"No," Mina admitted. Brad had suggested writing reminders on her hand to help her remember. The idea sounded great, but she realized she'd misplaced her marker when she got home last night. "I couldn't find the marker you gave me."

"Mina. What are we going to do with you?" Brad shook his head and returned to trimming the rose stems for the upcoming Marx wedding, which was just two days away.

"I guess it's good that I am an amazing floral designer." Mina smiled brightly, moving to the back of the store area where her workbench was set up.

The vibrant flowers spread across the butcher block counter made Mina smile, her fingers itching to start crafting. Much like her life, her workspace often was in complete disarray. The scared surface held remnants of stem clippings, leaves, and ribbons from previous floral arrangements she'd been commissioned to make.

Despite Kat's casual teasing, Mina knew Kat would never let her go. She had made quite the name for herself, especially within the bridal community. Her work being showcased in numerous bridal magazines made her one of the most sought-after floral designers in the Bay area. A position she didn't particularly care about one way or the other, but it allowed her to do what she loved, and for that, she was grateful.

With the Marx wedding fast approaching, the next few days were going to be tough, but she was up for the challenge. Tight deadlines always made the work that much more enjoyable. The anticipation of the formidable axe waiting to drop always got her heart rate up. Even though it drove

Brad crazy watching her work until the last possible minute to apply the finishing touches to an order due for delivery, she couldn't help herself. That was why he insisted on giving her tools to help her be more organized, but to his chagrin, they never worked.

She tried. Whenever Brad offered her a new suggestion to fix her little problem, she gladly accepted it, but nothing had made the least difference. She supposed she was destined to be the absentminded florist of Columbus Street.

Chapter Three

From the front seat of his boring gray sedan rental, Derrek Borup flipped through the file on his lap as he watched the floral shop. He had never been a fan of cars. At over six feet tall, cars had a way of making him feel cramped. There never seemed to be enough room for his legs, proven by the fact that every time he shifted his position, his knee inevitably would hit the steering wheel. Although he much preferred a truck or large SUV, he had to blend in with the endless lines of cars on the streets in San Francisco.

He'd already been sitting on his target for two days, and so far, he had seen nothing explaining why her folder was on his lap. The glossy eight-by-ten headshot of Mina Turner had the same captivating effect on him as the first time he laid eyes on her dossier. It didn't matter how often his gaze landed on her smiling face; his stomach would tighten, and longing, deep and unmovable, would burn with the need to meet her. His usual response to such feelings was to immediately make her acquaintance. By the conversation's end, he always left with a phone number and a date for the next evening.

That wasn't an option this time. Perhaps if he said it enough, it might sink it. Derrek studied her photo, an acquiescent smirk playing on his lips. He couldn't have this one, even though his body growled in protest. He wasn't used to denying himself anything. It was part of the deal he had made with himself thirteen years ago when he had joined the AOD project (Administer of Death). He understood what they were asking him to do, to kill and eliminate those who prey on the weak and desperate of society. But he also understood himself and what he would need to be able to live in the world and be what they needed him to be. He had made a pack, promising himself that when he worked, he worked and, when he was between jobs, well then, he could play. He could let loose and enjoy the sweeter side of life. And up until now, he had done a damn good job of separating the killer from the man.

His gaze fell again to Mina's face, his finger brushing over her lower lip. She was a beauty—anyone could see that. But there was more to her. There was something about her, something untouched by the world's dirt and chaos. She was pure, and it pulled at him just as hard as the heat surging through his veins. He wanted her—badly. The thought of running his hands through her hair, soft and thick as it looked, drove him crazy. His fingers twitched, craving the feel of her skin, her body beneath his touch. It was becoming an obsession, and he wasn't sure he could stop it.

His fingers tightened around the steering wheel, knuckles whitening as he fought the urge to go into the shop where she had spent the last two days. He bet she smelled incredible—clean and soft, maybe a hint of something floral. Sweat broke out over his brow as he struggled with the driving need to satisfy this particular desire. The thought sent a sharp jolt through him. Sweat prickled along his brow as he wrestled with the gnawing need to close the distance to satisfy this craving that had taken root deep inside him.

A bitter smile tugged at the corners of his mouth—he'd done this to himself. Indulging every fantasy hadn't been a great idea after all. Now, his inner beast was not satisfied, demanding more, demanding action. But he didn't have a choice. The proof lay open in his lap. The file was thin, but it was enough: Mina Turner, twenty-eight, San Francisco. Tied to the Petrov crime family, with connections stretching from San Diego to New York. The details were vague, but the message was clear—taking her out could send shockwaves through the Petrov network.

Scowling through the windshield, his sharp blue eyes bore into the glass door as if he could see through the building and straight to Mina. The dossier didn't fit the woman he'd been watching. He couldn't reconcile the woman who hummed eighties songs and petted every dog she encountered as a prominent member of a violent and ruthless crime syndicate.

Still, orders were orders. He'd do the job. But just because he had to kill her didn't mean he couldn't meet her first. Maybe taking her on a date that ended with a quick taste. That could work, he mused as the idea took hold. There were no restrictions on how close he could get to a target as long as he finished the job. And finishing wasn't a problem.

Drumming his fingers on the steering wheel, his indecision made him restless until he couldn't take it anymore. With a sharp exhale, he pushed the car door open and crossed the street. The job had taken its toll over the years, and he'd learned to shrug off the disappointment, telling himself he'd eventually be free to live on his terms. However, this time, he couldn't shake off the resentment. It clawed at him, raw and relentless. Of everything the job had taken from him, this was the one thing he couldn't stand. He had to meet her, talk to her, taste her...just once. Only then would he finish the mission. But first, he needed answers.

The short walk to Blossoms' door felt longer than it should have. Each step slowed his heartbeat, sharpening his focus as he drew closer to his quarry. Anticipation tightened his chest, coiling like a spring ready to snap. His jaw set as his hand curled around the handle, and he opened the door. Cold air smacked him in the face. The floral shop had a distinct chill inside he hadn't been prepared for. It was as if he had walked into a refrigerator. The stark difference sent an involuntary shiver down his body. Years of rigorous training and conditioning had him masking his sudden discomfort.

A practiced smile graced his lips as he entered. He took a quick look around his eyes, hidden behind the dark lenses of his sunglasses. The shop looked as he would expect. An intense, sweet, and almost overpowering scent of blooming flowers filled his nostrils. He slipped his sunglasses off, folded them over the collar of his shirt, and moved to the counter. A middle-aged woman stood talking with a customer he'd watched arrive over half an hour ago.

He couldn't imagine what anyone would need to discuss in a floral shop for that long. Dismissing the thought with a mental shrug, he wandered around the showroom, his eyes scanning the neatly arranged displays lining the glass shelves. A particular arrangement of deep red roses and some kind of exotic-looking flower drew his gaze. Before he thought better of it, his finger stroked the delicate petals, unable to resist their exotic allure.

"Can I help you?"

The clear feminine voice turned his attention. He looked up to meet the welcoming face of the woman who had stood behind the counter a few moments earlier. The man was gone, though he hadn't noticed him leave. A slight frown puckered his brow before he pushed it away, forcing his face to relax once more. "Yes, I believe you can. I need someone to help me design a floral arrangement."

The woman's face brightened. "Well, then, you have come to the right place. Why don't you come over to the counter, and I can show you some samples? Do you know what kind of flowers you would like to use?"

He allowed a faint blush to rise to his cheeks, tilting his head down just enough to seem embarrassed. Over the years, he'd worked hard to strip the southern drawl from his voice, knowing it could make him too easy to identify. But here it felt right, letting that smooth, honeyed drawl flow from his mouth. "I'm not sure," he said, his voice rich with a slow, southern warmth. "I want something special, something I couldn't just pick up anywhere. Do you know what I mean?"

"Yes, of course. You want that special touch of a custom bouquet. Come on over, and let's start by looking at some flower options. Then, we can go through our art book for inspiration."

His face relaxed into an amiable smile. "That sounds like a great plan. Thank you, ma'am."

It didn't take him long to realize he could waste the whole day flipping through the books—but that wasn't what he wanted. He wanted Mina beside him, her voice guiding him, her scent surrounding him. But nothing he'd said so far had drawn her out of the back room. His gaze kept sliding towards the doors, hoping to get a glimpse of her. He clenched his jaw, debating his next maneuver when the doors finally swung open. She stepped out, bright and cheery, her smile exactly as he'd imagined—warm, effortless, and impossible to ignore.

"Mina, how is it going? Do you need help?" The woman asked.

"Everything is fine. The vases Kaitlyn ordered are gorgeous. I had to make some minor alterations to the overall design to make them fit in the containers, but I don't think anyone will notice."

Derrek's breath hitched at Mina's sunny smile. He hadn't expected—hadn't anticipated—just how radiant she was. For a second, his purpose blurred, lost in the curve of her mouth and the words he couldn't quite hear. His golden brows drew together as her honey-colored eyes met his.

"Oh, I'm sorry. Here I am, rambling away. I didn't mean to interrupt."

"It's no problem." His gruff voice lost some of that easy southern charm he'd put into it earlier.

"I'm glad you're here." The woman explained, drawing Mina closer. "I was showing this gentleman some different flower options, but I think it would be best if you talked with him. He wants a custom bouquet made, and I think this calls for your particular style."

Derrek noticed Mina's slight hesitation and wondered at it. Her smile remained warm and inviting, but a flicker of shadow passed through her eyes—wary, assessing. Why? He hadn't done anything to put her on edge aside from frowning a bit. Surely, he wasn't the first man to scowl at her lovely face.

Maybe she could sense the predator in him. Did she know he wasn't what he seemed?

His job had taught him to read people—to recognize threats before they surfaced. Once, he'd walked into a convenience store just as a man, high as a kite, decided to rob the place. It had taken him all of thirty seconds to recognize the danger and neutralize it. His survival depended on instincts like that.

So, it stood to reason that someone tied to a notorious crime family would develop a similar intuition.

The thought hit harder than it should have. The idea of Mina being one of the bad guys twisted something deep in his chest. He didn't want to believe it. And that realization unsettled him almost as much as it annoyed him.

"Sure, Kat. I'll take care of him."

Mina's words had him arching a golden eyebrow. Exactly how did she mean to take care of him?

When her honey-colored eyes met his, a surge of raw awareness jolted through him, tightening every muscle in his body. It was instinct—primal, relentless. And it pissed him off. Frustration flared hot in his gut, a tight ache he couldn't shake. He wanted her—no question. The craving gnawed at him, and the fact that he had to ignore it felt like a punishment he wasn't sure he could keep enduring.

Chapter Four

M ina's gaze locked onto the man before her, a sharp awareness prickling her nerves. A flush of foolishness washed over her for stepping out of the safety of the back room. When immersed in the creative process, few things could break her focus, but the deep, soothing voice had drawn her in, unraveling her concentration. It washed over her like a wave, pulling her attention until she had to see who was responsible for the sound rattling her senses so completely.

Well, now she knew, and she wished she had resisted the temptation.

It took every ounce of willpower she possessed to meet the piercing heat of his gaze. Squaring her shoulders against the sudden urge to turn tail and run, she held out her hand in greeting. "Hi, I'm Mina. How can I help you?" There, that sounded professional, not like a woman on the brink of hysteria, which was exactly how she felt.

From a distance, she supposed anyone would merely think of him as an attractive, physically fit man, but up close, there was a primal intensity about him. He reminded her of a large cat, sleek and powerful, poised in calm stillness. For now, he seemed at ease, almost docile, but there was no mistaking the coiled energy beneath the surface. She could sense it, the lethal potential.

The stern line of his mouth curled up into a flirtatious smile, sending her stomach into somersaults. "Ma'am, it's a pleasure. I'm Chris, Chris Summers."

She sighed with relief, his name putting her at ease. There was something very safe in the sound of it. Even his voice carried a hypnotic and calming timbre, soothing her jittery nerves, a smile blooming on her face.

She'd never encountered anyone quite like him before. The pull she felt was undeniable, but it left her off balance—adrift, uncertain how to navigate the storm of feelings. It wasn't just his size; he certainly was big enough to make most men seem small. It was something deeper, something unspoken. An undeniable magnetism radiated from him, raw and electrifying, drawing her in with a force so powerful it left her breathless, powerless to resist.

"Like Kat said, I am looking to order a special arrangement, but I don't want anything that has already been made. I want this to be unique." Even though his words flowed with that slow, honeyed southern drawl, his eyes contradicted the laid-back sound. They locked onto hers with an intensity that made her insides twist and her pulse race. It dissected her, peeling back the layers to see past the mask she wore and into the depths of who she was. The thought sent a shiver through her, equal parts unsettling and electrifying. She couldn't understand why he would care. A man like him wouldn't want to see the truth of her—raw and unguarded, no man did.

To conceal her sudden discomfort, she pushed a catalog in his direction. "Do you know what kind of flowers you would like?"

He shook his head and leaned over the book, his body crowded into her space. A faint masculine scent tickled her nose. The smell so out of place amongst the flowers made her pulse jump. Her brow furrowed as he bent over, his golden hair catching the light. She couldn't remember another customer crowding her as Chris was. It was as if he were deliberately invading her personal space.

His head turned, their noses almost touching, making her breath catch in surprise. "What are your favorite flowers?" he asked, his eyes burning bright.

"Um..." Her mind went blank. She couldn't think of the name of a single flower. Her gaze dropped to the glossy pages and latched onto the first flower. "Lilies are pretty," Mina murmured, her cheeks flushed, avoiding his eyes, unwilling to risk rekindling the unsettling connection.

She couldn't make sense of the way this man unraveled her. It wasn't like men were some dazzling new experience. She'd encountered all types and ages and always kept herself emotionally distant. The hard lessons learned at her father's hand cured her of expecting much from men. They were convenient acquaintances, nothing more. Yet, here she was, her carefully built detachment slipping as if this man had reached past her defenses without even trying.

"If I wanted lilies, what other flowers would you recommend going with it?"

"I like to use hydrangeas and orchids for an exotic and dramatic arrangement. But if you want a more elegant look, roses pair well with lilies." She personally loved the striking potency of orchids with lilies, but this was his choice.

A playful grin spread across his lips, making her heart flutter. "Let's go with the exotic. I've always been a fan of rarities."

After finalizing a few last details, Chris left Blossoms, allowing Mina to return to work. But even after he was gone, his presence lingered in her mind. She kept replaying their brief, peculiar encounter, scrutinizing every moment, every word. Most of all, she couldn't shake her unsettling reaction to him—an unfamiliar mix of emotions that left her uneasy. She was surprised how he'd managed to stir something in her when no one else ever had. The encounter gnawed at her, leaving her both intrigued and unnerved.

Back in her safe space, she plucked a flower from the pile. Mina slipped the white blossom into the vase, then added another and another until the arrangement took shape. It was a good thing she'd already finalized the designs of the table displays because focusing on anything else was impossible. Her thoughts kept drifting, leaving her hands clumsy. Each time she lifted a rosebud, a thorn pricked her finger. She hissed under her breath, muttering a curse. Mina sucked on the pad of her thumb as she looked for another bandage. What was wrong with her? She'd been working with these blooms all morning without a single mishap, but now it was as if her coordination had vanished entirely.

"I see that the hunk left." Kat came in through the swinging doors. Her contagious smile drew one from Mina.

"Yep. About ten minutes ago."

"Did he ask for your number?" Kat's eyes sparkled with mischief as she wagged her eyebrows.

Heat flooded Mina's face. "Of course not. This is hardly the place for a man to ask for a woman's number."

Kat's expression fell in disappointment. She folded her arms over her generous bosom and demanded. "Why not?"

With a heavy sigh, Mina put aside the flowers she was assembling and twisted to face Kat. "Because Kat, men who come here are usually ordering flowers for a loved one."

"So?"

"So, that loved one is usually a significant other. You know, like a wife or a girlfriend." Mina finished with a note of impatience.

"And was Mr. Hunky Smile ordering the bouquet for a wife?"

"I'm not sure. He didn't say, and quite frankly, I didn't ask."

"Well, why not? How is he supposed to know you are available and interested if you don't tell him?"

Mina snorted. "Right, and how was that conversation supposed to go? *Hi, I'm Mina. I'm available and interested. Care for my number?* Or wait, I could have been even more direct and simply asked him out to dinner."

"There's no need to be so snide. I'm just trying to help you. I don't want you to have to spend this life alone." Kat gave Mina a searching look. "When was the last time you went on a date? Or meet up with friends to see a movie or have dinner? As far as I can tell, your life is limited to a five-block radius. I don't want you to wake up one day and have regrets."

Mina didn't want to look at her life. Granted, it had gnawed at the edges of her mind lately, but she wasn't ready to examine it. She preferred it to stay high on the top shelf, all the way in the back. Out of sight, out of mind. Regrets were something she knew all too well; to her, they were simply the price of living. And even though she understood Kat was only trying to help, the conversation left her squirming with discomfort she couldn't shake.

"What makes you think I will? You make it sound like there's no hope for me. Besides, how do you know if I am even looking for a relationship? For all you know, I could be in a relationship this very minute."

Mina frowned at Kat's abrupt and rather rude eruption of laughter. "What's so funny?"

"You." Kat snorted. "If you were seeing someone, you would've told me. Heck, you would have told the whole street by now."

"You think you know everything about me?"

Kat patted Mina on the shoulder, "Of course I do, and don't pretend like I don't. You know, I think of you as my little sister. I only want good things for you."

"And you think Chris Summers would be good for me?"

"Ah, so his name is Chris. Funny, I wouldn't have pegged him as a Chris."

"Really? And what name would you have picked for him?"

"I don't know. But he just doesn't seem like a Chris to me."

"Well, that's neither here nor there. Chris wanted to order some flowers for a woman in the hospital. He wasn't looking for a date."

"All right. I yield." Kat smirked at her. "For someone as laid back as you are, you sure are getting worked up. Are you sure you aren't interested in him?"

Not interested? How had Kat gone from Chris being unavailable to her not being interested? She wanted to laugh at its absurdity. Of course, she was interested; there had never been any doubt. Not when her pulse hammering away as it had. Not interested. It was absurd. Ridiculous even. No, the problem wasn't her lack of interest. It was something else entirely, and she wasn't ready to look closer.

"Kat, this conversation is pointless. It doesn't matter if I am interested or not. The problem lies in his availability, which evidence clearly shows he isn't."

Kat clucked her tongue. "It's the pessimistic attitude that lands you in all these challenging positions."

Mina wanted to argue with Kat's obvious and miscalculated assessment. It wasn't her negativity that led her into unfortunate situations—it was the men in her life who proved, time and time again, that they were better left alone. They'd shown her exactly how little she mattered to them, and she'd learned not to waste her time on those who couldn't spare even a sliver of theirs for her.

"I don't want to sound rude, but I need to get this done," Mina said, gesturing to the mess of flowers strewn over her workspace.

After a quiet, pensive look, Kat nodded and left her to work. Mina let out the breath she hadn't even realized she'd been holding. She loved Kat and Brad. They were both so generous and kind to her. It had been through their generous and attentive behavior that had helped to ease her into her life here. She loved this place, the smells, the sights, and the sounds, and it was all because they had taken her under their wing.

She supposed Kat did have a point. How would any man she met know if she was available if she didn't make an effort? But was that something she even wanted? Her track record wasn't exactly inspiring, and the thought of trying again felt more like a gamble than a fresh start.

First, there was her father. A man who put his work first, even before his wife and children, had set the example of what to expect from men. The countless nights she spent in bed, with the cover pulled up over her head, trying to block out the sound of her mother crying. Or how many times she had to listen to her mother's plea for time, time her father hadn't wanted to give.

Then, there was the one serious relationship she had in her third year of college. She'd trusted Dale, believing his promises that he was nothing like the man she'd grown up with. She'd opened up to him, sharing the pain and neglect her father had caused, and Dale had reassured her, claiming to be different. For a while, she believed him. But in the end, his lies cut even deeper than her father's indifference. At least she'd known what to expect from her dad—his distance, his detachment. Dale was supposed to be the one person she could trust, the one who would protect her heart. Instead, he shattered it. She didn't wait for excuses or explanations when she found him comforting her roommate in a way that left no doubt about what was happening. She packed her things, walked out that night, and never looked back.

Unfortunately, her impulsive side had left her with no recourse but to drop out of college just a year shy of getting her degree. Her dad had been furious, demanding she return and finish. But she hadn't been able to do it. Not when Dale and Brittney were there. She couldn't face them. Either of them. That was when she set out on her own. She'd learned a lot about herself and what she was capable of.

Now, Kat wanted her to open herself up to that kind of hurt again. Fear clamped down on her chest, squeezing the breath out of her. She pushed the fear away, squaring her shoulders as she picked up the rose, taking in its sweet aroma. There would be time later to dwell on her situation and consider what she wanted in life. But now wasn't the time. Now she had work to do.

Chapter Five

He shouldn't have gone in there.

His life, such as it was, had been full of regrets. But they all paled in comparison to the colossal mistake he'd just made. Derrek cast a dark glare over his shoulder. He'd asked for it. Hell, he knew the risk of getting too close to a mark, but he'd done it anyway. As any could testify, once was never enough. Now, he was paying for his impulsiveness. He should have left it alone and walked away, but no. He had to talk to her. Just once. Yeah, right. The joke was on him. He should have known once would never begin to satisfy him.

He hadn't expected her to be like sunshine cutting through the rain or for her eyes to hold a sparkle that made him forget why he was there. Her mouth...jeez. The photo hinted at the potency of her smile, but experiencing it firsthand, she took his breath away.

It was a mystery to him how she managed to conceal her other side. Despite knowing her true nature, he saw no hints of it. He couldn't understand how she could walk the line between two separate lives so convincingly. Who was he kidding? He knew exactly how she did it, the same way he did.

He swore under his breath, yanking the driver's side door open on his rental, using far more force than necessary. Derrek slammed his hand against the steering wheel, finding a twisted kind of relief in the pain that shot up his arm.

He didn't want to kill her. If he even had a soul left, it recoiled at the sheer injustice, every nerve in his body screaming in protest. He wanted her. He wanted her—more than he had ever wanted anything. Right now, nothing else mattered. However, the task demanded her death, a harsh reality that left him with no choice but to comply. His training demanded the order to be followed, no matter the cost. Gritting his teeth against the waging war inside, his hand tightened on the wheel.

The sound of his phone chirping from his pocket came as a welcome distraction. He slipped the burner out, reading the screen before swiping with his thumb. "Borup."

"Status?"

He closed his eyes, bracing himself against the cold voice that cut through the line—a voice he had come to dread over the years. It was hard to reconcile the woman speaking now with the one who had recruited him so long ago. Back then, her smooth southern drawl had been captivating. But that was before the years had hardened her—or maybe before he'd truly seen her for who she was.

"Located target. Learning routine and will initiate final directive when a clear opening is achieved." The words left his mouth with chilling detachment, but every syllable felt like a betrayal. A wave of raw, silent rebellion surged within him, desperate to take the words back, but he didn't dare. Refusal wasn't an option. If he said no, they'd send someone else—and then come after him.

His mouth set into a grim line as the weight of his reality settled in. This wasn't a forgiving group; too many secrets and too much at stake. There was no retirement plan, no way out. He often wondered what he would do if he ever decided to get out of the business. He somehow didn't see them simply letting him walk away. Not when he knew as much as he did.

"You are breaking pattern."

"No. The parameters mandate a slower approach."

"See that you don't take longer than necessary. The protocol will remain intact."

Typical.

His lips twisted into a chilling smile. She always had a way with words. He didn't need the reminder. "I understand."

When silence echoed in his ear, he tossed the phone aside in disgust. Ms. Abigail Weaver had a way of making her point clear without giving an outright threat. This time, the message was unmistakable: fail, and he was out. Permanently.

After starting the car, he merged into traffic, keeping a casual pace as he circled the block. His destination: the shadowed alley behind Mina's apartment building. He'd cased the place several times before and knew where to park while remaining unnoticed.

He knew about the two old men who sat like wrinkled guard dogs at the main entrance. Even though he found them harmless, they were sharp enough to remember a face. He'd already crossed paths with them when he first arrived in town, and if he tried the front door now, they'd undoubtedly mention it to Mina. That would shatter his cover, and for all his contingencies, he wasn't ready to burn this identity yet.

Not that he didn't have multiple others to choose from. Keeping his aliases intact was critical. Despite what Hollywood might suggest, crafting the kind of IDs he relied on was no simple task. Each was a masterpiece of deception, a tool that took time and expertise to perfect. The smallest misstep—a raised eyebrow, a passing comment—could render an identity useless, forcing him to start over. And he couldn't afford that kind of exposure. Not now.

Pulling into the alley, he killed the engine and slipped out, his movements calculated and deliberate. The back door had a basic deadbolt and no other security system. In under a minute, he had the door open and his lock-picking kit tucked in his pocket. He slipped through the door leading to the stairwell. Instead of risking a run-in with a tenant in the elevator, he opted for the five-flight climb up the stairs.

The hallway leading to Mina's apartment was clear. Even without direct sunlight, the hall was well-lit. Florescent lights spaced evenly cast a warm glow. He smiled at the rug in front of Mina's door, its message inviting him to make himself at home. It took him a few seconds longer to enter Mina's apartment, but only a few. With her door closed, cutting him off from the rest of the world, he allowed his guard to drop marginally. He never left himself completely relaxed. Not when the world wanted him dead just as much as his enemies did. He figured that if a person took as many lives as he did, it would only make sense for balance to be made.

Standing at the small entrance, he was immediately surrounded by the same sweet scent that had swirled around him while looking over floral arrangements with Mina earlier. The familiar smell brought flashes of smooth skin, captivating eyes, and her irresistible, smiling mouth.

Damn, he didn't want to kill her. Not when his body ached, and his hands itched to hold her. It had been a long time since a woman had gotten to him. Perhaps that's why Mina had managed to get under his skin so fast. Derrek forced down the rising war within him. He wouldn't allow little bouts of lust to thwart his mission. He had a job to do, and he was going to do it.

Derrek took a moment to accumulate himself with the woman who lived there.

Although she didn't have much space to work with, Mina did a hell of a job creating a comfortable place for herself. Derrek opened the door next to the entryway; his eyes skimmed over the colorful array of coats hanging in the closet. After looking through the few boxes Mina had crammed on the top shelf, he closed the door. A few steps into the apartment led him to a small dining table tucked against the wall. He snatched a red apple from a bowl of fruit that took up most of the surface. Taking a bite, he flipped through her mail, stacked haphazardly on the counter. He opened a few drawers in the kitchen and closed them again when none held any surprises. After a quick perusal of the inside of her fridge, he left the kitchen area and moved to the living area, where an overstuffed couch sat on an angle facing the television and the wide window.

As Derrek looked at the room, he could picture Mina sitting there, curled up with her feet tucked beneath herself. He imagined she would watch TV on sunny days and, when the sky was overcast, stare out the window, watching the steady drizzle of rain slipping down the panes. The image was far too alluring for him to dwell on. If he wasn't careful, he might find himself lost in the fantasy, maybe even putting himself on the sofa with her. Except, she wouldn't be curled into the corner; she would be snuggled against his side. He'd have a ball game on, and she would rest her head on his shoulder; all he'd have to do was turn a little, and his face would be buried in her hair.

No.

Pulling his hand away from the couch, he turned to the back of the apartment. His jaw straining under the force of his frustration. He had to stop this. She wasn't meant to be his, and if he continued to let her spin her web of illusions in his head, he wouldn't be able to complete the job. It did him no good to lose his head over a woman who was just as skilled as—if not better than—he was at playing the long con.

Along the short hallway leading to the single bedroom was a collage of photographs. All of them showed Mina in different stages of her life. Several of her young with an older woman Derrek assumed was her mother. He smiled at a picture of Mina laughing at the camera, holding onto an oversized beach hat as the wind rolled the edge backward. Then, his attention focused on one photograph. Mina had her arm around some guy's neck, and she was kissing his cheek. He glared at the photo, his stomach twisting. It took him a minute to recognize the feeling of jealousy. In alarm, he turned away. Jeez, what was wrong with him?

He forced himself to continue walking, resisting the urge to study the photos again. He had a job to do. The inanity did nothing to ease the acidic taste of envy burning a hole in his tongue.

Mina's bedroom was the epitome of feminine sanctuary. If he could capture sunshine, it would look like this. The soft hues of pink, orange, and yellow were splashed around the room in a kaleidoscope of happiness. He ran his fingertips over the fluffy, plush comforter and a velvety blanket folded at the foot of the bed. Her scent, what he'd thought had been the flower shop, but now he realized it was her, hung heavy in the air. Every breath brought images of her like flashes of radiant light to his mind.

He tore himself away from the bed, where the temptation to linger drove him crazy. His eyes fell on the dresser, where a bright pink handbag sat. It couldn't be that easy. He planned to return after she was asleep and plant a tracking device on her purse, but he might not need to. Heaven knew women loved purses. On the off chance that her wallet was inside, he looked through the bag, his fingers closing over a small leather object. The corner of his mouth quirked up as he flipped open the cover, revealing the cutest ID picture he'd ever seen. His crooked grin turned into a full-fledged smile. He hadn't thought taking a good license photo possible, but Mina surprised him yet again. In fact, she looked sexy as hell, her dark hair curled around her wholesome face. The camera had even captured the alluring twinkle in her eyes.

He shook his head to dislodge the sudden need to see her again. His eyes swung to the bedside clock. He'd spent too much time here. He needed to plant the tracker and get out before she came home. With nimble fingers, he slid the flea-sized tracker deep into the crevice of her wallet, where it would appear as nothing more than a speck of lint. Satisfied she wouldn't notice the device, he slipped her wallet back into her purse and left the apartment.

Perhaps he'd get lucky and track her to her contact. Then, there would be no question of her guilt. He only hoped that, with proof, killing her would be easy. The words didn't ring true even as he thought it.

Chapter Six

By the time Derrek let himself into the single-bedroom apartment, he'd sublet for two months; the computer had chirped at him twice. Being in his line of work made having a personal cell phone foolish. Years ago, he opted for the anonymity of a virtual phone. Now, when his mother or one of his few remaining friends wanted to "get in touch with him," they could leave a message on a secure server, which only he had access to. Every night, he'd habitually scrubbed the voice files so if someone ever managed to crack through his firewalls, there wouldn't be much for them to find.

The burner phone he tossed onto the cluttered table was just for this job. It would be destroyed when he completed his mission, the same as all the others before it. Like his phone, his living situation followed a similar pattern. With every assignment, he rented another apartment and then moved on. Derrek spent most of his time in one random location or another, never knowing where the next mission would lead him. On the off times, during those transitional months when he was in between assignments, he had a small apartment in Austin twenty minutes from his parents' house. Being close made it easier to see his folks and allowed him to relax, even if only for a little while.

As a rule, he had no pets, no plants, nothing that needed tending. His apartment, which held only the basic necessities, looked as faceless as he felt. It was nothing like the haven Mina had created for herself. Derrek supposed it could be another layer of protection keeping her cover intact, but it seemed personal. The furnishings all matched her too well to be merely for her cover. Unless she'd done it on purpose. Perhaps she feared someone would investigate, and if her apartment resembled his, they'd realize she wasn't who she claimed to be.

For him, it wouldn't much matter. He was a man, a bachelor. No one would expect him to have a picture on the wall or a bedspread that matched the pillows. Mina, however, couldn't get away with sparseness. Whoever it was would see it for what it was: a woman with no ties who could walk away without ever needing to collect her possessions.

It did no good to fixate on something he had no control over. Like it or not, Mina was the target, and, in the end, he would kill her.

The thought pushed him into a bad mood. Like the best of thunderclouds, Derrek grumbled all the way to his computer. Tearing a chair away from the desk, he sat down and booted up the screen. As usual, his mother had left him a message. Rarely did he go a day without receiving at least one call from her. He let his head fall against the back of his chair, his eyes closing as he listened to the twang of his mother's voice.

"Derrek, honey, it's Mom. Have you been eatin' lean meats? I just read this article, which says it's not only good for your overall health but also important for your sperm quality. Now, I'm not sayin' I'm expectin' grandbabies today or even tomorrow, but sugar, the clock's always tickin', and when you're ready, you need to make sure everything's workin' like it ought to. If you catch my meanin'."

Derrek groaned, pressing his forefinger and thumb into his eye sockets. His mother had been after him for years to settle down and start a family. Lately, though, it appeared as though she was gearing up for an all-out assault. "Your daddy swears up and down that he only ate the leanest meats when we were tryin' for babies, and I ended up havin' four healthy ones.

But, honey, we were also a lot younger than you. You know, I've been giving this some thought, and I think you should add a little more garlic to your diet. It's supposed to help with fertility, and every little bit helps. Just don't go eatin' garlic on a date, you hear? I remember this one fella tried to kiss me after consumin' a whole loaf of garlic bread. It was awful! Don't worry, it wasn't your daddy – this was before I met him. Let me think...I met your daddy in eighty-seven, so it must've been in eighty-six, wait no, the fall of eighty-five. I remember 'cause it was cold outside, but not cold enough for a heavy coat."

He tilted his head and glanced at the clock. His mother had been talking for five minutes, and by the sound of it, she wasn't winding down anytime soon. Years of practice had taught him the fine art of half-listening. While her voice droned on in the background, Derrek's mind wandered—like it always seemed to—straight back to Mina. He shouldn't have spoken to her today. It was a mistake, one he couldn't undo even if he wanted to.

The talk of fertility sent his imagination racing, fueled by images and thoughts he couldn't control. He'd never been much for kids. His sisters had a few, and while he enjoyed them well enough, at the end of the day, he liked the solitude his life afforded him. However, the thought of having kids didn't make him panic as it usually did. With Mina, it didn't seem like such a trial, although he supposed it could just be the act of making babies that made the idea so tempting.

"Her name is Emilee. That's spelled with two e's at the end. Isn't that just the cutest thing? You make sure to let me know when you are comin' back in town, and your sister will take care of all the arrangements." Derrek dropped his feet to the floor, casting an incredulous look at the computer screen. He rewound the message a few minutes and then pressed play.

"I have the perfect girl for you." His mother's cheery voice proclaimed.

"Not in this lifetime." He muttered. Shutting off the recording. He'd probably catch hell, but he didn't care. No way was he calling his mom back now. Maybe next week; hopefully, by then, she'd be onto something new.

The second message was from Damian. He was one of the few guys he kept in touch with after training for the AOD project. Damian had excelled from the beginning, and since then, he often got the most challenging missions. Not that Derrek minded. Damian was more than welcome to the suicide missions; he often wondered if Damian would have been as willing to go on those missions had his relationship with Calista ended differently. Heartache made a person do strange things, and he'd seen the pain in Damian's eyes from the beginning. In a way, it had made him stronger, colder even. He had a remoteness about him now; that was a shame. The charismatic guy he knew over a decade ago had long since disappeared. Now, Damian was a person he didn't want to mess with. Even though they were friends, he couldn't shake the feeling if he found himself on the target list, Damian wouldn't hesitate to pull the trigger.

"Hey," Damian's calm and deliberate voice broke the silence. "We need to talk. Einstein missed the answer. You know the number."

After listening to Damian's vague message, it was too hard to ignore. He had Derrek's number in that regard. Dangle a carrot, and he was bound and determined to follow it.

"King."

Derrek grinned at the crisp bite of Damian's tone. "What's happening, brother?"

"It took you thirty minutes to call me."

"Yeah, I just got your message. I had to stop in to plant a tracker."

"I know, Chris," Damian said. His voice held a clear, sardonic edge. "That's why I thought you would call me back thirty minutes ago. You're late."

Derrek tried to ignore the flurry of alarm. "How did you know what name I am using?" He asked, his brow dipping over his nose as he tapped the keyboard. "And how do you know where I was?" He heard a distinct snort.

"It's my job to know things."

"Not about me."

"Sure, it is. We may be working on different assignments, but you're still my responsibility. As the team leader, I should always know where my teammates are."

Derrek didn't like the way his statement made his stomach turn. This was a side of Damian he hadn't seen since all those years before they understood what they were being conditioned for. "That was years ago. You aren't responsible for me anymore."

"I suppose you are calling because you want the details about what happened to Clint?"

That caught his attention, pulling Derrek away from their previous discussion. Damian used the art of distraction masterfully. "Yeah, last I heard, he was somewhere in the Middle East."

"He was, but his target turned up two days ago, alive and well."

"So, Clint failed? Can't say I'm surprised. It was bound to happen at some point. It's a miracle he's lasted this long." Derrek surmised.

"No more than Peter or Eric. All three of them scraped through training by the skin of their teeth. They weren't cut only because they have a certain usefulness."

"Yeah, how would you know what they would be useful for?"

"Like I said, any good team leader knows where all the players are at all times."

Derrek grunted. "Well, is he dead? Did his mark take him out before he had the chance to do the same?"

"My opinion, yeah, he's dead. Now, whether or not AOD is willing to openly acknowledge that, your guess is as good as mine. Speaking of AOD, I hear your assignment is giving you trouble."

A flash of irritation crept into Derrek's voice. "She isn't giving me trouble. I'm supposed to make it a clean kill, but I can't do that without a clearer picture of her routine. I need more time before I make a move." Scowling at the computer screen, he looked over his files. He didn't like feeling defensive, but this conversation had a way of crawling under his skin.

"You're approaching three weeks. No job is supposed to last longer than that."

"Yeah, if the illustrious Abigail Weaver doesn't like my way of doing things, then she can come out here and do it herself."

"Calm down, man. No need to get all worked up. You got this. Just don't drag your feet."

"Oh, I'll get the job done; don't you worry about that." Derrek's mouth compressed into a thin line. Yeah, he'd get the job done. All he needed was to catch her in the act, then the kill wouldn't be as complicated. He could pull the trigger and watch the light fade from her eyes without feeling the whisper of doubt.

Chapter Seven

Mina woke to the relentless drumming of rain against the windowpane. Each sharp tap reverberated in her chest. The world beyond was a smudged watercolor of buildings and trees, blurred by the downpour. A shiver coursed through her as if the storm weren't outside but seeping into her bones.

Determined to make today better than yesterday, she rolled out of bed, the floor cool beneath her feet. Yesterday had been a disaster—her mind had been too scrambled in thoughts of Chris to focus. She'd botched two centerpieces for the Marx wedding and a frustrated Kat, who had finally shooed her away, telling her she was done for the day and to go home and get some rest.

The cruel irony was she hadn't slept at all. Instead, she'd spent the night tangled in restless thoughts about the woman who'd received that stunning bouquet from Chris. Was it his wife? His girlfriend? There hadn't been a ring on his finger, but that didn't mean anything. He could still be taken, and the idea made her feel foolish and guilty for her wanton daydreams. She should have asked him – she'd done it countless times with other clients, never giving it a second thought. But with Chris, the words stuck in her throat, the possibility of hearing he belonged to someone else left her hollow and deflated.

Mina sighed, her fingers skimming over hangers as she sifted through her closet, each outfit suddenly feeling dull and uninspired. For so long, she'd focused on healing, convincing herself she was content that she had everything she needed. Yesterday had fractured something deep inside. Chris had awakened a yearning she hadn't realized was there, a quiet hunger for something more. Her father had taught her long ago that men couldn't be trusted. They used women when it was convenient and cast them aside when they were in the way.

It wasn't until she started working for Kat and Brad that Mina saw what genuine love in a marriage could look like—steady, kind, and real. Their bond made her wonder, just for a moment, if she'd been too quick to dismiss the idea of love entirely. Even their shining example wasn't enough to erase the scars of her past. She saw the potential but had spent too many years watching the fallout of being unloved. The risk of opening herself up never seemed worth it. Not until Chris.

Mina stared at her reflection in the bathroom mirror, and what she saw twisted her stomach into a tight knot. She barely recognized the woman staring back at her. She used to take pride in her appearance when bold, vibrant colors filled her wardrobe. And the shoes—oh, how she'd loved her high heels. Sexy, flirty, unapologetic. Her collection had once been a source of joy, but now it sat tucked away, gathering dust along, much like the version of herself that seemed so distant now.

It wasn't that she didn't dress to impress now—she did, but in quieter, less noticeable ways. Only now did she realize how much she had muted her femininity, almost as if she'd been trying to erase it. She'd spent years hiding the very essence of herself, the part she'd been taught to despise. The thought left a bitter taste, an ache for all the times she'd let herself shrink instead of shine.

No more. She refused to let the past dictate the woman she was becoming. A newly emboldened sense of purpose propelled her to the closet, where two boxes sat in the shadows. She pulled them out, brushing away a light layer of dust, and dug through them, unearthing some of her favorite outfits. The desire to wear them was almost overwhelming, but the dank, musty scent of years in storage clung to the fabric, making her wrinkle her nose. She grabbed a large reusable bag and stuffed it full. The dry cleaner would be seeing a lot of her over the next few weeks.

With her clothes in hand, she grabbed her purse and headed out the door. It was time for a new beginning. Things were looking up for Mina, beginning today.

Mina breezed into Squeeze almost an hour later than usual, the scent of rain following her in. She shook the droplets from her coat and flashed a bright, almost too-bright smile as she approached the counter. Jenny glanced up in surprise, her eyebrows lifting. "My, what have you been up to?" she asked, her voice laced with curiosity.

Mina beamed, her face glowing as she sauntered up to the counter, doing a little turn as she approached. "I went shopping. Do you like it?"

"Like it? Girl, I *love* it!" Jenny exclaimed. "You look like a ray of sunshine – exactly what we need on a dreary day like today. What brought on this sudden transformation?" With a quick, practiced motion, she filled a plastic cup with lemonade

Mina shrugged, setting her purse on the counter. "I don't know. I just woke up wanting a change."

"If change was what you were after, you nailed it. Honestly, I'm wondering why you haven't dressed like this before. Not that your other outfits weren't cute, but this feels *so* you."

A faint blush crept up Mina's cheeks. "I used to dress this way but was trying something different for a while. I decided it wasn't working for me."

"I'm glad you went back to your old look. It suits you."

Mina smiled tentatively. "Thanks." Hoping to steer the conversation away from her appearance, she added, "Kat said I left my phone yesterday."

"You sure did," Jenny chuckled, pulling out the clear bin with Mina written in big bold letters. "I put it in here. It should have a charge left from yesterday."

Mina fished the phone out of the container and slid it into her pocket without checking the battery. Phones were such a nuisance. She could never remember where she'd left the stupid thing, and honestly, the only people who ever called her were her parents. If that wasn't the pinnacle of social failure, she didn't know what was.

After paying for her order, she grabbed the tray of drinks and a bag of sandwiches. Seeing as it was almost lunchtime, she hoped the bribery of food would ease Kat's irritation over her tardiness. With a bit more hop in her step, she made her way to Blossoms, weaving around puddles and sidestepping the occasional pedestrian. The rain had settled into a light drizzle, but she kept her umbrella up, knowing it could change at a moment's notice.

Her gaze wandered to the shop windows, her thoughts drifting back to Chris. Not that they had ever really left. She stopped to admire a bright orange bowl on display, wondering if it would look nice in her kitchen. A movement in the corner of the glass made her heart lurch. Chris? She spun around, certain she'd see him across the street, but he wasn't there. Her eyes swept over the faces of the people walking by, her disappointment almost painful.

The bowl forgotten, she trudged toward Blossoms with a heavier step. Her eyes darted to the reflections in each passing window, hoping, despite herself, that she might catch a glimpse of him once more.

By the time Mina strode into Blossoms, Kat was in a tizzy. "Where have you been?" She demanded, hands on her hips. "I've been worried. Did you get your phone from Jenny?"

"Yes, I did. Sorry, I had to run a few errands before coming in. They took a little longer than I expected." Mina held up a white paper bag, grinning. "But, I brought food."

"Oh, well, in that case, all is forgiven."

They laughed as Kat snatched the bag out of Mina's hands and pulled out the food inside. Around a mouthful of gourmet sandwich, Kat said, "The Marx wedding needs to be finished by tomorrow. Do you think you have a handle on this? Yesterday, you were a little...off after taking that man's order."

Mina rolled her eyes, but her blush gave her away. "I'll be fine. It shouldn't be a problem getting it done tomorrow." Toying with the straw wrapper, Mina struggled to face Kat. "Sorry, I ruined so many of the lilies yesterday. Were you able to use them in the bridal bouquet?"

"Most of them. There were only a couple that were a lost cause." Kat gave Mina a pointed look. "Just be careful with the rest of the inventory earmarked for the Marx wedding. There isn't a lot of surplus left over."

"I understand. I'll be careful." Before Kat could remind her again about yesterday's disaster, Mina grabbed her drink and sandwich and made a beeline for the back, where the Marx wedding centerpieces awaited her.

It wasn't until she went to put her purse in her cubby that she realized it was no longer on her shoulder. After looking around, she groaned, remembering the last time she used her wallet was when she bought lunch. With a resigned sigh, she picked up her phone and called Jenny.

Derrek sat outside Blossoms, tapping at his laptop. The tracker he'd slipped into Mina's purse showed her more than two blocks away, yet he'd just seen her walk into Blossoms a few minutes ago. She must have found the tracker. It was the only thing that made sense, and it pissed him off.

This only proved Mina wasn't who she appeared to be.

He only stuck around so long, hoping to prove this whole matter was all a mistake—that Mina was nothing more than a single, attractive floral designer living a quiet life in San Francisco, not a criminal moving within the dark circles of society. However, his plan had backfired. The longer he watched her, the more suspicious her behavior seemed.

This morning, when he'd trailed her, she'd stopped—he thought—to admire something in a store window. But when their eyes met, he knew. She'd seen him. The possibility was a punch to the gut: maybe she'd known he'd been following her all along.

He usually faded into the background, unnoticed. He'd taken every precaution to stay out of her line of sight. So how had she spotted him? He should have remained invisible, yet when their gazes locked, something inside him tightened—an unspoken force that stole his breath.

He couldn't make sense of it. It was something deeper, a magnetic pull he couldn't explain, one that had been haunting him since their first conversation.

Who was he kidding? Mina had him by the short hairs the moment he laid eyes on that damn glossy headshot.

A humorless smile played at the corners of his mouth. Nothing good ever came from mixing women and work. It was the only explanation for how she kept outmaneuvering him.

It looked like he'd be sneaking into her apartment tonight, after all. She might've found the tracker in her wallet, but she wouldn't find the others he planned to plant. She'd better enjoy her cunning now because she wouldn't escape him so easily again.

The light in Mina's bedroom window flickered out just after midnight. Derrek sat across the street, the dark interior of his car holding him in an impenetrable shadow. He parked just beyond the halo of the streetlamp, granting him the anonymity he needed. Over the past hour, traffic had dwindled to almost nothing—just the occasional car or lone pedestrian about every twenty minutes. The street would be completely deserted by three a.m., except for him.

Leaning back in the bucket seat of the rental car, he let his head settle into the headrest. His eyes fell to half-mast as he waited for the street to settle for the night. He had one chance to get the trackers placed and get out unobserved. If she caught him, he would have to kill her, and it wouldn't be the nice clean hit he was commissioned to do.

He lifted the tape from his watch face, checking the time before concealing the glow. These precautions were tedious but necessary. The irony wasn't lost on him. He could end it all tonight, here and now. He'd already played out several scenarios—ways to get the job done and be gone from San Francisco before anyone noticed. But every plan was met with resistance from the voice in his head, listing reasons why it wouldn't work. Frustrated, he gave up and returned to his original plan: placing three trackers.

Derrek watched a car drive by, the beam of light from its headlights flashing in his review mirror seconds before driving past. He checked his watch, noting the time, mentally clocking the interval between the car and the last time he'd seen anyone else filter by. As he predicted, the street had become nearly deserted. Another hour and he'd be able to finish the job tonight.

He didn't particularly care for waiting. It left too much time for his mind to wander, and tonight, it refused to stay on the job. Instead of focusing on his strategy—how to get into her building and apartment without being seen—his thoughts kept drifting back to those sparkling brown eyes the color of amber. To soft lips curling into a smile he wanted to taste. Irritation welled up inside him, his fists tightening. This wasn't supposed to be difficult. But the thought of her—so close yet out of reach—made his stomach churn.

What little light illuminating the night sky disappeared behind a heavy cover of clouds. Fat drops of water hit his windshield in lazy concession. The rhythmic sound brought on a sudden desire to sink into a couch with a warm body tucked next to his. His eyes closed as he pictured himself on Mina's couch, with her soft, subtle body snuggled against his side. The image was too tempting, and the feelings that stirred within him were too alluring. Derrek shut the thoughts down, turning his gaze to the apartment building. His restless gaze swept the street one last time.

The onset of rain was a blessing. It would drive potential stragglers indoors and obscure the view of anyone who may happen to look outside. He was good at blending in. After years of being invisible, he didn't have to work hard at it. It had become second nature. The need to operate in oblivion was how he'd survived this long. But he couldn't be satisfied with that any longer. He didn't want to be invisible. He didn't want to live his live his life in the background. The sour taste of discontent curdled his stomach.

It hit him suddenly: this couldn't continue. The solitary existence he'd forced himself to live no longer was an option. When he finished this job—his expression turning grim—he would walk away. He'd set up a contingency plan years ago on the chance he needed to leave the life. It seemed the time had come. He would start over again. And if he played his cards right, he might even be able to pick up the pieces of his old relationships. Maybe spend the holidays with family instead of alone.

Chapter Eight

Derrek slipped into Mina's apartment building the same way he had before, his movements swift and practiced. A heavy, suffocating darkness filled the alley behind the building. Overhead, a dented metal light fixture flickered weakly, its glow barely stretching beyond the worn door it hung above. The flickering bulb buzzed softly, its sound unnaturally sharp in the predawn silence.

He pulled out a penlight, its beam reduced to a razor-thin thread by black tape. Clamping it between his teeth, he angled the light toward the keyhole. His fingers worked swiftly, flipping the lock and opening the door in under six seconds. A personal best—not that it mattered. The basic lock had hardly been a challenge.

The stairwell to the right of the door stood empty. Derrek paused at the base, his foot hovering over the first step, ears straining for any hint of movement. Nothing. He moved, his pace swift but cautious, halting at the fourth-floor door. He remembered the hinges squeaked from his last trip and eased the door open in slow, measured increments.

A faint squeak broke the stillness. He froze, holding his breath. Then, in one smooth motion, he pulled the door open the rest of the way. This time, it closed behind him without a sound, the offending squeak mercifully absent.

Mina's door was six down on the left, the hallway lights burning bright despite the early hour. Derrek walked with purpose, his movements steady and unremarkable—acting nervous was a surefire way to be noticed, and he had no intention of being remembered.

Her locks proved more of a challenge than the building's exterior door, but nothing he couldn't handle. Nine seconds and a brief fumble later, he slipped inside. He paused by the door, letting his eyes adjust to the darkness. Having been here before, he didn't need to rely on sight to navigate. Faint light from the street filtered through the sheer curtains in the window, casting the furniture into soft, shadowy shapes.

Derrek's eyes swept over the room, a faint smile tugging at his lips as he took in the trail of clothes strewn across the floor. It was almost like tracking her movements in reverse—shoes kicked off by the door, her jacket draped carelessly over the couch. His fingers brushed over the fabric. Her bra, a pink lacy confection, lay discarded on the armchair near the kitchen. He moved further in, pausing at the armchair near the kitchen where the pink, lacy bra lay abandoned.

He stopped at a pool of fabric on the tile floor near a stack of mail. But it wasn't the unopened envelopes that caught his notice. His lips curved in satisfaction as he spotted her phone resting in its glittering pick case on the charging dock. Mina couldn't have made it any easier for him. *Atta girl.* He thought with a note of appreciation.

He lifted the phone, checking for hidden alerts that might signal tampering. Satisfied, he slipped off the glittering case and set it aside. The new trackers AOD had developed were impressively discreet and practically invisible. He was among the first to use them in the field, a fact that usually brought a flicker of pride, though tonight it was absent.

His hand dug into his pocket, pulling out the micro-sized trackers. He slipped the tweezers from the case and lifted one tracker, placing it over the screw left of the charging port. Designed to blend seamlessly with the phone's hardware, it looked identical to the existing screws. Only someone trained would ever notice the difference. As he affixed the device and tested its functionality, a flicker of hesitation crossed his mind. His gaze wandered back to the discarded clothes and the quiet intimacy of her space.

He shook off the prickling unease, refocusing on the task at hand. In under three minutes, the tracker was in place, the case reassembled, and the phone returned to the charging dock exactly as he'd found it.

He moved to her coat, draped over the couch. Placing a tracker on clothing wasn't ideal—too many variables, too much unpredictability—but Mina had managed to slip past him too many times. He felt fairly safe putting a tracker on her coat. It was the only one he'd seen her wear.

It was a frilly thing. He didn't know how it kept her warm. Lifting it, he searched for the pocket, and a soft floral scent wafted up to him. He paused, caught off guard by its sweetness. *Focus.* The sharp rebuke in his mind pulled him back. Now wasn't the time to appreciate the alluring smell that seemed to follow Mina around. Not when the slightest mistake could compromise the mission. It would do him no good to become distracted, especially now when he needed to pay attention to what he was doing.

A soft light burst through the darkness as he folded the tracker into the pocket seam. Instinct took over. Derrek spun on his heel, sliding soundlessly toward the support pillar a few feet away. He ducked out of sight, pressing his back to the cold cement. He held still, listening for any sign of Mina's position. His mind raced, replaying the last ten minutes. He tried to pinpoint the sound that had alerted her to his presence. She was good, better than he expected. Granted, she wasn't as good as Damian, but few were.

With his eyes closed, he could almost track Mina's progress through the apartment. The faint hiss of running water from the second bathroom broke the silence. A flush followed, and then darkness returned as the light clicked off. He held his breath, body taut, as he waited for her next move. His pulse hammered in his ears, a mix of adrenaline and anticipation. His blood pumped hot through his veins.

He counted off her steps and knew the minute she moved through the kitchen. He pictured her selecting a weapon. He tensed, ready for the lethal attack that should come any second.

Any second now.

He stood in stunned silence, almost weighed down in disappointment. Instead of her steps drawing her closer, she moved away, receding to the bedroom. The unexpected move left him uncertain about what to do next. He couldn't make sense of what had just happened. Mina should have confronted him by now. By all accounts, his job should be finished. He felt a strange satisfaction that it hadn't ended too soon.

Mina continued defying expectations, an enigma in a world where he rarely encountered surprises. The uncertainty of her next move exhilarated him in a way he hadn't experienced in years. For the first time in what seemed like forever, he felt truly, undeniably alive.

Mina lay in bed, staring at the ceiling as sleep eluded her. She turned her head, glaring at the clock beside her bed. She spent the night wrestling with her sheet. Every time her mind slipped into sleep, she was pushed into vivid and disturbing dreams.

Chris haunted those dreams, his image circling her mind like a ghost she couldn't banish. The alluring blend of sandalwood, musk, and his intoxicating scent filled her nose. At one point, she swore the smell was more than just a dream, but in the room with her.

She woke to use the bathroom, but that tantalizing scent tickled her senses. Drawn by some unseen compulsion, she moved to the kitchen. The empty space greeted her as she knew it would, but the disappointment still hit hard. Frustrated with herself, she returned to bed, burying her face in the pillow.

There was no point in holding onto a man she met once and would probably never see again. It would be best to put him firmly out of her mind. Besides, she didn't know how many more sleepless nights she could handle before fatigue turned her into a walking zombie.

Luckily, it was Wednesday—aside from Sunday, it was her only other day off. With nowhere to be and all day to get there, Mina let herself loll in bed for a little longer than usual. Her perpetual can-do attitude prevented her from lingering too long. The day was gorgeous. The only rain in the forecast wouldn't roll in until late afternoon.

She hurried through her morning routine, eager to be outside in the sunshine. On the fridge, she had an ongoing list of things that needed her attention. Wednesday was her favorite day to tackle a few of them, choosing the ones that felt most satisfying to cross off. Over a bowl of cereal, Mina ran a finger down her list, looking for anything that caught her fancy.

"Drop off dry cleaning."

She could do that. The dry cleaning bag she hung in her closet was certainly full enough.

Returning to the list, Mina's eyes paused at "Visit the kennel." Her heart immediately seized onto it. She loved animals, and if she didn't live alone in a building with a strict no-pet policy, she might have been tempted to adopt one. Instead, she lived vicariously through others. She settled for visiting the Second Chance Animal Shelter a few blocks away. The day manager, Elijah, always let her come in and hold the puppies. The thought of all those sweet faces waiting for attention made her heart swell. Yes, this was exactly what she needed, some unconditional love.

Mina headed to her closet, pulling on a pair of snug yoga pants and an oversized sweater, the kind that made her feel wrapped in a blanket. With the promise of sunshine, she left her jacket at home. Grabbing her dry cleaning, she made her way to the door, her hand hovering over the door knob. Shoot, her purse.

She would have smacked herself on the forehead if her hands weren't full. One of these days, she was going to figure out why she could never remember to grab things on her way out. She walked to the table, where her purse usually sat, but it wasn't there. Frowning at the empty spot, she tried to remember the last time she'd seen it. When nothing came to mind, she shrugged. It wasn't like she needed any money yet. Payment wouldn't be necessary until she picked up her dry cleaning; for now, she had time to find it.

By the time she reached the street, Wednesday morning was in full swing. People milled around, their faces intent. Mina moved through the crowd, juggling her dry cleaning from hand to hand, murmuring apologies when her bag bumped against someone. But even the grumpy crowd couldn't bring her down. The sun was high, the breeze soft—it was a good day.

Bayside Drycleaning was a family-owned business that had been part of the neighborhood long before the artisan movement took hold. Thankfully, the artisan community embraced small businesses like Bayside, and the shop continued much as before. Although the couple who started the company still hung around, it was their granddaughter,

Sandra, a sweet-faced redhead, who had taken the reins. She was passionate about the artisan direction, working to shift the company toward natural, environmentally friendly products and away from harsh chemicals.

Mina joined the line that stretched from the door across the storefront. She smiled at the man ahead of her and then turned to the street, watching the bustling crowd. The faces of strangers always interested her; what was their story? What made them smile or, more often, frown?

An elderly woman joined the line behind her, carrying a load twice the size of Mina's. "We just got home from a two-week cruise." the woman said, offering a pointed look at the bundle in her arms. "Otherwise, my bag would be half this amount." She admitted in a paper-thin voice that carried a note of a Midwestern drawl.

Mina turned, smiling. "Wow. Where'd you go?"

"This time, we did the Mediterranean."

"This time? Do you take cruises often?"

The woman's face brightened. "Oh, yes. It's the only way my husband and I travel anymore."

"Really? I've never been."

"You have to try it. Everything is included, and the only extra thing is the excursions, but my husband and I rarely do those now. We did in the beginning, but the older we got, the harder it was to keep up. By the time the excursion was over, we would both be so tired that we couldn't make it to dinner. That's when we decided to stay on the boat. Sometimes, we'd get off to shop for a bit, but never more than a couple of hours."

"It sounds lovely. I imagine having someone to travel with makes the trip even better," Mina surmised, imagining what it would be like to travel with someone. She had always wanted to try out cruising but never did—not when she would have to go alone.

A surprising urge to cry formed a lump in her throat. She blinked hard, willing the tears away. This was ridiculous. So, what if she didn't have anyone to take trips with? That was just *right now.* She had her whole life ahead of her, and she refused to believe she would spend it alone. Somewhere out there was a man tailored made for her. She just had to find him.

As if summoned by her thoughts, Chris appeared across the street. He was sitting at a table, reading a book, a half-eaten muffin beside him. Mina froze, momentarily caught off guard by his presence, before her senses snapped back into focus.

The older woman spoke again, pulling Mina's gaze away from Chris. "You don't have to have someone to travel with. I have taken a few cruises without my husband. You know how men are. Anyway, there are always plenty of people to talk to."

"I suppose that's true." Mina conceded, her eyes drifting back to Chris, only he wasn't there. The table he'd been sitting at was now occupied by a different man. Much older and not nearly as attractive. Where the half-eaten muffin had sat now held a tray laden with food and a large straw cup. Mina frowned at the people across the street. Her gaze searched for Chris even though he appeared to be gone.

"I'm sorry, but did you see the man sitting at the table over there?" she asked the older woman, gesturing to where Chirs had been.

"You mean the gentleman in the blue shirt?"

"No, not him. There was another, in a black shirt and dark sunglasses. Did you see him?"

The woman shook her head. "No, sorry."

As the line moved toward the door, Mina refused to turn her back on the crowd. She had seen him. She knew it. Even though he seemed to have disappeared, she wasn't imagining things. He had been there. The way he stared at her, a lingering heat in his gaze, drew her attention to him. He'd been watching her in that odd way of his. She couldn't put her finger on what it was, but there was an intensity she couldn't ignore.

At the counter, she smiled at Sandra. "I have a pile for you today."

"Great. Any stains? Concerns?" Sandra pulled each item out, taking a quick look before setting them aside.

"Nope. Just the usual treatment."

Sandra typed into the tablet on the edge of the counter. "Okay. I can have these ready by Friday."

"Perfect," Mina grinned. "I'll see you then."

Sandra handed Mina a printout of the items she'd dropped off. "Don't lose this," she warned.

Mina bit the inside of her cheek to keep from giggling. "I won't."

"I mean it."

"I know."

Sandra sighed; snatching the ticket back, she pinned it to the corkboard behind the counter. "I have it. I'll see you Friday."

"Thanks, Sandra," Mina said, her lips twitching.

"Yeah, yeah." Sandra waved her off. "Next."

Instead of heading out the front, Mina slipped through the back exit. On her way out, she paused by the office door to exchange a few words with Sandra's grandmother. She was a delightful woman with a passion for soap operas. She spent most of her day crammed in the small office, binge-watching her favorites.

"What is John up to these days?" Mina asked, leaning against the doorframe.

Roberta didn't even glance up. "Shh, this is the best part," she murmured, eyes glued to the screen.

Mina chuckled softly. "Sorry," she whispered, tiptoeing away.

The back door was down the hallway, next to the bathroom. Mina pushed the heavy metal door open, digging into the tote she had dangling on her arm. The man she was looking for was huddled in a cardboard house he had built over the summer. A thin sheet hung over the opening, blocking most of his body from view.

"Tommy, are you in there?" Mina asked, pretty sure the shoe, held together by duct tape and twine, belonged to him.

"Whose asking?" The cankerous reply lost a little of its thunder, muffled by the cardboard.

"Mina. Got something for you." She shuffled through her bag, pulling out a couple of cans of food and a secondhand sweater she'd picked up.

After some shuffling and some unruly moans, Tommy emerged. His clothes, no longer showing their original color, having been stained and dirtied beyond repair, hung off his reed-thin body. He looked thinner than she remembered, his skin pale and sickly, and her heart constricted.

Mina smiled softly. "Hey, Tommy. How've you been?" She had met Tommy a year ago, quite by accident. Sandra showed her a new product and then had her go out the back door, which led to an alley Tommy had made into his home.

Since then, whenever Mina dropped off her dry cleaning, she made a point of bringing a little something extra for Tommy. A man who reminded her so much of her father. Not so much in appearance but in how he completely disregarded the world and those who lived in it.

He squinted at her, his face a mixture of wariness and gratitude. "What'd you bring me this time, girl?" His voice was hoarse, his body unsteady as he reached for the items.

Mina held up the cans and sweater. "It's getting cold out here; I thought you could use a little something warm."

Tommy snatched the sweater, fumbling to put it on. Mina stepped closer to help, but he jerked back, snapping, "I can do it."

She nodded, pulling her hand back. "Sorry. Where should I put the food?"

"I'll take them. Don't want no body messing with my stuff. I got a system. I don't want you in the way."

She forced a smile, his smell making it hard to breathe. She pulled air in through her mouth but almost gagged. The taste of it lingered, bitter and sharp, as she staggered back a step, her stomach churning.

"Well, I've got to get going. I'll see you later." Mina moved away, drawing closer to the other side of the alley, which would lead her to the street where the Second Chance building was located.

Tommy grumbled something she couldn't make out and figured he had already moved on. Taking his distraction as a green light to leave, Mina walked at as fast a pace as her short legs would allow. In moments like these, legs that stretched to the ceiling would be useful.

She didn't know why she felt compelled to bring things for Tommy. When she tried to analyze it, nothing made sense. But the impulse was there, undeniable, even without a logical reason.

She supposed it had something to do with her need to hold puppies and make friends with everyone she met. She was clearly trying to fill a void, albeit in a misguided way. If any of this was working, she wouldn't be dreaming about a man she met once and had now seen or maybe not seen on the streets twice. She was losing it.

Shaking her head, she headed for Second Chance. Perhaps it was time for some deep reflection.

Chapter Nine

Derrek sat at the café table, idly eating his muffin as the crowd moved past him. A gap would appear, every so often giving him a clear view of Mina. The only tracker she carried was the one he'd planted on her phone. The others were still pinging from her apartment building, except for the one in her wallet, which she'd left at Blossom the day before.

It didn't matter to him which item she carried as long as she had one. With the number of trackers he'd placed, losing her shouldn't be a problem. This job, however, was proving to be more expensive than usual. Between the space he'd rented and numerous trackers, a call from accounting was inevitable.

He hadn't anticipated Mina. She wasn't a typical mark. Mina had already proven herself to be more cunning than any previous job. She challenged him in a way that shocked him back to life. For too long, he'd been living on autopilot, carrying out his assignments with the detachment of a machine. But Mina... she'd shaken him awake. Every time she outmaneuvered him, she rekindled a thrill he hadn't felt in years. She wasn't just a job anymore—she was a mystery, a spark of life in a world that had gone dull.

As the crowd thinned momentarily, his eyes locked on her. She stood in line, chatting with an elderly woman. Then, as if sensing his gaze, Mina looked up. Their eyes collided, and an electric jolt shot through him. His muscles coiled, every instinct sharpening. This was the moment. Would she run?

The air between them vibrated silently, stretching tight as a wire. A shot of adrenaline surged through him like a jolt of caffeine. Derrek sat tense, alert, and ready. He thought she might bolt for a second, but then her attention shifted back to the old woman.

Derrek took advantage of her brief lapse in attention. He swiped his muffin from the table and slipped into the crowd. Using the continuous flow to elude detection a second time.

Not willing to risk being seen again, Derrek took a position inside a nearby bookstore. He stayed near the window, angled just enough to maintain a clear view of the dry cleaner. His position provided him with a direct line of sight but left him imperceptible to her. He shifted to a more comfortable stance and stood watch. Occasionally, he picked up a book, flipping over the back cover to avoid suspicion.

When Mina disappeared into the dry cleaner, he checked his phone. The tracker confirmed her position still matched. Minutes ticked by—five, ten, fifteen—and an irritating itch began to crawl up his spine. Where was she?

He glanced at his watch, then at his phone again. The signal still placed her at the dry cleaner. Maybe she was chatting. Mina had a penchant for talking to strangers, an odd part of her ruse he hadn't quite wrapped his head around. He couldn't understand what she hoped to achieve by wasting time on casual conversation.

When the door to the dry cleaner swung open, his eyes snapped to it. The older woman Mina had been talking with earlier exited. Derrek's brow furrowed. That woman had been behind Mina in line. By now, Mina should've been out, too.

The itch turned into a full-blown warning. He checked his phone again, frowning at the screen. The tracker still placed her inside, but something felt off.

Derrek hovered in indecision, a nervous energy thrumming beneath his skin. He could go to the cleaners and see if she was still inside, but if she was, he would have to come up with some reason for being there. He didn't want to blow his cover, but a gnawing worry whispered that it might already be too late for caution.

What if she had found the tracker on her phone after all? Maybe going to the dry cleaner was a way to lose him. She could have put the tracker on anything inside the cleaners and then slipped out back.

Derrek rushed to the exit, cursing himself for the oversight. He should have anticipated Mina knowing about alternative exit points; he always accounted for it in his plans. Swearing under his breath, he paused at the curb, waiting for a break in the traffic. A bitter smile tugged at his lips, twisting his expression between amusement and irritation. This was precisely why getting too close to a mark was a bad idea—it clouded judgment and made room for errors.

It was stupid mistakes like this that cost people their lives. She was likely meeting one of her contacts now. Her entire charade was designed to throw him off her trail. Derrek dodged through the traffic, ignoring the impatient blare of horns. His blood pumping hot through his veins. He strode to the glass door, yanking it open with such force it rattled in its frame.

"Hey, buddy! There's a line," an older man grumbled, gesturing toward the waiting customers.

Derrek barely contained his irritation, his jaw tightening as he turned to the man. "I'll only be a minute," he said, his voice clipped but controlled. He stepped inside, letting the door swing shut behind him.

His gaze swept past the young woman behind the counter to the rows of hanging clothes. Among the various garments, his eyes locked onto the bright pink sweater Mina had held earlier. Relief flickered briefly, but it was gone as soon as he scanned the room. She wasn't here.

The woman behind the counter gave him a wary, speculative look.

"Do you have a bathroom?" Derrek asked, leaning in slightly, his tone just casual enough. He caught the flicker of hesitation in her eyes, the subtle shift of someone debating whether to be honest. He added a sheepish grin for good measure. "It's kind of urgent, if you know what I mean."

Her lips twitched into a fleeting, uncertain smile. "Uh, sure. Down the hall, to the left. Third door."

"Thanks," he said over his shoulder, already striding toward the hallway. The urgency to find Mina—to get the answers he needed to finish the job, pushing him to hurry.

Derrek stopped to open every door, peering beyond for any sign of Mina. The only other person there was an older woman engrossed in some television show. She hadn't even bothered to turn around when he poked his head through the open doorway.

Wherever Mina had gone, it was clear she wasn't here anymore. A green exit sign glowed over a closed metal door toward the back of the hallway. His jaw tightened, determination hardening his features as he moved toward it.

He eased the door open, wincing as sunlight flooded his vision. Raising his arm to shield his eyes, he scanned the alley, the butt of his pistol nestled in the palm of his hand.

A homeless man stumbled out of a makeshift cardboard home. His clothes sagged from his gaunt frame. "What are you doing to my home?" The man hollered. His face set in a belligerent scowl.

"Easy, old man. I'm just passing through," Derrek said, his tone measured but firm. He studied both ends of the alley. The one end would have led Mina to the bookstore where he had been waiting. She might have slipped by without him noticing, although he liked to think he was more observant than that. The other end opened onto a completely different street, likely a better option for evasion.

A calculating smile curled his lips as he holstered his gun. If he had to bet, Mina took that route. It would offer her the best chance of evading him, although it wouldn't be for long. He moved toward the far end of the alley only to be brought up short by the homeless man. A flare of impatience had him scowling. "Is there a problem?"

"Hand it over," the man demanded, extending a grubby, dirt-streaked hand.

Derrek was flabbergasted. The old man was trying to rob him. It was so absurd he almost laughed. "Get out of the way, old man."

"Not until you give me the stuff."

Folding his arms, Derrek studied the man. He could easily make him move. It wouldn't take much effort, but he didn't want to hurt the guy. "What stuff are you referring to?"

"Food, clothes, stuff." The man said with a hint of impatience.

"I don't have anything with me."

The man frowned, his confusion evident in the deepened dirt creases of his forehead. "What do you mean, you ain't got nothin'? She always brings me things. Anytime she uses my home. You want to use my home; you bring me things." He stubbornly explained.

Derrek's attention sharpened, zeroing in on the man. "She? There was a woman here before me?"

"She brings me things." He said again, pulling at the arm of the sweater he wore.

"Did she bring you the sweater?" Derrek prodded.

The man nodded, his focus solely on his sleeve. "She gave me food." His head shot up as if the reminder of food had reignited his memory. "Did you bring me food?"

"No," Derrek said. Then he remembered the half-eaten muffin he'd shoved into his jacket pocket. Pulling it out, the napkin he'd loosely wrapped it in fell open, revealing the crumbling pastry inside.

In a swift move, the man snatched the muffin from his hand and turned his back, hunching over the food as if it were a coveted prize. "Which way did she go?" Derrek asked.

With a subtle nod, the man gestured toward the far side of the alley, in the direction leading to the bookstore. Derrek frowned in puzzlement. "Are you sure?"

"What did you bring me?" The man asked. His yellow teeth curled into a snarl.

Uninterested in repeating what had just happened, Derrek took out his phone. He suspected it would still show the dry cleaners, but what was the harm in verifying? The blue circle moved on the screen, pulsing a block and a half away, moving in the opposite direction the homeless man had pointed. Excitement pounded in his chest, a rapid rhythm that quickened his pulse. He just knew she was meeting her contact. This time, he had her. She couldn't escape him twice. By tonight, he should be on his way home. With his questions confirmed, there was no reason to linger. All except one. Why had she given the old man a sweater?

Mina laughed, turning away from the eager licks of a soft pink tongue. She crooned to the puppy, a loving yellow lab with warm chocolate eyes and a thick, velvety golden coat. Snuggling the wiggling body on her lap, she scratched behind his ears. "If I could take you home, I would," she admitted with a whisper. At the sound of her voice, the puppy seemed to take it as an open invitation to renew his efforts to lick every part of her face. "No, boy," she giggled; her attempts to calm him were futile.

She held his cold, wet nose against hers, peering into his beseeching gaze, and her resolve wavered. Perhaps coming to the kennel today hadn't been her brightest idea. She was feeling a little more susceptible than usual. She could blame it on her father for not calling or even the chill of her empty apartment, but neither was the cause. She wanted someone to come home to, another living, breathing soul she could snuggle with and share her worries. As the puppy wriggled closer, nuzzling against her cheek, a lump formed in her throat.

That was the problem with filling your life with friends; you couldn't fill the empty parts. Mina wanted a partner, someone to share her burdens, someone to confide in, someone to love. Chris's face flashed in her mind, sparking a deep longing. Of course, she had to meet the man of her dreams only to find he was already taken. Life had a cruel sense of humor.

The kennel door squeaked, pulling her from her thoughts. Mina turned, her smile brightening when Elijah entered, carrying a bucket of food. Ducking under the low frame, he shifted sideways to squeeze through, his broad shoulders brushing the edges. The kennel erupted in a chorus of excited yaps and eager paws dancing in anticipation as Elijah made his way down the line.

"You sure have a way with animals," Mina observed with a cheeky grin.

Elijah scoffed. "Anyone walking around with a scoop of food can work miracles."

"I don't think so," Mina said, her smile widening as Elijah scowled down at her. "If I had to guess, I'd say these little guys love your cuddly nature. To them, you're nothing more than a giant teddy bear."

Elijah snorted but didn't reply, continuing to fill the feed dishes. Dogs of all shapes and sizes rushed to their meals, tails wagging in a flurry of motion. Between scoops, he patted a head or scratched a side, his large hands surprisingly gentle. He still wore that same impatient, grumpy look she remembered from her first visit. Back then, she'd been intimidated, certain he'd snap at her. But it hadn't taken long to see past the growl to the kindness in his actions. It was just his way, she thought and smiled.

Elijah's gaze flicked to where she sat. "I see you found Red."

"Red?" Mina looked down at the puppy sprawled across her lap in a sleepy heap. "Why do you call him Red?"

"His nose," Elijah said. Moving to the next dish. "It's got a bit of red compared to his brother."

She lifted the puppy from her lap, holding him higher for a better look. "Wow, will you look at that? I didn't even notice. What does that say about me?"

"I'm not surprised," Elijah said with a shrug. "For someone who walks around with their head in the clouds, I doubt if you would notice a man bleeding on the street."

"Hey! I am not that bad," Mina protested, crossing her arms. "I'll have you know I saved a butterfly during that awful storm last Sunday. It was heroic."

"It's not the animals I'm talking about," Elijah replied.

Mina's cheeks warmed. Maybe she wasn't as good at hiding her little problem as she thought. If Elijah had noticed, who else had? She'd need to work on that—it wouldn't do for anyone to see what was beneath the surface. Clearing her throat, she set Red down. The puppy whimpered, circling her feet and nudging her ankle.

"Are you going to take him home with you?"

She looked down at Red's upturned face. "I wish I could. He's a sweetheart, but I am not allowed to have pets in my apartment." A sharp pang of regret had her leaning down to pick him up. She rubbed his ears and buried her face in his silken coat. Coming here today had been a mistake. She was more emotionally raw than she'd realized.

"I could hold him for you," Elijah offered, his voice gruff but kind. "Maybe for a week or so. Give you time to think about it."

Startled, Mina looked up. "I don't know," she said hesitantly. "What if he misses out on a family with kids? He deserves all that fun and chaos." Her fingers absently traced patterns in Red's fur. "I wouldn't want to take that chance away from him."

"Families like that are a dime a dozen. If he missed out this week, there will be another next week."

Mina hoovered between indecision. She had never let herself think of getting a pet, not when she would have to move. After all, she was gone at work all day. What would he do while she was gone? "I don't know." Worrying her bottom lip. She stroked his fur.

Taking the decision from her, Elijah said, "I'll give you two weeks. If you decide you don't want him, I'll put him back into the adoption pool."

"Won't you get into trouble?"

He snorted. "Not likely."

Mina bit the inside of her cheek, running her finger over Red's nose. "Okay. Deal. I'll let you know either way in two weeks."

She helped Elijah put Red back in his kennel and left the shelter, promising to check back soon. Once outside, she couldn't stop the daydreams from filling her mind. She could see Red curled up on her couch, his nose resting on her leg as she read beside him.

The image warmed her heart, but reality quickly tempered her daydreams. Pets weren't technically banned in her building, but they came with extra fees and a mountain of paperwork—proof of vaccinations, registration, and the like. And then there was the practical side. Nine hours alone each day? A puppy needed space to run and play, not a cramped apartment and fleeting walks in the park.

Still, the pull to take Red home was stronger than ever. She'd visited the shelter dozens of times, but she'd never been tempted like this before. Was it because of her father? She didn't want to admit it, but his recent silence gnawed at her. He hadn't responded to her texts, and when she called last night, he didn't answer.

She considered calling Braxton. Her brother always seemed to know what was going on with their father. But her relationship with Braxton was even worse than the one with her dad. She sighed, scowling at the ground. No wonder she shied away from men. After all, she'd learned early they couldn't be counted on.

Then, like a beam of sunlight breaking through clouds, Chris's face appeared in her mind. She must have it bad for him because he had a way of showing up in the most unusual places. It was as if her mind was imposing him onto strangers. Twice now, she'd thought she'd seen him. Maybe it was just her imagination, but her heart seemed intent on convincing her mind that not all men were the same.

A smile full of hope and dreams spread across her face, drawing one in return from a woman she passed on the street. Perhaps, if she ever saw Chris again, she'd let him know she was available. Who knows, maybe he could prove her wrong, which wouldn't be such a bad thing.

Chapter Ten

Derrek kept one eye on the flickering dot on his phone, the other on the street. His heart thudded with anticipation, the steady rhythm a reminder of how close she was—fifty yards. Ten seconds, fifteen tops, and he'd have her.

She was meeting her contact. He knew it.

But damn, it disappointed him.

He didn't want it to end, not yet. Not when there was so much more he wanted to know. None of it had anything to do with the job, of course. It wasn't about intel or strategy anymore. Something about Mina had gotten under his skin, shaking loose a part of him he thought was long dead.

His brow dipped over his nose in consideration. He couldn't recall the last time any emotion had stirred him enough to get a response out of him. For years, he'd lived in the void, untouchable and unshaken until now. The realization hit him hard, his step faltering, but he shoved it aside. Distractions were not an option.

Derrek darted across the street, slipping between honking cars and drivers' frustrated yells. His gaze flicked to the red brick building holding his query, which had no windows on the bottom floor. Closed dock bays lined the side facing him, their black doors sealed tight. He skirted around the side, boots scraping on uneven pavement, scanning for another way in.

The only door he'd found was on the far side, topped with an old-fashioned lamp that swayed feebly in the wind.

Too exposed. Too risky.

Unable to find a way in without drawing attention, Derrek melted back into the crowd, ducking into a shaded alcove. His dark sunglasses hid his gaze as he focused on the building's only exit. The crowd moved around him, a murmuring sea of faces, oblivious to his presence—just the way he liked it.

When a blonde in a snug sweater passed by, flashing him a playful smile, Derrek met it with a quick, cocky grin. His gaze followed her for half a beat, no longer. The moment she disappeared into the crowd, his attention returned to the door, only to see it swing shut.

A sharp jolt shot through him. His body coiled tight, senses sharpening. His eyes swept the crowded street, scanning for Mina through the blue of moving bodies.

Ignoring the impatient horn blares, Derrek rushed across the street. The acrid stench of burned rubber stung his nostrils. He pushed through the crowd, his heart beating faster, matching the rhythm of the chase. Adrenaline surged, pulling an unexpected smile from the firm line of his lips.

He'd get her yet. Given enough time, he got everyone.

A sharp creak cut through the street noise, snapping his attention to the building's entrance. He watched as the door swung open, his pulse quickening. Identifying Mina's contact was too valuable to ignore.

A burly man stepped out, the flame tattoo on his arm curling up to wrap around his neck. Gray hair cropped close to his scalp and a menacing expression carved into his face made him look every bit as dangerous as Derrek suspected.

Derrek's phone was already in hand. One quick snap of the camera, and he saved the image. Never once did he break his stride as he pursued Mina.

After a quick look at the photo, he called Damian. If anyone could ID this guy, it was him.

"King." Damian's deep voice cut through the ring.

"Hey, man. It's Derrek. I need a favor."

"Don't you mean Chris?" Damian's tone was laced with a dry edge of amusement.

Derrek rolled his eyes, biting back a curse. "Yeah, right, Chris. Can you help me or not?"

He scowled, his eyes narrowed, at a man who stepped in front of him, cutting off his line of sight. Muttering under his breath, he moved around the obstacle. The tension in his muscles eased only when Mina came into view. She darted through the crowd as lithe as a deer. He quickened his pace, his heart pounding. It was by pure luck that he still had eyes on her. She could've slipped away while he'd been distracted.

Damian's low chuckle grated in his ear. "What's the problem? Your little dove hasn't flown the coup, has she?"

"No. I have eyes on the prize. It's for something else."

Derrek's mouth pressed into a thin line, frustration simmering beneath the surface. He didn't like letting on to Damian that Mina was a challenge to track. She had the maddening ability to vanish just when he thought he had her pinned.

"Oh? And what might that be?"

"I've got a photo I need to be identified."

The pause on the other end was deliberate. Damian always did enjoy making him squirm. "Sidestepping protocol, are we?"

"Because it isn't part of the order, and you know how they feel when we overcharge."

"I suppose your resources weren't an option," Damian said dryly.

"My resources aren't nearly as handy as yours. Besides, why use one of my hard-earned IOUs when I can use one of yours?" Derrek grinned unabashedly as Mina paused at a window. His muscles tensed, but she moved on without glancing his way.

"I see." Damian's calm tone pulled him back. "It may take a day or two. I'm in the middle of my own little side project."

Derrek's brow lifted. Damian, the dutiful soldier, rarely strayed from sanctioned jobs. His unwavering obedience and objectivity earned him the best assignments. A side project was unusual—and intriguing.

Sometimes, a little playful ribbing is too good to pass up, friend or not. The corner of his mouth twitched as Derrek smothered a laugh, unable to resist tugging on the tiger's tail. "Side project? You?"

"Don't read into it."

"Anything I can help with?" he offered, meaning it.

"No, not yet. That might change, but I've got it handled."

The uncharacteristic edge in Damian's voice made Derrek pause. "This doesn't have anything to do with a siren's call, does it?" Calista's name went unspoken, but the implication was clear. Granted, it had been years ago, but she still seemed to have some kind of hold over Damian.

A tense silence stretched between them. Derrek winced. He had no business poking that bear, particularly since he was doing his fair share of tempting fate.

"And if it does?" Damian's tone was ice.

"And nothing. It doesn't change anything," Derrek replied firmly, glaring at the street. A passing grandmother's cheerful smile crumbled under the weight of his frown, making him curse.

"Good. I'll get back to you in a day or so," Damian said, cutting the call before Derrek could reply.

Mina suddenly stopped and turned back, forcing Derrek into an open doorway. He swore under his breath, pressing himself into the shadows until she passed. Only then did he slip back onto the street. A barely controlled frustration simmered beneath his surface.

He followed her for several blocks, alternating between keeping her in sight and tracking her through the device hidden in her wallet. She moved like someone who knew the risks of standing still—doubling back, pausing unexpectedly, and weaving unpredictably through the streets.

If he had to guess, she was delivering information—probably time-sensitive—to someone in the Petrov crime family. Derrek watched her seamless ease, envying her ability to stay a step ahead without seeming paranoid. He couldn't find any rhyme or reason for the route she took. She turned left, then right, and even backtracked a few times as if she sensed she was being pursued.

Her natural cunning abilities forced him to follow her at a more sedate pace. She would have stumbled over him at least half a dozen times by now at his usual range. He'd narrowly missed being seen by her when she had stopped mid-track and spun on her heel, heading straight toward him. He'd ducked into a building before she caught a glimpse of him.

His phone vibrated in his hand, allowing him to obscure his profile. His eyes briefly read the screen, groaning inwardly as he said, "Hi, Mom. Now isn't a great time."

"That's okay. I only had one thing to tell you, and then you can get back to your work." Derrek laughed, trying to cover the sound with a cough. "I hope you aren't getting sick, Derrek. I heard just yesterday that there's an outbreak of some new virus. You know it's one of those animal ones. It is always the animals. I keep telling your father he needs to get rid of those chickens, but he refuses. When we wind up sick in our beds dyin' from some kind of chicken feather disease, I'll find comfort in bein' able to tell him, 'I told you so.'"

"Mom, I'm fine. Healthy as a horse." He knew he was asking for trouble but couldn't help himself.

"Horses are carriers too, you know. All animals are. You stay away from them. Especially rats. Yuck. Or do I need to remind you of the disaster they created in Europe?"

"I hope you aren't referring to the plague."

"Of course. This is serious stuff. And you're washing your hands, right? Not just after the bathroom...How is that going, by the way? Everything shootin' off as it should be?"

Derrek pressed his forefinger and thumb into his eyes. The pressure relieving the headache he could feel building in his head. "Yes, Mom." He answered absently. His gaze followed Mina's progress. She paused at a shop window, and he let his attention return to the voice ringing in his ear.

"...healthy bowel movements are just as important as changing the oil in your car."

He pulled the phone away in horror. "What on earth are you talking about, Mom?"

"Goin' number two. Haven't you been listenin'?"

"Mom, I thought you had one thing you wanted to tell me. I sure hope it wasn't to discuss my use of the porcelain throne." Derrek cut in exasperation creeping into his voice.

"Really Derrek. I don't know why you are always so quick to get off the phone with me. I'll have you know that your sisters love talkin' with their mother. Where I went wrong with you, I'll never know."

"Mom," Derrek pleaded.

His mother's sigh wasn't a great sign. It meant she was now upset with him and would be until he apologized and gave her at least an hour of his time, either on the phone or in person. Since he was in the middle of a job, it meant he was in for a long chat. Maybe there would be a good game on to help pass the time, he mused.

"I was calling to let you know I am takin' a trip with a few of my girlfriends. You know Gabby and Philis?"

"Sure." He didn't, but that would only add to his mother's irritation, and an hour's penance was enough for him.

"Anyway, I'll be gone for five days. I'm leaving your father home alone. I have your sisters checkin' in on him. Naomi is goin' to stop by before she goes to work. Lillian will swin' by after school pick-up. I want you to call him durin' lunch or before bed. I'll let you decide which you prefer."

"Mom," Derrek moaned. "Dad is a grown man. He's been taking care of himself for years. I think he can handle being alone for a few days."

"You wouldn't say that if you came home more often. Why, the other day, he had ice cream for breakfast. Image that. When I asked him what he was doin', he told me he was in the mood for somethin' sweet. For breakfast!. That man is goin' to be the death of me."

"I don't think Dad will appreciate—"

"Son, trust me to know what I am talking about. Now, are you going to do this for me or not?"

Derrek's gaze followed Mina as she slipped further away from him. His gut clenched. "Sure, Mom. I'll give Dad a call."

"Every day," she pressed.

He made a muffled sound of agreement, ending the call with their usual statements of love. He shook his head. At least one silver lining had come from the conversation. His mother was going out of town. Five days without her hovering wasn't a bad deal, considering how distracted he was. He tucked his phone in his pocket and followed his Mina with grim determination.

Chapter Eleven

What should have been a thirty-minute walk had stretched into nearly an hour. Derrek shook his head in disbelief as Mina's backward trek through the heart of the artisan district led Mina straight to Squeeze.

He found himself caught between wanting to laugh at the situation's absurdity and fuming over the colossal waste of time. If this little game of hers was for his benefit, he wasn't amused. Still, he couldn't deny her skill. She had a knack for throwing him off, and even with his usually sharp sense of direction, an hour of shadowing her had left him slightly disoriented.

A reluctant smile tugged at his lips. As frustrating as it was, he had to hand it to her—Mina knew how to keep him on his toes.

She was a tease, no doubt about it. But something about her lingered in his thoughts, a pull Derrek couldn't shake. She was driving him crazy in all the worst—and best—ways.

Stepping off the sidewalk, Derrek crossed the street. He didn't realize his intent until he pulled the door to Squeeze open. He slipped inside, sauntering in with the practiced ease of someone who hadn't just endured the most invigorating and maddening chase of his life.

His eyes landed on Mina immediately. She was leaning over the counter, looking at something—he had no idea what. The woman on duty was talking with her as she filled plastic cups.

Derrek moved to the end of the line. In the few minutes it had taken him to follow Mina inside, four other people had joined ahead of him. He didn't mind the wait; it gave him time to breathe, to recalibrate. More importantly, it created the illusion that he hadn't been trailing her.

He snorted quietly at the thought, drawing a curious glance from the young couple in front of him. He coughed and turned his head, feigning disinterest. She was making him sloppy—scattered in a way he hadn't felt in years. This constant topsy-turvy behavior had turned him upside down.

He scowled at Mina's back. His gaze lingered on the appealing way the fabric clung to her backside. His eyes slid to her feet She shifted on her tiptoes, leaning over the counter with an effortless grace that drew every eye in the room, including his. When she rose, she held a bright yellow claw-like clip; she smiled wide and laughed.

The sound rippled through the air, light and warm, capturing the attention of everyone in line. Her voice possessed that undeniable talent, shattering his focus on more than one occasion. And now, he realized, he wasn't the only one affected by her. Derrek's jaw tightened as he scanned the room. This realization stirred something dark within him.

While part of him was relieved to know he wasn't alone in his fascination, another part, a darker side, resented the other men finding pleasure in her sound. He didn't want to share her light, her sweetness, with anyone. A primal part of him, the side he didn't acknowledge, yearned to scoop her up and disappear, to keep her light all to himself. Maybe, just maybe, she could help him find what he'd lost.

But those were dangerous fantasies, best left buried. He wouldn't let himself go there.

He smiled when Mina approached him. She hadn't looked up. Her attention was fixed on inserting a straw into her drink. Derrek shifted his stance, blocking her path just enough to force her to raise her gaze. He turned his head slightly—not so much as to obscure himself completely, but enough to suggest their meeting was entirely by chance.

He should have known better.

A sudden splash of icy liquid soaked his right side, the sticky beverage seeping through his shirt and dripping down his arm. It pooled on the floor around his boot, cold and unpleasant.

Mina let out a surprisingly colorful curse, her hand flying to her mouth as her amber eyes widened in shock. A faint pink flush flooded her cheeks, making the dusting of freckles along her nose stand out.

"I am so sorry." she blurted, grabbing a handful of napkins and dabbing at his chest. Her movements were frantic but oddly endearing. When her gaze finally locked with his, recognition flared. "Chris—uh, I mean, Mr. Summers! Are you all right? I can't believe I did that. I wasn't watching where I was going." She giggled, a nervous, almost hysterical sound, as her cheeks darkened further. "No surprise there, but I don't usually run into anyone. I mean, not physically. I suppose you weren't paying attention, either. So, this is both our fault. Don't you think?"

Derrek's lips twitched as he watched her ramble, amusement flickering behind his steady gaze. She hadn't changed—still a whirlwind of energy and contradictions.

He lifted a brow, his tone deliberately calm. "How so?"

"Well, if one person is always aware of those around them, situations like these would be avoided. But if both parties aren't doing their due diligence, we end up with a mess like this one," Mina explained. She continued to flutter around his body, dabbing at the rivulets of lemonade left behind.

Derrek tried to focus on her words, but having her close, feeling her hands move over him, was damn distracting. "I'd argue that the person carrying the drink should be the one watching where they're going," he said, a teasing edge to his voice.

Her blush deepened. "True. But isn't it everyone's responsibility to help each other?"

"And how exactly would you like me to help you?" Derrek couldn't resist asking. A teasing smile played at the corners of his mouth as he looked into her earnest face.

"Forgive me?" Mina said in a breathless whisper.

"Only if you have dinner with me," he said, the words slipping out. He knew, even as he spoke, that he was making a mistake.

Her eyes widened, and for a heartbeat, he wanted to take it back. He didn't want to make her uncomfortable. Even if it made little sense. She was his mark. He was supposed to make things permanently uncomfortable for her.

He forced a smile as the woman at the counter handed him a towel. "Forget I said that."

"Okay," Mina said softly, almost at the same time.

Derrek stilled. His heart lodged in his throat. "Wait. What? Did you just say yes?" He studied her face, searching for any sign of doubt. "Are you sure? I don't want to make you uncomfortable."

Mina took the towel from his hand, her fingers brushing his, and dabbed at his body again. His muscles constricted under the tender ministrations. "If you are willing to risk dinner with a klutz like me, I would love to."

He wanted her to look at him. Watching the top of her head gave him no clue as to what she was feeling. Was she nervous? Excited? Her voice sounded strained, as if she were struggling to breathe. If she had doubts about going to dinner with him, he wanted to see the evidence in her eyes.

His hands stilled the restless movement of hers. The contact against skin made Mina look up, her lips forming a startled 'O'.

He studied her face, allowing himself a moment to indulge in the pleasure of having her close. "You don't have to?" he said softly, hating every word as it left his mouth. "I was only kidding."

Hurt flickered in her amber eyes before her gaze dropped to his chest. He wanted to lift her head, to force her to look at him. He wanted to demand that she tell him the truth so he could be done with the whole mess.

"Of course. I didn't think you meant it," she murmured, her voice quieter now. "Besides, I couldn't promise your next shirt wouldn't meet the same fate." All traces of laughter faded from her expression.

When she made to move around him, he caught her arm in a light hold. He didn't want to scare her off, nor did he want her to leave without making sure she understood. He flashed her his best smile and let his southern drawl flow like honey. "If that's the case, I'll schedule an appointment with my dry cleaner. I think they'll look forward to a challenge. It's been too long since I brought them something they would have to put a little effort into."

Her eyes sparkled, the tension leaving her shoulders as she laughed softly. "Rest assured, if they can't deliver, I know Sandra will have any blemish out without breaking a sweat."

"Well, in that case, I don't see why we can't have dinner."

"Are you sure?" A hint of uncertainty flickered in Mina's eyes as she asked.

"Are you free tonight?"

"Yes."

"Sinclar's at eight?"

Her smile, bright as sunshine, flashed with excitement. "Sounds perfect."

Mina spent the six hours before her date oscillating between excited anticipation and paralyzing dread. She even threw up once—an unfortunate habit she'd developed growing up under the scrutiny of a father obsessed with studying human emotions.

The first time it happened, she was ten. She and her brother had argued over who won a board game, a silly disagreement that escalated into screaming and name-calling. Her mother had tried to mediate, but Mina had stormed off, unwilling to listen. Before she could retreat to her room, her father intercepted her and led her into his office.

To this day, she couldn't say what his intent had been. His probing questions and calm demeanor had unnerved her. By the time she left, her stomach churned so violently that she barely made it to the bathroom. Ever since, any surge of strong emotion—anger, excitement, fear—threatened to send her running for the toilet.

She calmed her nerves by working on a puzzle. She didn't care how quirky it seemed; piecing together tiny fragments of an image was the only thing that quieted the storm inside her. Something about the focused, deliberate process brought her back into balance.

Over the years, she'd learned to recognize the early warning signs and take action before the nausea set in. But there were days, like today, that blindsided her—when no amount of preparation could stop her body's involuntary reaction. That's why she always kept a puzzle close at hand. Since she never knew what might set her off, it was better to be prepared for anything.

Her mother had first suggested it. After reading, painting, and knitting failed to keep her anxieties at bay, her mother pulled out a thousand-piece puzzle of a colorful field of flowers. She dumped the contents on the dining table and told Mina to start with the edges.

That's what she did now, sorting out the straight edges. The seven-hundred-and-fifty-piece puzzle she'd found at a secondhand bookstore featured a cozy cabin tucked in the trees, surrounded by woodland creatures with adorably curious faces. The box had caught her eye immediately, but it wasn't until tonight that she felt the need to open it.

She had been working on the puzzle for over an hour, her pulse finally slowing to a steady rhythm. The familiar rhythm of sorting and piecing had soothed her frayed edges—until the sharp chime of the doorbell shattered her calm. She glanced at the clock on the stove as she went to see who was at her door.

"Crap," she muttered, her heart leaping into her throat. Thirty minutes until her date, and now she worried again.

Mina rose to her toes, peering through the peephole. On the other side, a man stood holding a messenger bag slung over his shoulder.

"Can I help you?" She asked through the door.

The man pulled an envelope from his bag. "I have a courier letter for Mina Turner."

With a smile of apology, she unlatched the chain and opened the door, stealing a peek at the name stitched into his shirt. "You never can be too careful."

"Not a problem," he replied, holding out a tablet. "Sign here, please."

Mina signed, watching the courier retreat down the hallway before closing the door. Turning the envelope over in her hands, the handwriting was unmistakable—her father's.

Torn between opening it now or setting it aside, she hesitated. What could he possibly need to say in a letter that couldn't be said over the phone? Before she could decide, her phone rang.

The shrill tone startled her, and she took it as a sign. Rushing to answer, she froze when an unfamiliar number flashed across the screen. A wave of unease washed over her. Maybe it was the letter or the memories the sight of his handwriting stirred—but her father's voice echoed in her mind.

Sometimes, the worst people appear to be the most harmless.

A shiver raced up her spine, leaving her skin prickling with goosebumps. She clutched her arms, trying to shake the eerie feeling. Now wasn't the time to dwell on cryptic warnings or unsettling memories. She was late enough as it was.

She tossed the envelope onto the counter and resolved to deal with it later. Whatever it was, it could wait.

Chapter Twelve

S inclar's defining characteristic was a never-ending line snaking out the door. Even on a slow weeknight, the energy was just as palpable as any other evening. The hum of conversation and the clink of glasses spilled onto the sidewalk. Derrek stood just outside the entrance, leaning against the red brick wall. His arms folded across his broad chest, his body radiating a silent warning to stay away.

Frustration whittled away his patience. His jaw tightened as he scanned the faces in the crowd, and each passing minute dragged his mood further into the gutter.

Where was Mina?

His gut twisted, a nauseating blend of impatience and dread. This was a mistake. He shouldn't have asked her to dinner. Nothing good could come from this, and he knew it. The mission was already teetering on the edge of failure, and here he was, throwing another complication into the mix.

His muscles tensed as his gaze caught a cascade of long brown hair, its distinct wave setting it apart in the shifting crowd. A frantic, pounding rhythm filled his ears as his heart thudded against his ribs. Why did she have to be so damn perfect? His frown hardened, his gaze boring into the crowd as if he could will her away—or maybe draw her closer. He wasn't sure which.

Then, she emerged a vibrant streak of color amidst a sea of gray. At that moment, he knew why he'd waited. She had the power to light up his world, to ignite something deep inside him that he thought had burned out long ago. He moved toward her, drawn by an invisible but potent pull. His usual scowl softened into a genuine smile.

"I was beginning to think you changed your mind," Derrek teased, slipping an arm around her waist as he guided her through the crowd.

Mina's laughter did wonders for lifting his spirit. "I'm not *that* late," she countered with a cheeky grin. "What time is it, anyway? Five after?"

"Try, eight-thirty."

Her eyes widened. "That can't be right!" She pulled her purse off her shoulder, digging through the pockets, her brow furrowing. "Oh, fiddlesticks."

An amused grin curled his lips. "Fiddlesticks? I didn't realize I was taking out Miss Daisy."

Mina nudged her elbow into his side, humor dancing in her eyes. "Haha. I think I forgot my phone."

He leaned closer, the faint floral scent of her perfume making his head spin. "Does that happen often?" he asked, his voice low.

She turned slightly, their noses almost touching. A faint blush bloomed on her cheeks. "No, not usually."

The spell broke as the hostess appeared, her polite smile ushering them forward. Derrek followed, acutely aware of Mina's soft footsteps trailing behind him.

Derrek scanned the room, his gaze sweeping over each face. He didn't linger on anyone too long, but his mind registered every detail: postures, expressions, exits. Habit, more than paranoia, dictated his choice of seating. Pulling out Mina's chair, he saved the spot next to the wall for himself.

Settling into his seat, he angled his body, ensuring a clear view of the room. He picked up the menu, but his focus wasn't on the list of dishes. His mind lingered on Mina's comment.

"Did something happen?" he asked, his voice casual, though his eyes were sharp, watching her every reaction.

Mina blinked, her expression blank for a moment. "Happen?"

"To forget your phone. Was something distracting you?"

"Oh! Right." Her lips pursed as she studied her menu. "No, not really. Honestly, I don't even remember where I had it last."

"I'm sure it'll turn up." He thought briefly about checking his phone to track it but dismissed the idea. It didn't matter if she was lying, not now, anyway.

"It usually does," she said absently, making him chuckle. "Did I say something funny?" she asked, raising an eyebrow.

"Not at all. So, what looks good to you?"

"The chicken sounds nice, but I don't like sun-dried tomatoes." She wrinkled her nose.

"You could just ask them not to add it," he said simply.

"I know, but I hate to be difficult."

He leaned back, momentarily stunned, a crease forming between his brows. "You think that's difficult? It's their job."

Her cheeks flushed a delicate pink. "Well... doesn't it make more work for the kitchen staff?"

Amused, he grinned. "If you want the chicken, order it without tomatoes. I promise they won't mind."

Before he finished speaking, she was already shaking her head. "I couldn't."

"You can," he countered, bemused to see the mulish shape her mouth had taken.

"What looks good to you?" she asked, scanning the menu. A slight frown played on her lips.

A broad smile spread across his face, crinkling the corners of his eyes. "I guess we're through discussing chicken?" His tone was teasing, but his gaze sharpened as he watched her.

The server arrived, breaking their playful standoff. He set a dish of dipping oil and warm bread in the center of the table. "Can I start you with something to drink?"

Mina ordered water with lemon, and Derrek followed suit. Before the waiter left, Derrek asked, "Quick question, how hard is it to leave sun-dried tomatoes off a dish?"

He cast a glance at Mina as he spoke, gauging her reaction. Would she laugh, get annoyed, or show a flash of impatience? He didn't even know what answer he wanted.

The server smiled. "Not hard at all. We'd be happy to accommodate."

Derrek shot Mina a triumphant look as the waiter walked away. "See? No big deal."

Mina gave him a mock frown, but her lips twitched, betraying her amusement. "You're impossible." She said, popping a piece of bread in her mouth.

He laughed, but his stomach dropped when Mina abruptly pushed her chair back. "Wait, you're not leaving, are you?"

Her lips twitched, fighting a smile, and the small gesture eased the tension knotting his chest. Her gaze dropped to her blouse. A wet blemish spread over her right breast. "No, I'm just going to the restroom," pointing to the stain. "I don't suppose you know where it is?"

"No idea, but we can ask." Derrek raised a hand to flag down a passing busboy.

Mina reached for his arm, her voice hushed. "Don't ask. Please."

He tilted his head, studying her, "Why not?" She didn't answer, merely shaking her head, her cheeks flush.

He couldn't see a reason why she would be upset about it. Turning back to the busboy, he ignored her silent plea. "Hey, man, where's the restroom?"

The young man, barely eighteen, adjusted the tray balanced on his hip. "By the entrance, west side of the doors."

"Thanks," Derrek said, then turned to Mina. "Did you catch that?"

"Yes, I'll be right back," she said with a fleeting smile.

Derrek watched her weave through the crowded restaurant, heading in the opposite direction from where the busboy had indicated. Amused, he leaned back in his chair, trying to decipher her movements. She stopped briefly to speak with a server, then followed the waitress toward the restrooms, her path looping by their table on the return trip, waving cheerfully as she passed.

A small grin tugged at Derrek's lips as, without thinking, he raised his hand. He shook his head. Amused, he sipped his water as he watched the restroom door close behind her.

Five minutes passed. Then another five. An inexplicable unease settled in his chest. He shifted in his chair, trying to push away the irrational worry.

When Mina finally reappeared, he let out a quiet sigh of relief. It was a fleeting feeling. He'd barely begun to relax, the tension easing from his shoulders, when she turned and headed toward the exit. He couldn't believe she was rabbiting. He pushed his chair back, ready to follow, when she reentered his line of sight. Mina's face flushed as the hostess pointed back to their table, a sheepish smile on her face as she retraced her steps.

While she slid into her seat, Derrek hesitated. He didn't know if he should bring up what had just happened. Admitting he'd watched her every move would only invite questions he wasn't ready to answer. On the other hand, if that little detour had been a deliberate act for his benefit, she'd done a damn good job of making him second-guess everything he thought he knew about her.

Before he could decide, the server returned to take their orders.

"Aren't you going to order the chicken?" Derrek asked a hint of challenge in his tone.

Mina folded her menu, her eyes sparkling with the promise of retribution. "I was planning to. Without the sun-dried tomatoes, please."

He gave his order, handing his menu to the waiter. As the server walked away, Derrek leaned back, a faint smirk tugging at his lips. "See? That wasn't so bad."

"Not at all," Mina agreed, her grin unwavering. "But if the chicken comes out dry, I blame you."

"Fair enough," he chuckled. The amusement faded as he studied her. Every smile and glance seemed so genuine. She gave no indication of being anything other than what she appeared to be.

Their eyes met, and the conversation stilled. The weight of her gaze pulled at something deep inside him, a connection he couldn't quite name. For a fleeting moment, he allowed himself to imagine what it would be like to kiss her, to hold her, to—

Derrek jolted as if physically shaking off the thought. Shifting in his seat, he averted his gaze, focusing on the table.

"Is something wrong?" Mina asked, concern creeping into her voice.

He forced a casual tone. "I spoke with Tommy today. He had nothing but good things to say about you."

That was a lie. He hadn't spoken to Tommy Petrov. He'd never even been near the man. But he needed to gauge Mina's reaction to see if her connection with Tommy was as close as it was supposed to be.

Her face brightened, the worry in her expression melting into a bright smile. "You did? I didn't realize you knew Tommy. He's such a dear man—though he can be cranky sometimes."

Derrek arched a brow, disbelief flickering across his face. "You think Tommy is a dear man?"

Mina's cheeks colored. "Well, in his way. He has his moments. How do you know him?"

"I wouldn't say I know him. It's more of a casual acquaintance."

"That makes sense," Mina said with a small laugh. "I've known him for almost two years, and he's still grouchy every time I see him."

Derrek leaned in, his gaze narrowing. "When do you plan to see him again?"

She tilted her head, thoughtful. "Probably in a week or so. He tends to get extra cranky if I bring him things too soon after the last time."

Derrek's stomach twisted at her words. He kept his expression neutral, but inside, anger simmered. They were casually discussing her delivering to a known crime family as if it were as mundane as dropping off groceries. She hadn't specified what she brought him, but his imagination filled the blanks: drugs, weapons, people—it didn't matter. It was all rotten.

"Distribution problems?" he asked, forcing the question past the bile rising in his throat. He didn't know what she would say but knew it would only deepen the hole she had dropped herself in.

Mina laughed, light and unbothered. "Tommy isn't exactly the sharing type."

Derrek's jaw tightened, his voice dry. "I don't suppose he would be."

When their food arrived, the conversation shifted to lighter topics. Mina beamed over her chicken, declaring it the best she'd had in ages. He couldn't say the same for his food. It was like chewing on flavorless cardboard, the texture as unpleasant as sawdust in his mouth. He forced himself to swallow every bite. All the while, he was firmly aware that Mina was exactly what her dossier proclaimed her to be.

When Mina took the last bite off her plate, Derrek set his fork down. He stood, tossing his napkin onto the table. "I'll walk you home." The irritation in his voice surprised even him, but he couldn't help it. The night had been a slow burn of frustration. Mina was perfect. Except, she was a criminal, and the oath he'd sworn to the AOD ensured he could never be with her.

Moving to her chair, he pulled it back so she could stand. She smiled up at him, her face glowing with happiness. He froze when she rose onto her toes and pressed a quick, chaste kiss to his chin. The warmth of her lips lingered on his skin, a tingling reminder of how much she affected him.

"Thanks for dinner. I had a lovely time," Mina said, her voice light and sincere. She smiled at the waiter, thanked him for his service, and started toward the exit.

Derrek followed close behind, his mind a storm of conflicting thoughts and his body tense with unspent energy. They murmured farewell to the hostess, and Derrek held the door open, letting Mina step out into the cool night air.

He turned left, expecting her to walk alongside him, but when he glanced down, she wasn't there. He spun around, half-expecting she'd slipped away.

Instead, he spotted her walking in the opposite direction. With a few quick strides, he caught up and wrapped his hand gently around her wrist. "Where are you going?"

Mina blinked up at him, her expression puzzled. "Home. Why?"

Derrek tilted his head in the opposite direction. "Isn't it that way?"

She paused, looking down the street, first one way and then the other, before meeting his gaze with a sheepish smile. "Oh, you're right. It's so hard to keep your bearings at night, don't you think?"

He didn't think so but wasn't about to say it.

Whether it was an impulse or a need to ensure she stayed by his side, he slid his hand into hers, their fingers intertwining. The subtle flutter of butterflies in his stomach caught him off guard, deepening his frown.

His thumb began to stroke the back of her hand, the movement unbidden yet strangely soothing. He had no control over the gesture—or the chaos of emotions rioting within him. The thought of pulling away felt as unthinkable as inflicting pain on himself. He didn't want to admit how much he craved this small connection, these fleeting moments with her.

Her gaze flicked up to him, her expression curious but guarded. If Mina noticed the shift in his demeanor, she chose not to comment. Her silence was a gift he didn't deserve but gladly accepted. Sharing his thoughts with her wasn't an option.

He just needed to get her home. Then, he could focus on the next steps, on making plans. But the thought of extinguishing her light, of breaking something so vibrant and untainted, filled him with a deep, simmering anger—at her, at himself, and at the impossibility of it all.

He was spoiling for a fight, and he pitied the man who got caught in his crosshairs.

Chapter Thirteen

M ina bit back a sigh as her building came into view. If only she
lived a little farther away—just a few more blocks to delay saying
goodnight. Her date with Chris had been wonderful, far better than she'd
dared to hope.

Even though he'd had a few grumpy moments, they hadn't bothered her.
She could hardly fault someone for having feelings, unlike her father, who
used to lecture or even threaten her whenever she expressed the slightest
hint of emotion.

Chris was different. Vibrant, full of life in a way she found irresistible.
She couldn't help but respond to him, his magnetism drawing her in. It was
the only explanation she had for the spontaneous kiss. A moment of pure,
bubbling happiness that had slipped past her control. How she wished she
could read minds, or at least his! She still didn't know what he thought of
her impulsive act. His expression revealed nothing.

She cast another furtive look in his direction. He hadn't said much on
the walk home, but his thumb brushed over the back of her hand in a
gentle rhythm that sent warmth coursing through her. The unexpected
connection was thrilling yet comforting, a silent understanding resonating
deep within her—a feeling she wasn't ready to let go of.

When they reached the entrance of her building, she hesitated, expecting him to say goodbye. Chris, however, opened the door, beckoning her forward, his eyes twinkling.

"Chris, you don't have to," she began, her voice tinged with gratitude and uncertainty. "I mean, if you have somewhere else to be—"

Her words faltered as his hand slipped to her waist, guiding her forward with gentle but firm pressure. A jolt of warmth shot through her at the unexpected contact, causing her breath to catch.

He flashed her a slow, knowing smile, his drawl as smooth as honey. "You know," he said, his voice low, "a real gentleman would ensure you got home safe. Guess I'll have to try and live up to that."

Before she could respond, a familiar voice cut in.

"Well, well," came Edgar's gravelly tone as he appeared at her side. His wrinkled eyes narrowed suspiciously at Chris. "Back again, are we? Did you decide on a place, then?"

Mina blinked, caught off guard. "Oh, no. Edgar. This is Chris, my *date*. He doesn't live here."

Edgar snorted, unconvinced. "I know that. He was here a week ago looking at the vacant apartment on two. That one's gone now, but others are open on three and five."

Mina shot Chris an apologetic look, mouthing, *I'm sorry.* He seemed to be taking it all in stride. His smile remained in place, and he didn't appear annoyed.

Abel joined the fray before she could explain further, clapping a heavy hand on Chris's shoulder. "Hey, Simon. Decided to rent after all? Just don't pick my floor. I don't need you stomping around all night."

"No, Abel." Mina groaned. "This is Chris. We met at Blossoms a few days ago."

Abel folded his arms and squinted. "I don't forget faces. He doesn't have all the hair now, but those eyes? Same guy."

Edgar stepped closer, mimicking Abel's stance. "Yep. That's him. No doubt about it."

Mina rubbed her temples. "You've been sitting by the front door too long. *This is Chris.* Not Simon!"

The two men exchanged stubborn glances, then shook their heads emphatically. "He's Simon," Edgar insisted.

Chris's wry grin never wavered. "Gentlemen, this has been fun, but I must get Mina home." He leaned down to whisper in her ear, "Shall we make a break for it?"

Mina giggled. "Chris is right. I need to get to bed." She kissed Edgar and Abel on their cheeks, hoping to defuse the situation. "I'll see you both in the morning."

Edgar frowned. "I don't like you going off with Simon here. A man who doesn't even know his name? That's trouble. What do you think, Abel?"

Abel scratched his chin. "I say we toss him out on his ear." He took a step toward Chris, and Mina's stomach tightened.

She quickly laced her fingers with Chris's, giving them her brightest smile. "I'll be fine, I promise. Goodnight!"

Chris tugged her toward the elevator, the tension in his hand betraying his otherwise calm facade. As the doors closed, he murmured, "You've got interesting neighbors."

She moaned. "You have no idea." Reaching for the button panel, Mina paused when she saw the number four already lit. "How did you know I live on the fourth floor?"

He flashed a sheepish grin. "I didn't. I just wanted to get out of there as fast as I could. Lucky guess."

"I'd say," she replied, trying to ease the awkwardness. "Maybe you're psychic." Her attempt at humor landed flat. The corner of his mouth twitched, but his smile no longer reached his eyes.

Without Edgar and Abel's antics, the elevator ride felt oddly subdued. Chris had let go of her hand the moment the doors closed, and the absence of his touch was sharper than she'd expected.

She glanced at him, unsure if she should say something—anything—that would turn the night around. Her thoughts drifted to Edgar and Abel, their behavior replaying in her mind. She'd never seen them act so bizarre, insisting Chris was this "Simon" person. The whole thing was ridiculous—why would Chris pretend to be someone else just to look at the building? Better yet, why would anyone?

Thankfully, it hadn't seemed to faze him. Any other man might have bolted at the first sign of bedlam, but not him. He hadn't argued or made a scene, even though he had every right to. Instead, he'd stayed calm, letting Edgar and Abel play their part as self-appointed sentinels.

She glanced at him again, gratitude softening her expression. "Thanks for not making a big deal out of all that. Edgar and Abel can be...a lot."

Chris's smile returned, faint but genuine. "They're harmless. Dedicated, though—like they're guarding the gates of something sacred."

Mina laughed, some of the tension easing. "They'd love that. It'd justify all the door-staring they do."

The elevator ride ended too soon, the doors sliding open to the softly lit hallway. Her mind raced for a way to recapture the easy connection they'd shared earlier. She didn't want the night to end like this. She had hoped he might ask for a second date or, at the very least, kiss her goodnight.

Chris stepped out of the elevator, his stride unhurried as he turned toward her apartment. With a sinking heart, Mina followed, her hopes crumbling with each step.

"I had a wonderful time," she said, forcing cheerfulness into her voice.

Chris glanced over his shoulder, a small smile tugging at his lips. "Me, too."

He stopped at her door. Another lucky guess, considering the twelve possibilities. She frowned at the gold-plated number. Had she mentioned her apartment number during dinner? She couldn't remember doing so.

Standing so close to him now, Mina hesitated. She couldn't bring herself to open the door, not yet. Everything about the moment felt incomplete. She twirled her key around her finger, fidgeting; she shifted her weight. Avoiding his gaze, she feared what she might see there. She tried to gather her courage, but the heavy and unrelenting silence pressed down on her.

When she finally dared to look up, her breath caught at the heat in his eyes. Chris stepped closer, his hand threading through her hair and cradling the back of her head. His thumb tilted her chin, his face lowering until his lips hovered above hers.

"I know this evening didn't end as smoothly as I planned," he murmured, his voice low and intimate. "But I'd like to kiss you goodnight."

Mina couldn't speak. The intensity of his gaze and the warmth of his hand left her dizzy. She managed a small nod, and his grip on her hair tightened slightly, sending a shiver down her spine. Gasping with surprise and pleasure, she rose to meet his mouth. When their lips met, her world fell away. Her heart hammered in sync with the chaotic swirl of thoughts and emotions overwhelming her.

Her hands trailed up his chest, slipping around his neck as she melted into the warmth of his embrace. Helpless, she clung to him as his kiss filled her with a sense of surrender. Left breathless, her mind was a muddled haze of longing and disbelief. Her eyes were slow to open, only to find his expression guarded. A wave of disappointment washed over her, sending a chill down her spine.

"I have to go," he said, his voice distant, almost strained.

Confused, she furrowed her brow, a knot of worry tightening in her chest. His voice was strange. She couldn't put her finger on what was different, though.

"Okay. Thank you again," Mina replied, though her hands lingered at his shoulders until he stepped back, forcing her to release him. She mumbled an apology, heat flooding her already burning face.

Chris studied her for a moment longer, his face unreadable. She didn't know what he was waiting for. Maybe he wanted her to open her door before he left. Mina slipped the key into the lock, turning it until the click broke the awkward silence. She glanced back, unable to conceal her hopeful expression.

He made a low, frustrated noise, dipping his head to graze her lips with his. She barely had time to process the fleeting kiss before it was over. Without another word, he turned and strode to the elevator, his movements fluid but laced with tension. His gait reminded her of a large cat sulking away after being denied a meal.

Mina watched him go, her heart a tangled mess of emotions. She couldn't imagine what upset him or why he seemed so distant now. Perhaps he had been hoping for an invitation inside. She hadn't seen again the predator-like intensity she'd noticed when they first met until tonight, and it unsettled her more than she cared to admit.

As she closed her apartment door, she realized what had been off about his voice—he'd spoken without a Southern accent.

Derrek rode the elevator down to the bottom floor, cursing himself, cursing Mina. He shoved an impatient hand through his hair. What had he been thinking? He laughed a harsh chuckle at the mess he'd made.

Maybe he could steal her away. There were plenty of places to disappear. Not forever. Just until the people he worked for had new priorities, and the Petrov family forgot about her.

He had money stashed away. Enough to buy a remote place in some forgotten corner of the world. He'd been thinking about leaving the business, anyway. A man can only do this for so long before it starts to eat away at his soul.

He had reached the point of no return. If he had any hopes of having normalcy, family, or children, he needed to walk away before he crossed the line. Perhaps that was why Mina meant so much to him. His soul had recognized her as his saving grace, the light at the end of the dark, impenetrable tunnel he had created for himself. She represented his chance at redemption.

Time was running out for Mina. If he didn't finish the job, AOD would send someone else. He had to make a decision soon. Otherwise, there wouldn't be another opportunity.

The elevator dinged, and the doors opened to reveal Edgar and Abel, standing shoulder to shoulder, their arms crossed, expressions grim. Despite the night's frustrations, a grin tugged at Derrek's lips. He still couldn't believe he had forgotten about them. It was the only explanation for the fiasco that had happened. If Mina had paid attention to those two old men, his cover would surely have been blown. It was a stark reminder of how much she was affecting him.

"Gentlemen," Derrek nodded, stepping forward, only to have them shift to block his path. He hadn't dealt with this kind of stubbornness since his granddad, and now he was facing it twice over. Life had a funny way of repeating itself.

Memories of being fifteen, hormones blazing, and a cocky grin as he rolled his granddad's old truck down the lane. The twin girls next door had been all the encouragement he needed to borrow the truck for a little joyride. The plan had been perfect—blanket, crackers, and a stolen bottle of his grandma's cooking wine. They had been hungry for adventure, and well, he'd just been hungry. He'd coaxed a kiss out of the sisters and thought he'd died and gone to heaven. He'd been convinced he was invincible until he'd driven into the irrigation ditch. The sound of shattering glass and his granddad's fury still made his stomach clench.

"You're not going anywhere until we get a few things straightened out," Edgar said, his tone as sharp as his narrowed gaze.

Derrek swallowed a sigh, memories of his granddad flashing in his mind again. That man had been just as unyielding. He almost heard his voice: *Don't let a pretty face lead you into trouble, boy.*

"Straightened out, huh?" Derrek crossed his arms, forcing himself to stay calm. "What might that be?"

"Mina," Edgar snapped, jabbing a finger into his arm. The unexpected force made Derrek wince.

"She's a sweet girl," Abel said, his fists clenched. "We've taken a liking to her, and we don't want her getting hurt."

"What makes you think I'm going to hurt her?" Derrek asked, unsure if he would like the answer.

Abel stepped closer, his voice low but firm. "Because you're hiding something, Simon—or whoever you are. Don't think we didn't notice you skulking around here last week."

Derrek bristled. He could argue, but Edgar cut him off with a raised hand.

"Save it," Edgar said. "Just know this: Mina's got a kind heart, and I won't stand by while someone like you tramples all over it."

Their words stung more than Derrek wanted to admit, echoing his granddad's warnings from years ago. Maybe they were right. Maybe he wasn't capable of giving someone like Mina what she deserved. The thought twisted in his gut. Suddenly, his idea of running away with Mina didn't hold the same appeal.

Tired and worn, Derrek brushed past Abel and headed for the door. "Don't worry," he said over his shoulder, his voice cold. "It was just a date. I wasn't planning on calling her again, anyway."

The door closed behind him, but the bitterness of his own words lingered.

Chapter Fourteen

Derrek shook the water from his coat, cursing under his breath. He'd barely left Mina's apartment when fat raindrops began splattering on the pavement, quickly building to a torrential downpour that drenched him to the bone. If he hadn't been so absorbed in his thoughts, he would have noticed the storm brewing and got off the streets before the first raindrops fell. This served as yet another reminder of how completely Mina had managed to knock him off balance.

He hung the soaked garment on the hook by the door and left a trail of wet clothes on his way to the shower. A deep chill settled in his bones, but it wasn't from the rain. A persistent, maddening itch crawled beneath his skin, a sensation he couldn't quite grasp. Something about tonight didn't sit right, and no matter how many times he ran through the evening in his head, the pieces refused to fit.

Under the pounding heat of the shower, Derrek leaned into the discomfort, hoping the scalding water would shake loose the elusive detail nagging at him. Mina's performance tonight had been flawless. The "lost on the way to the bathroom" routine was expertly executed, right down to involving the restaurant staff. Mina had a way of playing the doe-eyed victim to perfection. He could almost admire her craft—if he hadn't been the target.

He couldn't figure out what she was playing at. Her warm, amber eyes had radiated a sincerity that was almost impossible to fake. And that kiss... Derrek closed his eyes, his mind replaying the moment. Sweet, unguarded, electric. He'd nearly forgotten his mission altogether, tempted to lock the world out and lose himself in her. A grim smile curved his mouth. She was irresistible, and the thought of letting her go was impossible.

Damn it. Derrek ran a hand through his damp hair. He wanted her more than he cared to admit, but that desire was clouding his judgment. He couldn't afford to be reckless, not with AOD breathing down his neck. If Mina wasn't who they thought. If they were wrong...

He kept returning to running away. It was the only option. He could have her packed and gone within twenty-four hours if she was willing. He just had to decide. Was she worth risking his life for? A part of him screamed *yes!* But the other part of him, the cold, ruthless part, kept him from jumping in with both feet.

It all came back to the troublesome concern that nagged at his mind, a thread that, if he could find the right one to pull, would lead him to what wasn't right.

Derrek stepped out of the shower, steam curling around him as he halfheartedly dried off and wrapped a towel around his waist. The bathroom mirror, fogged and streaked, reflected his moody expression, but he barely glanced at it. As the chirp of his computer pierced through his thoughts, he abandoned the idea of getting dressed and moved toward the desk. His curiosity flared as he powered up the system, hoping Damian had already had the information he'd been waiting for.

Damian's voice filled the room, brusque and to the point.

"I ran your guy, Elijah Cumbers. Retired Navy, now working at an animal shelter. Squeaky clean. If someone fed you this lead, it's garbage. Listen, be careful. I got that itch beneath my shoulder blade. You know, the one that tells me when shit is about to hit the fan. Make sure you get the hell out of town before it does. I don't have time to come and save your ass."

Derrek deleted the message with a scowl. The message disappeared from his inbox. He drummed his fingers on the tabletop, his gaze falling on Mina's open file on the coffee table. Moving to the couch, her face smiled up at him, serene and disarming. He picked up the folder, flipping through the pages, his gut tightening as his eyes paused at Tommy Petrov's name. The "Dear man," Mina so warmly referenced. However, the report painted a different picture: charming, smooth, and never one to lose his cool. He was the schmoozer the family called in to handle deals. Nowhere in the file did it indicate him as temperamental or "grouchy," as Mina put it.

And then there was her travel history. Derrek frowned at the list of remote, treacherous locations she'd navigated in recent years—places he knew well, having been to some himself. Unlike the structured grids and navigable streets of the US, these areas had no roads, let alone names. Survival there demanded sharp instincts, precision, and an unerring sense of direction. It wasn't just difficult—it was the kind of challenge only someone with exceptional skills could overcome. Yet today, Mina had wandered, turning the wrong way down streets she should have known and known well.

Derrek leaned back on the couch, a frown furrowing his brow as a chill of unease washed over him. He had initially thought she was toying with him, trying to get him to slip up. The hoops she'd made him jump through to avoid being caught had grated on his nerves, leaving him simmering with irritation.

His mind flashed back to the restaurant. Her flustered wave, her hesitant steps, and her flushed face as the server guided her to the restroom. She had first turned toward the exit before doubling back to the table. Perhaps it was a mistake. The thought sparked a growing sense of alarm, and he sat upright. Could AOD have gotten it wrong? They were rarely, if ever, mistaken. But if Mina wasn't the intended target, then who was?

The questions gnawed at him. He needed to know where the information had come from. So far, nothing proved she'd done what she was accused of. Yet, there was also nothing to fully clear her. If it was truly a mistake, though—if AOD had sent him after the wrong person—then he wouldn't have to kill her. He could get the right file, complete the mission, and leave her untouched. Everything would be fine.

He shoved the folder aside and stood, his heart hammering. He stormed to the bedroom, dropping the damp towel onto the floor. Jerking on his clothes, his movements lacking the usual finesse.

Despite everything, a nagging uncertainty, a cold knot of doubt, remained in his gut. Something wasn't adding up, and the clock was ticking. If he didn't act now, he might lose his chance to uncover the truth—and protect Mina from a mistake that could cost her life. He was on the edge, and he knew it. If only he could recall what it was that bothered him.

Mina's brow furrowed as the steady, detached voice of her father's voicemail played. She ended the call with a frustrated sigh, scowling at her phone. Three attempts, and still no answer.

She set the phone down on the counter with a little more force than necessary and opened the cupboard, pulling out a ceramic bowl. If ever there was a night for ice cream, it was tonight. Opening the freezer, she scanned her options, seesawing between the refreshing, cool, mint chocolate chip and the sweet reliability of vanilla swirled with salted caramel. Vanilla won out. It was simple, comforting, and exactly what she needed.

Far from satisfied, she rummaged through her refrigerator for the finishing touches: chocolate syrup, whipped cream, and maraschino cherries. Who said she couldn't go all out even if comfort was the goal? Glass clinked as she assembled her creation, a mountain of sugary solace piled high in her bowl.

With her newly loaded dessert, Mina returned to the couch, where her father's letter lay waiting like an unanswered question. She sighed, sinking into the cushions as she placed the bowl on the coffee table. Her gaze lingered on the familiar handwriting scrawled across the pages, unable to resist the pull of those strange, unsettling words.

She had read it twice already, and still, it troubled her. If it was supposed to explain his missed Sunday call, it failed miserably. Apologetic, yes, but cryptic in a way that made her stomach twist. She still wasn't sure what he was trying to say, and the more she thought about it, the more disturbed she felt.

Her father had never been one for nostalgia, least of all about the years before the divorce. Whenever she tried to recall a joyful moment from her childhood, he'd quickly change the subject, treating the past like a forbidden space. That's why the letter felt so out of character. Two pages of rambling, handwritten no less—his pristinely formed script wandering across memories she hadn't thought of in years.

The focus of his letter was a family trip they'd taken to her grandfather's beach house near Sea Ranch three or four years before the separation. They had only been there once, but it was her favorite family vacation. She could still remember the sun on her skin and the gritty, damp sand between her fingers as she searched the shore for seashells.

Her father, though, had spent much of that week lost in his thoughts. He'd been in one of his inexplicable moods, rambling about things she hadn't understood at the time. He talked endlessly about human behavior and how the world's expectations often clashed with the expectations we set for ourselves.

And then there was Icarus. He had been fixated on the myth, recounting it so often that she'd stopped paying attention. She'd dismissed his ramblings as one of his moods—just another odd layer of the trip. It wasn't until reading his letter that she even remembered that detail.

"The world will tell you to soar," he had said one evening as they sat on the deck, the heat of the day fading with the orange glow of sunset. "But no one talks about the fall. Do you know the story of Icarus, Mina?"

She had nodded, her mind half on the shells she'd collected that day. "He flew too close to the sun, and his wings melted."

"Exactly," he'd said, his gaze distant. "The world celebrates the flight, but it's the fall that matters. That's where you learn who you really are."

"Did he die?" She'd asked, her gaze drawn by a flock of seagulls diving towards the water.

"He did. Just as we all must, some are blessed with a long life where others are cheated of time." Her father mused. "It is those who can stop those who steal time that will right the balance."

A breeze from the sea chilled her skin. She rubbed at the sudden chill in her arms. "How do you steal time?"

Her father's eyes dropped to hers. His face held a hollow, distant gaze. "Killing."

The stark memory had her shuddering. It was one of many conversations she'd had with her father. The memories were nonsensical, leaving her with a cold, empty feeling instead of the cozy warmth she craved.

Now, he was asking her to recall something specific from that week, something that, according to him, she needed to remember. But the letter gave no real clues, only vague hints and a sense of urgency that left her unnerved. She had tried, over and over, to fill in the gaps, but her mind came up blank.

Mina leaned forward, picking up the letter again, the paper crinkling under her fingers. There was something buried in her father's words—something important—but without him to guide her, she couldn't piece it together. She stared at her phone, willing it to ring, the silence around her as maddening as the gaps in her memory.

She dropped the letter onto the coffee table, tired of looking at the thing. Even her father's silly puzzles could only hold her attention for so long. Inevitably, her thoughts drifted to Chris.

With a sigh, Mina pressed her spoon into the softening ice cream, the cold sweetness doing little to soothe the rising need his memory stirred. The man could kiss—there was no denying that. Even now, just thinking of those breathless moments outside her door sent a delicious shiver down her spine. His touch had been electric, leaving her both dazed and dangerously hopeful.

But then he had left. The memory of his retreat hit her like an unwelcome jab, the sharp sting of disappointment curling in her chest. She'd replayed it too many times already—the way he'd pulled away abruptly, his face a mask of indifference. The warmth of his presence was replaced with a chill that lingered long after he was gone.

She'd hoped he would stay, if only for a little while, so they could have talked. She hadn't mustered the courage to ask him to stay before he was halfway down the hallway. Maybe Edgar and Abel's embarrassing scene had soured the mood. Or perhaps she'd been wrong to believe that kiss had meant more than a fleeting moment.

Now, hours later, the questions still circled her mind, each one unanswered. In a single evening, her life had unraveled into one uncertainty after another. Her gaze fell to the discarded letter, its crumpled edges a silent reminder of the father she couldn't reach and the man who had left her standing in the doorway. First her father, then Chris—would men ever stop breaking her heart?

Chapter Fifteen

Mina had barely stepped into Squeeze when Jenny swooped in, hooking her arm and dragging her toward a table. Amidst Jenny's rapid-fire questions, Mina couldn't help but laugh as she grasped Jenny's shoulders. "Slow down. I can hardly follow you."

"Stop torturing me. Tell me everything," Jenny demanded, her eyes wide with excitement.

"Okay. Okay." Mina blushed. She hadn't broadcasted her evening plans, but Chris had asked her in front of Jenny, so there wasn't an option of keeping it a secret. "Ask me your questions again, but one at a time. You were giving me whiplash, throwing them at me all at once."

Jenny clasped her hands, squealing in delight. "Did you meet him here, or did you know if from before?"

"I met him at Blossoms. He was buying a special bouquet."

Jenny leaned closer, a sly grin on her face. "So, there's a history."

"If you call one business a history, sure."

"Come on now, it had to have been more than a mere business meeting." Jenny implored with a sly smile. "I saw the way he was looking at you. Even before you bumped into him."

Mina blinked. "He was?"

"When he was standing in line. He only had eyes for you. I could feel the sizzle behind the counter."

"Are you sure?"

Jenny turned, calling over her shoulder, "Hey, Collette, didn't you say that guy was checking Mina out?"

Collette poked her head out from the kitchen, a towel in hand. "Oh, absolutely. He couldn't take his eyes off her. I haven't had a man look at me that way since I met Scott." Collette added with a wistful sigh.

"Focus, Collette," Jenny snapped, though her tone was teasing. "Shouldn't you be watching the bacon?" She turned back to Mina with a grin. "See? Told you it wasn't just me who noticed. So… was there flirting before you bumped into each other? Or was it all part of a master plan?"

Mina's face burned. "Of course, it wasn't! And I think you're exaggerating how he looked at me."

"Not a chance," Jenny said, waggling her eyebrows. "Now spill. I need details, Mina. Don't leave anything out."

"I made a mess of his shirt."

"To which all the women here were most grateful," Jenny quipped. "Did you get a look at those abs? So flat and—"

"Reminded me of Scott's firm tush when we first started dating," Collete called out from the kitchen.

Jenny rolled her eyes. "We've all seen Scott, Collette. You're not fooling anyone." She scowled at the closed door before turning back to Mina. "Anyway, as I was saying, we were all delighted with how nicely that soaked shirt clung to his body. It's been a while since a man like that walked through our doors."

Mina sighed. "Is there a point to this?"

Jenny leaned back with a smug smile. "Just making sure you know how lucky you are. Men like him don't come around every day."

"I know," Mina replied, her voice tight and her expression grim. She was painfully aware of how rare good men were. Chris had seemed like he might be one of them, but now... she wasn't so sure.

Jenny tilted her head, studying her. "Good. Now, where were we? Oh, right—how did this date even happen?"

Spotting a couple walking in, Mina seized the opportunity to escape the awkward conversation. "I don't want to keep you..." she started.

Jenny glanced over her shoulder and frowned at the intrusion. "Oh, my. You're right. Wait right there."

"But I have to get to work," Mina argued, standing to leave.

"No, you don't. I called Kat and told her what was going on. She said to take your time."

Mina raised a skeptical brow. "She did?"

Jenny grinned. "Well, after I promised her a sandwich."

"And there it is," Mina said, laughing.

It took almost an hour for Mina to answer all of Jenny's questions—partly due to the steady stream of customers and partly because Collette kept interrupting with quips about her husband, Steve. From the way Collette described him, Mina was eager to meet the man. He sounded like quite the hunk.

True to Jenny's word, Kat wasn't upset at all about her tardiness. Especially once she got her hands on the sandwich Jenny had sent with her.

"I know you already told Jenny everything, but now it's my turn," Kat said, shooing Mina toward the back. "Brad, cover the front!"

Once Kat had settled on a stool, she unwrapped her sandwich and took a bite. Swallowing a moan of pleasure, she grinned. "So worth it."

Mina laughed, sitting on the stool at her workstation. She never thought she would get tired of talking about Chirs but found the more she replayed the night, the more ridiculous it all sounded. These kinds of things didn't just happen to people.

"Okay," Kat said, leaning in with a curious gleam. "Spill. I didn't believe Jenny when she called this morning, but she wasn't kidding, was she? Who is this guy? It's not like you to go out with someone you just met."

Mina toyed with a rose stem, unable to hold Kat's stare. "It's not. I mean, he wasn't. Do you remember that man that came in earlier this week? The one who ordered a special bouquet?"

Kat's eyes widened. "The tall, dreamy one, with blonde hair and a sexy southern drawl? I didn't realize he had asked you on a date. You made it sound like you weren't interested."

"I wasn't," Mina said quickly, then relented at Kat's skeptical look. "Okay, maybe I was. But he didn't ask for my number, so I thought that was that."

"And running into him at Squeeze was just a happy accident?"

"It seems so," Mina replied, though the coincidence still nagged at her. Her father's voice echoed in her memory, warning her never to dismiss improbable odds as mere luck. What had he called it? The hand of another interfering in your life? She shook the thought away.

"Well?" Kat prompted. "Tell me, how was it? Where did you go? Did he ask for a second date?"

Mina couldn't help smiling. "It was wonderful. He took me to Sinclair's, and we talked for hours. He even asked about Tommy."

Kat's brow wrinkled. "Who's Tommy?"

"Oh, you know, the homeless guy behind the dry cleaners. I bring him food sometimes."

"Right," Kat said, nodding. "But how does Chris know about him?"

"You know," Mina said, frowning slightly, "I don't think he said."

Kat waved it off. "Doesn't matter. What about the end of the night? Did he walk you home?"

Mina's smile softened. "He did. It was lovely. The streets were quiet, and he held my hand the whole way. But..." She hesitated, her brows knitting.

"But what?"

"Well, Abel and Edgar were acting strange. They kept insisting Chris was someone named Simon."

Kat tilted her head. "Why would they think he was Simon? Did they meet him already?"

"That's the strange part," Mina said, shrugging. "They claimed he came in last week to look at the apartment for rent."

"What did Chris say?"

"Nothing. He just smiled and led me to the elevator. I could tell he was annoyed, but he didn't say a word to embarrass them, which I appreciated. If I'm being honest, though, I was irritated too. The whole scene kind of ruined the moment, you know?"

Kat gave a thoughtful nod. "So...did he ask for a second date?"

Mina's shoulders sagged. "No. And worst of all, he didn't get my number. Even if he wanted to call, he couldn't."

Kat frowned in sympathy, resting a hand on Mina's knee. "Oh, Mina, I'm sorry. That's such a bummer."

Mina forced a weak smile. "Me too."

"Well, if it's meant to be, he'll find you again."

"Maybe." Mina's gaze drifted to the flower in her hand, her father's words echoing in her mind: *Never mistake an improbable event for mere luck; instead, recognize it as a sign that someone—or something—is interfering.*

Mina wound up working later than planned. Not that she had any place to be, but she hated walking home at dusk. The shifting light made the shadows seem alive.

She pulled her coat tight against the biting wind, her steps quickening as she moved through the crowd. People brushed past her with heads down, and she veered closer to the buildings, trying to stay out of the flow. Her nerves were already frayed, her date with Chris an endless looping in her mind, the promising start, and the sting of his abrupt departure.

All she wanted was to get home, where she could replay everything, piece by piece, and figure out what she might have missed. Lately, her thoughts kept drifting to her father—maybe it was his letter or because she couldn't reach him. Either way, her father's words lingered, unsettling but persistent. He used to tell her things, things her mother had asked him not to say. Those fragments of advice, once cryptic, felt heavier now, waiting for her to understand their meaning.

A hand shot out as she passed a shadowed gap between two buildings, clamping around her arm. She was dragged into the dark before she could scream.

A gloved hand smothered her mouth. Butter-soft leather pressed against her skin as she thrashed in a panic, her heart hammering against her ribs.

"Shh," came a husky whisper near her ear. "I'm not going to hurt you."

Her breath came in sharp bursts as she stilled, trembling. The hand eased from her mouth.

"I just want to talk. If I let you go, are you going to run?"

She shook her head though the lie burned in her chest. The second she was free, she'd bolt. All she had to do was reach the street and someone would help her.

The grip on her arm loosened, and she took a step toward freedom. Before she could move more than a foot, an iron band wound around her waist, pulling her hard against a solid wall of muscle. She withered. Her scream was trapped once more by an unrelenting hand.

"Tsk, tsk." His low chuckle brushed her ear, sending a shiver down her spine. "Let's try this again. I will let you speak, Mina, but don't scream."

Her stomach flipped. Mina? How did he know her name?

The hand left her mouth. She struggled to turn to look at her captor's face. "How do you know me?" She demanded, her voice shaking. "Why did you grab me?"

"I told you—we need to talk," he replied. "This is life or death, and I need to know I can trust you to tell me the truth."

"And scaring me to death is your idea of a good strategy?" she snapped, glaring at the brick wall.

"Tell me about Tommy Petrov."

"Tommy?" She tried to turn, but his arm tightened, locking her in place. "What do you want with Tommy?"

"That's not your concern. Just tell me what you know."

Her mind raced. Mina struggled to understand what this man wanted with Tommy. She hesitated, terrified of risking Tommy's life. Perhaps he had gotten himself into some kind of trouble.

He must have grown impatient waiting for her reply because his other hand wrapped around her throat, holding her tightly against his chest. His hand flexed, causing her to wince. "Tommy," he reminded, his tone low and warning.

"I—I don't really know that much," she stammered. "I didn't even know his last name until last night. He lives in the alley behind the dry cleaners I use. Sometimes, I bring him food and clothes. That's it. Why? What has he done?"

The man laughed softly, the sound chilling. His warm breath stirred her hair. "Tommy Petrov does not live in an alley."

"I don't know what to tell you," she said, her voice cracking. "The only Tommy I know is an old homeless man who is cranky and likes baked beans!"

Mina gasped as the man's arm tightened. Her chest burned the life being squeezed out of her. "Are you saying you don't work for the Petrov family?" The man demanded. His voice, a rasping growl, made her tremble.

She tried to shake her head but couldn't move in his grasp. "What? No! I don't know anyone named Petrov. I'm a florist—I work at Blossoms for Kat and Brad Moore."

For a moment, silence hung between them, thick and suffocating. Mina's breath hitched. Any second now, she was sure he'd kill her.

His grip on her throat shifted, his thumb brushing her pulse, making her shiver. The hold around her waist eased, and his arm moved up her body until it rested beneath her ribs. His fingers wrapped around her arm just above her elbow. Despite her fear, her heart skipped a beat.

Her mouth parted. She wanted to scream at him. Instead, what came out was a whispered plea. "What do you want from me?"

"Everything."

In one fluid motion, he spun her out of the alley and onto the crowded street. She stumbled, bumping into a passerby.

"Sorry," she muttered, turning back toward the alley.

It was empty.

Chapter Sixteen

By the time Derrek unlocked his apartment door, he was fuming. He hated being used, and the growing suspicion he was being manipulated by some unseen puppet master only fueled his frustration.

The day had gone wrong from the beginning. After spending most of last night reviewing every detail, replaying every encounter, and recalling every conversation, his mind and heart remained at war. His mind saw deceit in Mina's every action, while his heart only saw kindness and sincerity.

After he'd exhausted every memory, he'd reluctantly gone to bed. Only to spend the remainder of the night staring up at the ceiling. Memories of the heated kiss they shared flooded his mind. He'd let himself imagine what it would have been like to follow her inside her apartment, to hold her, to prove the connection between them wasn't just in his head.

By dawn, he had given up on sleep and started reaching out to his contacts. There had to be more to the story than he had been told. Somewhere, there had to be the information he was looking for. Determined to prove his theory, he'd spent the day calling in favors, digging for answers. His FBI contact had sent over what little she could find, but the file on Mina Turner was heavily restricted. All it revealed was the bare minimum: a name, a few addresses, and nothing about the Petrov crime family.

Each dead end only fueled his frustration. By mid-afternoon, he'd given up on his contacts and decided to go directly to the source. He'd tracked Mina through the device in her coat—her purse was still at Squeeze, and her phone hadn't left her apartment.

He still couldn't understand why she'd left her things at these seemingly random places, if not to throw him off her trail. That was a question for another day.

When he finally found her and pulled her into the alley, he wanted to reveal himself and explain. But he'd needed answers and knew fear was the only way to get them.

Derrek pressed his fingers to the keyboard but paused, his jaw tightening. The memory of her trembling in his arms haunted him. He'd imagined her trembling in his arms countless times. But never thought fear would be the cause. He slammed his hand on the desk, trying to forget Mina's terrified expression. Short, sharp breaths escaped him as he fought to control his anger.

His computer chirped, providing him with a much-needed distraction. He typed in his password and hit play. Damian's voice tore through the silence. "What in the hell do you think you're doing?" He barked. "Of all the stupid ass stunts. I can't believe you have made it alive this long. Brother, you call me the minute you get this." The line went dead, silence falling heavily around him.

Derrek swore, blistering the air with his temper. If Damian knew, that meant it was only a matter of time before the cold-hearted bitch found out. By then, he'd be on marked time. Pushing to his feet, he paced the small confines of the room. His movements jerky as he struggled with the urge to run.

He'd already been thinking about running and had worked out most of the obstacles. The only remaining problem was Mina. He still couldn't be sure she would leave with him, but the longer they stayed, the greater the risk she was under. Things were heating up, and unfortunately, not in the way he wanted.

His gaze dropped to his phone. As if on cue, it rang. He snatched it up, not bothering to check the caller. Only two people had this number, one of which was on vacation. "Chris," he snapped, not wanting to hear another lecture from Damian on living his cover.

"Chris? Derrek, honey, is that you? This is Mom. Were you expecting a call from someone else?"

Derrek groaned, pressing his fingers into his eyes. "Mom, now isn't a good time."

"Why am I not surprised?" His mother complained. "It never is a good time with you. How are you supposed to meet a nice girl and settle down if you don't make the time for it?"

He ignored the non-too-subtle jab about marriage. Resigned, he collapsed on the couch, stretching his legs to rest on the coffee table. "I thought you were on vacation."

"I am, and we are having a wonderful time."

Derrek winced at what sounded like a loud crash in the background. "Where are you, Mom?"

"We're in the hotel. We're getting ready to head out, and I wanted to call and tell you before I forget."

He grunted, turning the television on with the volume down. "Dad's fine." He said, figuring that was the reason for the call.

"I know that. I just talked to him before I called you."

"If you are calling him, then why am I supposed to?" Derrek asked, his voice tight with exasperation.

"Because your father will tell you if something's wrong. He only talks about the good things with me," his mother explained. Then, as if she were turned away, she spoke again, but he couldn't understand what she said.

Derrek pinched the bridge of his nose, muttering under his breath. "Mom," he said with a slight whine. "I can't understand you. Are you talking to me?"

"No, dear. I was talking to Gabby. She can't decide what to wear tonight. I told her the red dress, but she thinks it's too daring."

If Gabby still looked like he remembered, he doubted what she wore would matter. The woman was a personification of every homemaker cliché. As much as he loved his mother, he had more important things to do. "Mom, I've got to go. Can I call you later?"

"Wait! I've got a message for you." His mother shuffled something on the other end of the line, then came back. "Alex Hill called the house phone yesterday. He spoke to your father. He wanted to know where you are and if he could get in touch with you. Your father gave him the special number you told us to give out if anyone tried to find you, but I thought you should know. Just in case it was important."

Alex Hill, if that wasn't a blast from the past. He hadn't seen or heard from him in over ten years. Not since the mission they were sent on shortly after completing the AOD training.

"Derrek, is that okay? Did we do it right?"

He could hear the uncertainty in his mother's voice and felt a twinge of guilt. He never wanted this life to touch his family, but even the best-laid plans have their holes. "Yes, Mom. Don't worry about it. I'm sure he will reach me if he needs me."

"Good." His mother said with a sigh. Her usual chipper tone returned. "Now, I've got to run. We are going to this hot new bar." She admitted with a giggle.

His brow furrowed, scowling at the television, no longer seeing the screen. "What do you mean you're going to a bar? I don't think that's such a good idea."

He could practically hear her bristling with indignation. "Oh, no, you don't. I am a grown woman, and I can do as I please. We'll be careful; besides, I doubt there will be all that many men around."

Derrek snorted. No men at a bar, yeah, right. "What makes you say that?"

"Because, Derrek, the waiters are men," she giggled, "and their uniforms are something only a certain type of clientele would enjoy."

He couldn't believe his mother giggled. Not only her, but he could hear a course of laughter in the background. He probably shouldn't ask. Some things were better left alone, but this was his mother, and if he had to hop on a plane to save her from some dangerous, hair-brained idea, he would. "What type of uniform?" He questioned, already dreading the answer.

His mother broke into uncontrollable laughter. He pulled the phone from his ear and waited for her to collect herself. "Mom?" He groaned, her mirth ringing in his ears, before attempting again. "Mom?"

"They wear jeans and suspenders."

Oh, well, that didn't sound too bad. Why his mother found suspenders so funny was beyond him, but what the hell. She was having a good time, and that was all that mattered. "Oh, okay. You have fun."

She giggled again, this time appearing to make an effort to suppress the sound, which caused him to frown. "What's so funny?"

"I don't think you understand. Suspenders and jeans are *all* they wear. The men carry around axes while they take orders. You can even try throwing a hatchet at a target. Doesn't that sound fun? It's called Lumberjack."

"Lumberjack?" He echoed, a mixture of disbelief and resignation washing over him. "You're telling me you're going to the *Lumberjack?*"

His mother's laughter bubbled again, this time joined by distant giggles. "Don't be such a stick in the mud, Derrek. It's a themed bar! It's all in good fun."

Her response left him speechless. If she got in trouble, he wouldn't have far to go. She referenced a bar no more than three miles from his apartment. His mother was in San Francisco.

"It's about time," Damian growled into the phone by way of greeting.

"Yeah, well, I had something personal to take care of," Derrek muttered, not wanting to delve into the intricacies of his relationship with his mother. "What is this all about?" He asked. He decided to play it off as a simple misunderstanding, his voice carefully even, a practiced calmness in his tone.

"Don't pull that shit with me. You and I both know what this is, even if you want to pretend like it isn't."

"And what if it is?" Derrek argued. "It's not like you haven't gone down this road before."

"Not with a mark." Damian snarled.

Derrek swore, threading his fingers through his hair. "How bad is it?"

Damian grunted with approval. "Not as bad as it will be. You have a few days, a week at the most, to finish the job. Then, AOD will send someone else in. You won't want to be around when that happens."

"And if I don't want to finish the job?"

"You're dead. You know the risk. We all did when we signed on. Don't let a pretty face destroy your life."

Ever practical, Damian had a way of breaking the facts down to only the essentials. Derrek's mouth pressed into a grim line. "Does it matter if I don't think she's guilty?"

Damian snorted. "No, not to those who gave you the assignment. They want her dead. Are you going to do the job or not?"

"What would you do? If you knew the person didn't do what they were being accused of?"

"The mission. I'm not paid to ask questions."

"Maybe you should. For example, why is Mina targeted but doesn't live like someone who works around the law? Or why her file is restricted. Who has the capability of locking someone's information up that tight?"

Damian cursed, then said, "Let me look into it. Don't do anything until you hear from me." He paused before stressing, "And I mean *anything*."

"Yeah, sure," Derrek muttered. Then, he remembered his conversation with his mother. "By the way, has Alex tried to get a hold of you?"

There was a lengthy pause before Damian said, "No. Why?"

Rubbing a hand at the back of his neck, Derrek said, "He called my parents' house looking for me. They gave him my encrypted message service number, but I haven't heard from him."

"I see. Don't do anything. All right?"

"All right." Derrek relented.

After Damian hung up, he dropped his phone on the table. Standing at the window, Derrek peered out to the street below. All those people moving about, going on with their lives, unbeknownst to the lethal predator that stood five stories above them. His mouth curled into a critical smile. He'd wait to hear from Damian, only to see if he could learn the truth. Then he'd make his move. He just needed to decide what move that would be.

He looked out over the horizon; a deep unease, a feeling of wrongness prickled his skin like a thousand tiny needles. His mind turned to Mina. Always to Mina. His hands curled into fists as he braced his weight against the window. The glass was cold against the evening breeze. He hated what he did to her today. It twisted at his insides. The next time he held her, he would make sure it wasn't in terror. He never wanted to see that fear in her eyes again.

He couldn't explain how she had come to have such power over him. She held him captive. Already, he was contemplating doing things he had never dreamed of doing. If only he knew for sure, she was innocent, and the façade she presented to the world wasn't a façade at all. Then, as if a light flickered on in his mind, he realized what had been bothering him. The one thing that hadn't added up.

Every move Mina made could have been calculated, a performance designed to deceive him. Every move except one. When she'd hesitated outside of the restaurant, uncertain and confused, she hadn't been faking. That moment had been real.

The truth struck him with the force of a physical blow: Mina didn't know her way home.

Chapter Seventeen

It had been three days since she'd seen Chris. Mina sighed, clipping the stem off of another rose. The red blossom landed atop the growing pile, her hands moving on autopilot. So what if he hadn't called yet? He would... eventually.

She tightened her grip on the shears, pushing aside the sharp sting of disappointment. It wasn't fair to hold Chris to a higher standard. She had plenty to occupy her. Work had never been busier. Between events and private orders, she barely had time to breathe.

If only staying busy could cure lovesickness. She stifled another sigh and snipped off another stem, pretending the pang in her chest wasn't there.

The backroom door swung open. Kat walked in, her arms full of white button poms and pink dianthus. "Hey, Mina," she said, laying the flowers on the back counter. Glass clinked as she lined the vases along the wooden surface. Kat glanced over her shoulder before turning back to her work. "Are the roses almost done?"

"Almost," Mina replied, signaling with a quick tilt of her chin. "You can start assembling with those. I'll be ready to help in fifteen minutes."

"Good. We need to work fast. I have two more arrangements to go out first thing tomorrow morning. Looks like it's going to be a late night. Are you up for it?"

Mina sighed. "Yeah, sure. It's not like I have anything else going on."

Kat raised an eyebrow. "You've been sighing quite a bit today. Everything okay?"

Mina straightened, the shears biting through the thick rose stem with a satisfying snap. "Of course." A painful smile stretched her lips, the muscles in her cheeks screaming in protest.

Kat tilted her head. "You sure you don't want to talk about it?"

Mina hesitated before shaking her head. "No. It's nothing."

"He still hasn't called?" Kat asked, worry creasing her brow.

The words stung more than Mina expected. "No," she admitted, blinking back sudden tears. "It's no big deal. He didn't promise he would."

Kat frowned. "True, but if he wasn't interested in a second date, he shouldn't have kissed you."

The memory of the heated kiss brought a rush of warmth to Mina's face. "He wasn't the first guy to kiss me and disappear."

Kat turned to Mina, her face a mask of irritation.

"Why do you keep defending him? You don't owe him anything."

Mina shrugged. It was a fair question, one she couldn't answer. Her rushed defense of Chris seemed illogical, considering he offered her nothing. Her only excuse was the inexplicable connection they shared. No matter the outcome, she couldn't ignore her undeniable attraction when they met, a pull that resonated deep within.

"I don't know. I just... I thought we had a connection..." Mina let the sentence trail off.

Kat softened. "How about this: give him a week. If you don't hear from him, we'll go out, and you can trash him all you want—no judgment."

Mina laughed through her tears. "So supportive of you."

"Always," Kat said with a grin.

Fresh tears sprang to her eyes. "Is it terrible that I hope I don't have to take you up on your offer?"

"Of course not," Kat said, her face full of compassion.

"I just want what you and Brad have." Mina admitted, a pang of envy making her wonder, "How did you get there?"

With a patient look, Kat gently took Mina's trembling hands in hers. "Don't let what you see fool you. Brad and I have been together for years. Things have not been easy, and they still aren't. We work hard every day to stay together. Each morning, as I wake, I silently renew my commitment to Brad and the life we've built together. And there are days when I can't stand him when life feels unbearable, and I resent the hell out of our marriage, but even on those days, when I am at my lowest, I kiss him goodnight and go to bed hopeful that tomorrow will be better."

Mina didn't attempt to stem the flow of tears; instead, she rose to her feet and embraced her friend. Despite Kat being her boss, Mina always felt a deeper bond between them. Kat was like the older sister that Mina had never had.

Brad entered the backroom, took one look at them, and spun on his heel.

"Hold it right there!" Kat called out.

Brad groaned but stopped and turned back. "Yes?"

The expression on his face was priceless. Mina pressed her fingers to her mouth, stifling a laugh. She almost pitied him, but watching the exchange between him and Kat was far too entertaining.

"Mina thinks it's only fair to give Chris a week to call before writing him off. I think she shouldn't bother. What do you think?"

Brad hesitated. His gaze darted between Kat and Mina. "Uh... do I have to answer?"

"Yes," Kat said with a mischievous grin. "You're the only guy here. Give us a man's perspective."

Brad sighed, rubbing the back of his neck. "Honestly? I don't think I should get involved. This is between her and... Chris, was it?" He looked at Mina, who nodded.

"And to be fair," he continued, giving Kat a pointed look, "neither should you. Let's just get back to work. I'd like to go home at some point tonight."

Kat rolled her eyes but chuckled. "You're no fun, Brad."

Mina draped an arm around Kat's shoulders. "It's okay, Kat. Maybe he's right. Besides, when we go out to bash Chris, you can throw in a few jabs at Brad, too." She added with a wink.

Brad rolled his eyes. "Whatever makes you happy."

Before Kat could respond, the bell over the door jingled, drawing their attention.

Using the distraction to his advantage, Brad indicated the front. "I'll just go see who that is," he said quickly, darting out like his pants were on fire.

Derrek shifted in the front seat of his rental car, lifting his coat collar higher. Not that it did much to hide his face, but it was better than nothing. What was with teenage girls these days? Heat rose in his face as he scowled at the group gathered outside the ice cream shop across from Blossoms, their giggles drawing unwanted attention.

The gaggle of schoolgirls blatantly watching him did nothing for his anonymity. He still couldn't believe one had blown him a kiss. He had to catch himself when the corners of his mouth twitched in a reluctant grin. The last thing he wanted was to encourage them. Shooting them a darker scowl, he turned back to his phone.

Mina's purse and coat pinged inside Blossoms, but her phone still registered at her apartment. He shook his head, a rueful smile tugging at his lips. She'd drive him crazy. It was an invigorating job, keeping tabs on her. She certainly kept him on his toes.

Derrek glanced at the clock on the dash. Damian's call would come at any minute; with it, he'd know what to do. Whisk Mina away or kill her. The thought churned his stomach.

Damn. Derrek's grip on the steering wheel tightened, his knuckles turning white. How had his life come to this?

A car pulled to the curb a few shops down. There was nothing inherently suspicious about it, but the hair on the back of his neck prickled. His eyes narrowed as he stared hard at the windshield. The interior was too dark to make out anything more than shadowy shapes.

His pulse steadied, falling into the rhythm of preparation. His fingers drummed a restless beat on the steering wheel. Instinct screamed for him to move, but caution kept him in the car. His eyes scanned the street for his opening, his guard up. Something was about to break loose.

A vibration pulsed through Derrek's skin as his phone beeped, a sudden, sharp disruption in the quiet.

"Derrek," he answered, voice sharp, forgetting to use his code name. He realized he was in trouble when Damian didn't correct him.

Damian said in an urgent tone, "They're coming."

Though already harboring a sickening suspicion, Derrek asked anyway. "Who?"

"AOD. Abigail sent her pet. Get Mina, get her now, and get out of there. You're blown."

Derrek's blood thundered, ringing in his ears as the urgency of the situation made it hard for him to remain in the car. Every instinct screamed at him to get to Mina. "Is she clean?" Derrek asked. He had to know to be sure. If nothing else, he had to know if he was right.

"Yeah, she's clean. But you've got to move. Now. Call me when you're clear." Damian hung up.

Derrek slipped the phone into his pocket and forced himself to wait. He took one last long look at the street. The parked car down the block still hadn't stirred. No movement. No sign of a threat. Not yet.

He stepped out of the car and into the street, weaving through traffic until he reached the sidewalk in front of Blossoms. Every nerve was on edge, the hairs on his neck practically vibrating. His gaze flicked back to the car. Still no movement.

Pushing the thought aside, he turned toward the shop. His priority was Mina. Everything else could wait.

He shoved open the door to Blossoms, shooting a glare at the bell overhead as it signaled his arrival. The flower shop looked exactly as it had the last time he was here—down to the overwhelming floral scent that made his nose itch.

Only Mina was absent. He told himself not to panic—she was probably working in the back room, just like she had been the first time he'd met her. But his instincts didn't care for logic. A tightness coiled in his chest, and a desperate need roared through him, ready to tear the place apart to find her.

A middle-aged man came through the back entrance. Derrek recognized him immediately as Brad, the shop owner. Mina had spoken glowingly of him, and Derrek's background check confirmed there was nothing shady about the guy.

Brad smiled as he approached the counter where Derrek had once sat with Mina, choosing flowers. "Can I help you?"

Derrek laid his hands on the cool surface, spreading his fingers wide as if the contact could control the war waging inside him. He knew Brad wasn't a threat, but his inner beast didn't care. Right now, he was an obstacle—another barrier between him and Mina. He forced down the primal urge to rip through anything standing in his way.

"Yeah, I need to speak with Mina," Derrek said, his voice tight.

Brad raised an eyebrow. "Is she expecting you?"

"No," Derrek ground out, his teeth clenched as he fought the rising urge to grab the man by the neck and force him to move faster.

"I see." Brad studied him for a moment, his expression unreadable. Then, without another word, he turned and slipped through the back door.

Derrek's patience was a thread stretched thin, every muscle in his body coiled and ready to snap. Then, like the sun breaking through storm clouds, Mina walked in. Confusion flickered across her face, but when her gaze met his, her smile bloomed as radiant and beautiful as ever.

"Chris!" she called, running toward him with unguarded joy. "What are you doing here?"

Relief surged through him as he clasped her hands, her warmth steadying him. But the sound of his cover name made him flinch. Lying to her was getting harder. The truth loomed like a brewing thunderstorm, and time was running out. When she learned who he was, he could only hope she wouldn't hate him.

"I need to talk to you." His voice was low, and his gaze flicked to Kat and Brad lingering in the doorway. "In private. Is there somewhere we can go?"

Mina glanced over her shoulder. At Kat's nod, she tightened her grip on his hand and pulled him into the backroom.

Derrek's eyes darted around, cataloging exits, assessing every detail. Heat surged through his veins—a mix of instinct and the thrill of her touch.

She stopped by a workbench covered with red roses. "What's going on?" she asked, her tone light but curious.

For a moment, Derrek just looked at her, savoring her presence. Two days apart felt like a lifetime. The last time he'd held her, she had trembled in fear—that memory clawed at him. He needed to replace it. The next time he thought of her in his arms, he wanted her trembling for an entirely different reason.

He slid an arm around her waist and pulled her close. Her hands fluttered to his shoulders, and her golden eyes wide with surprise.

"I missed you," he murmured, brushing his lips against hers.

She sighed into the kiss, melting against him, and for a few fleeting seconds, nothing else existed. But the danger lurking nearby forced him to end the kiss. Reluctantly, he pulled back, releasing his hold of her slowly, by degrees. Until only his hands remained on her arms. He couldn't bring himself to sever the connection, instead running his hands down to her wrists.

"Mina," he began, his voice rough, but the words wouldn't come. What? *You're in danger. I was here to kill you.* None of it would make her trust him; trust was the only way he could get her out of there.

He gazed into her golden eyes, shimmering with affection he didn't deserve. "Will you have lunch with me?" He finally asked.

"Now?" A look of disbelief crossed her face. "It's barely ten."

"Call it brunch," he said, impatience creeping into his tone. He wasn't being fair—she didn't understand the risk of waiting.

Her lips curved into a smile. "Sure."

Derrek wasted no time, grabbing her by the hand. He dragged her toward the door.

"Wait," she gasped, stumbling to keep up with him. "Let me grab my coat, and I should tell Kat where I'm going." She turned back as though to go do something.

He spared a moment's glance, "You can call her." He said over his shoulder.

Mina giggled, her hand circling his as she hurried to catch up with him. "Are you in that much of a hurry to spend time with me?" She teased.

Despite the urgency of the situation, a smile touched Derrek's lips. "Yeah, something like that."

He tucked Mina behind his back, pushed the door open, and stepped outside. His gaze swept the street, sharp and searching. A flicker of movement caught his eye—his stomach sank. Clint was already stepping out of the car down the street.

"Shit," he shoved Mina back inside.

"What's wrong?" she exclaimed.

Derrek didn't answer, ignoring Brad and Kat's questions as he maneuvered Mina to the rear of the shop. He opened the back door, relieved to find the alley empty. Turning back to Mina, he cradled her face in his hands. "Mina, you have to listen to me. I need you to meet me at the diner over on Sunset Boulevard. It's two blocks southeast of here."

Mina nodded, her eyes showing her confusion.

He kissed her—quick, almost bruising—the urgency making his touch rough, barely restrained. "Take the alley to the end, then head south two blocks. Turn left at Eighth Street."

She nodded again. "All right," she whispered.

He knew she didn't understand, but he kissed her again and shoved her out the door. Then he went to the front of the shop in time for Clint to come in. Kat gave him a suspicious look before smiling at Clint. "Can I help you?"

Clint smiled, but his attention was solely on Derrek. "Just looking around."

Derrek came forward. He grabbed Clint by the arm. "Let's take this outside."

"Where's your lady friend?" Clint asked with a sneer.

Brad stepped forward, his expression darkening. "Do you two know each other?"

Clint's sneer widened, but his gaze stayed locked on Derrek. "Oh, we've met."

Derrek tightened his grip on Clint's arm, forcing himself to stay calm. "Now, Clint," he growled, his voice low and dangerous.

Their gazes locked, the air crackling with tension.

Chapter Eighteen

Clint dipped his head in feigned surrender and strode toward the door. Derrek followed, pausing only at Kat's worried demand for answers. He glanced over his shoulder and forced a reassuring smile. "Mina's fine. Don't worry."

Outside, a heavy blanket of gray clouds smothered the sky, the air thick with a promise of rain. Derrek watched Clint with the wariness of a predator circling another. "What are you doing here?"

"Isn't it obvious?" A sarcastic sneer twisted Clint's lips. "I'm ordering flowers."

"Right," Derrek muttered, his jaw tightening. "You here on business?"

They both knew the answer, but Derrek needed to stall—Mina needed time to get clear. His mind scrabbled to find a way out. His gaze drifted across the street, landing on the group of teenage girls, each one holding a phone.

Derrek's eyes shifted to the car parked down the street, where a shadowy figure sat motionless in the front seat. His eyes narrowed as he glanced back at Clint. "Who's your friend?"

Clint didn't even blink. "Just me."

A cruel smile twisted Derrek's lips. "And I suppose the shadow in the front seat of your car is your blow-up friend Bunny?"

Clint's jaw twitched, and in a flash, he lunged forward with a jab aimed at Derrek's throat. Derrek sidestepped the strike, narrowly dodging. He clicked his tongue as he circled Clint. "Temper, temper. So, not Bunny, then. What about Mitch? He's always nearby when you're stirring up trouble. Did he tag along?"

Clint didn't bite, his scowl deepening, but his fists remained at his sides. So far, none of Derrek's subtle jabs had pushed him far enough to snap. Derrek's mind raced for a new angle. Then a memory surfaced—years ago, Clint fumbling embarrassingly at a knife-throwing target. He'd always been terrible at it, and Clint wasn't the type to work through his issues.

Derrek's smile sharpened, his head tilting. "You two playing with knives again? Didn't your mother ever teach you knives are for big boys who know how to handle them?"

Clint growled, charging at him with the force of a bull. Derrek dodged again, the narrow miss making his pulse spike. "Careful," he warned, nodding toward the girls across the street. "We've got an audience." Every single one had their phone out, recording their little exchange.

Derrek knew they couldn't keep this up. Sooner or later, someone would call the police. He had to lose Clint before that happened. Mina would almost be to the diner by now.

He studied Clint; the bulging vein over his right eye clearly showed how worked up he was. A few more well-placed verbal jabs and Clint would lose control. And when that happened, he'd make mistakes.

Killing him would be easy. After all, that was the name of the game. Derrek had ended more lives in his thirty-two years than the entire police force back home. The thought didn't bother him—if anything, he'd be doing the world a favor.

No, the problem wasn't killing Clint. It was what would come after.

There were rules.

Although AOD operated in the shadows, it thrived on discipline. Every operative swore to uphold five core creeds:

Rule One: Obey Kill Orders. No exceptions.

Rule Two: Don't Get Caught. Sloppiness was the fastest way to the grave.

Rule Three: Tell No One About Assignments. The fewer loose ends, the better.

Rule Four: Adhere to Mandatory Check-Ins. Loyalty had to be proven regularly.

Rule Five: Never Kill Another AOD Operative. No matter how much they deserved it.

Derrek's hand twitched, the urge to reach for the knife concealed beneath his jacket, almost overriding his need for caution. Even if Clint attacked, killing him wasn't an option. Not if Derrek had any hopes of making it out of this mess alive. AOD had sent Clint, and most likely Mitch, as backup despite Clint's denials. If Derrek killed either of them out in the open, AOD would retaliate. And when AOD came, it came with everything. No amount of skill could save him from that.

He watched Clint, noting the flicker of indecision that crossed his face. Clint glanced over his shoulder toward the car, where the shadowy figure remained unmoving. Derrek frowned, his gaze shifting between Clint and the car.

"Waiting for the green light?" Derrek asked, his tone dripping with disdain. "Just like any good lapdog, waiting for master's approval."

Clint's hands fisted at his sides as he took a threatening step forward, but he stopped abruptly, his posture stiffening. His shoulders squared, and his glare sharpened. A cruel sneer contorted his face. "Tell your little lady friend I'll be watching. She'll be alone sooner or later...and I'll have her then."

The threat shot straight to Derrek's heart. His blood roared in his ears as his hand moved instinctively. He slipped his knife into his palm in a flash of movement, hurling it through the air. The satisfying thud as the blade embedded itself in the meaty part of Clint's shoulder sent a fleeting rush of vindication through him.

Clint howled in outrage, tearing the knife free and tossing it to the ground. Blood seeped through his jacket as he staggered back. His face contorted with fury. "You'll pay for that." Clint bellowed, spittle falling on his chin.

"Pay for what?" Derrek asked his voice light, mocking. "A scratch?" He lifted a brow. "Why don't you run back to your master and lick your wounds?"

Clint's chest heaved with barely restrained rage, his breath ragged and uneven. He stormed toward his car, spewing a litany of curses. Revenge burned in his glare as he cast one last seething look over his shoulder, his eyes promising retribution.

Derrek backed away, never taking his eyes off Clint. His heart hammering with the need to hurry. He'd bought himself time, but eventually, Clint would find him again. And their next encounter might not end as well.

When he was far enough, Derrek pivoted and slipped into the shadows of the alley. The moment he was out of sight, dread surged through him, icy and relentless. Clint backing down didn't sit right. His instincts screamed that something was off.

Maybe it wasn't Mitch in the car after all. But if not Mitch, then who?

All this time, he thought he was the one stalling—but maybe he was the one being played. The entire encounter replayed in his mind, this time seeing it for what it was: a ruse to keep him busy while the wolves circled Mina.

A shudder rippled through him, but he shut it down before it could take root. No. He couldn't let fear control his decisions.

He had to believe she was okay, that she was waiting for him at the diner, alive and safe. If nothing else, he had to hold on to that one truth; otherwise, there'd be nothing left to fight for.

Mina followed the narrow alley, trying to breathe through her mouth. About halfway down, an obnoxious stench hit her, growing more intense with each step. She grimaced, pulling her jacket over her nose as if it could shield her from the odor. Whatever it was, she didn't want to know. Some things were better left a mystery.

Like Chris.

What had that been about? She couldn't stop replaying their encounter, his sudden appearance throwing her off balance as always. Mina smiled to herself, sidestepping a pile of soggy cardboard boxes. Her heart still fluttered from seeing him. He had a way of making her pulse race and her common sense take a back seat.

The things he asked her to do were crazy, but she'd do them every single time—if Chris was the one asking.

Despite the interruption to her work, a surge of joy had filled her at the sight of him. That thrill, the undeniable spark, was still there. But as the excitement began to fade, confusion took its place. What was he up to?

Mina's steps slowed, her thoughts tugging her further away from the stinking alley and deeper into the web Chris always seemed to spin around her.

As the end of the alley approached, she sighed with relief, her pace quickening. The fresh air hit her when she finally stepped onto the sidewalk. "Now," she muttered, brushing off her jacket. "What did he say? Go right to Eighth Street? Or left to Sunset? Where even is Sunset?"

She glanced up and down the unfamiliar street. Most of the buildings were charming old apartments, the kind you'd expect in San Francisco. A tall Victorian-style building caught her eye, its elegant trim momentarily pulling her thoughts from where she was headed.

Caught up in the intricate details of the buildings around her, Mina wandered forward, her gaze darting from one enchanting sight to the next. As she walked by a hotel, her fingers brushed over the ornate trim.

Just as she passed a shop window, something divine caught her eye. Her steps slowed, and her breath hitched. There, displayed beneath soft lighting, was the most stunning pair of boots she'd ever seen. The rich leather seemed to glow, and the bold design added a touch of hellishly sexy allure.

For a moment, everything else faded. All she could think about was how perfectly they'd pair with her new skirt, how they'd make her feel when she wore them.

Excitement bubbled as she pushed open the door. The shop exuded an upscale vibe, a little too fancy for her taste, but the promise of the amazing boots drew her forward. A large crystal chandelier in the entryway cast rainbows across the space. Ornate trim adorned the walls, creating a Victorian-inspired modern design.

She browsed the clothes displayed on the antique mirror tables, her fingers brushing over fabrics as bold colors caught her eye. Before she even reached the boots, she'd already filled a bag with two tops, a soft pair of jeans, and rich chocolate-brown corduroy pants.

A floral skirt with crimson poppies caught her eye, but of course, they didn't have her size. Her smile faded, but only for a moment. It was too good of a day to let something so small cast a shadow. There were still treasures to uncover, and Mina wasn't about to let a single disappointment hold her back.

"Can I help you find something?" A friendly voice interrupted her thoughts.

Mina glanced up to see a saleswoman at her elbow. Fingering the soft fabric of the skirt, Mina smiled sheepishly. "I love this, but I don't see my size."

"I can check in the back." The woman tilted her head, giving Mina a once-over. "Let me guess—are you a four?"

Mina laughed. "Yes. Good guess."

"Oh, honey," the saleswoman said with a grin, "when you've been doing this as long as I have, it comes naturally."

While the saleswoman disappeared toward the back, Mina continued to wander through the store. She loved shopping. There was something grounding about being able to touch things, to feel their texture in her hands.

She picked up a scarf, not because she intended to buy it, but because the fabric looked so soft. She rubbed her palm over the material and immediately pictured the stuffed puppy her father had given her during their summer vacation at Grandpa's house.

The gift had been surprising because it was the only time her father had chosen something for her on his own. Her mother had taken care of birthdays and Christmases. Not that it mattered; gifts had never been important to her. She would much rather have time, which was the one thing her father never gave freely.

Maybe that was why Red had tugged at her heart so much the other day. An ache deep in her chest swelled with longing. Mina brushed the moisture from her eyes. She hadn't realized until now how much Red had reminded her of that little stuffed puppy.

Frowning down at the scarf, she hesitated before placing it back on the table. She didn't need it, especially not for the sake of some long-buried memory. With icy resolve, she turned her back and headed to the shoe section, more determined than ever to get her hands on those boots.

Of course, when she passed a display of glittering gold jewelry, she had to stop. And who was she to turn away a pair of dangling earrings and a delicate bracelet with interlocking circles that would look fabulous on her. Then she spotted a pair of men's socks with a bear on top of a mountain with the words "No Beariers." They were so cute, and so what if she thought about giving them to Chris. It didn't mean anything. They were useful. Everyone needed socks. Right? She worried her bottom lip.

And then, there they were as if a halo of light ascended from heaven, leading her; she found the boots. A surge of overwhelming joy filled her, overshadowing every other thought and feeling. She couldn't swear it, but she thought the boots vibrated in her hands, calling to her.

"Ma'am," the saleswoman reappeared, holding a skirt in her arms, "Good news, they had your size."

Mina beamed. "Fantastic! I don't suppose you could see if you have these beauties in my size?" She held up the boots with reverence.

"I can go check—"

"That won't be necessary."

A deep male voice cut through the moment. Mina jumped, her heart skipping a beat as she spun around, eyes wide. "Oh, Chris. You scared me." She gasped, pressing a hand to her heart.

Her smile faltered.

Chris loomed over her, his towering frame and stormy expression making her pause. Funny, she hadn't noticed how tall he was before, but anger always had a way to make a person appear bigger, didn't it? The cord in his neck strained as if under immense pressure.

Despite his foul mood, Mina's heart danced at the sight of him. Rising on her toes, she brushed a kiss to his chin. But her smile faded as she tilted her head and studied his face. "I thought we were meeting at the diner."

His teeth bared in what she supposed was meant to be a smile, though it resembled more of a snarl. Still pleased with his efforts, she rewarded him with one of her own.

She didn't know what had him so worked up, but the tightness in his jaw and the rigid set of his shoulders told her he was barely holding it together. Whatever it was, his restraint was commendable.

"Oh, good. You do remember. Here I was thinking you were lost or confused." He said between clenched teeth.

His accent was gone again. Maybe it had something to do with his moods. She didn't realize a person could gain and lose an accent at will. She met his icy stare and realized he was waiting for a response.

"I'm not lost," she explained, nodding as his skeptical gaze pinned her. "I followed your directions, but I couldn't remember which way to go once I reached the street. Then I saw this beautiful building…"

Her words trailed off when Chris slipped the bag of clothes from her shoulder. Frowning, she reached for it. "I was going to buy those."

Chris's pointed stare stopped her short. "How? You don't have your purse."

Mina's hand dropped as realization hit. "Oh, snap. I wonder where I left it."

"At Blossoms," he said flatly.

"Oh. Well, I can pay with my phone," she said brightly, glancing at the saleswoman, who nodded in agreement.

Chris's incredulous expression darkened. "You don't have your phone."

"Oh," she murmured, sighing as her gaze fell on the boots she'd been so excited about. "I guess I won't be buying anything today after all." Her forced smile wavered. "I can always come back. I'm sure you'll still have my size."

Chris swore under his breath, snatching the bag and boots from the saleswoman.

"What are you doing?" Mina asked, her eyes wide.

"Buying this stuff," he muttered, stalking to the counter.

Warmth bloomed in her chest as she skipped to keep up with him. "You don't have to," she said out of politeness, though her eyes sparkled with gratitude.

"I know," he replied curtly.

Her grin widened. "Oh, by the way, those boots were the display pair. I need an eight."

Chris shot her a dark look before turning to the saleswoman. "I need these in an eight. You've got five minutes."

Chapter Nineteen

D errek shook his head as he glanced at the three bags she carried, disbelief still clouding his thoughts. The day had spiraled into a complete disaster. After confronting Clint, he raced to the diner where he was supposed to meet Mina. But she hadn't been there.

Every muscle in his body screamed as he fought to smother the panic tightening around his heart. Rage coiled in his gut—he wanted to rip through the place but couldn't risk drawing attention. Forcing his temper down, he questioned every worker, describing a pretty brunette with a perpetual smile and sparkling honey-colored eyes. No one had seen her.

He should have expected it. Following Mina always came with its own set of surprises. But he hadn't anticipated that she wouldn't be where he asked her to be.

He would have stuck to protocol if he hadn't let emotions cloud his judgment. He should have checked his phone first to track her location. Instead, all he could think about was getting to Mina before Chris did—a mistake that cost him precious time. Time he couldn't afford to lose in this race against the clock. He couldn't lose her. Not now, not when he'd just found her.

His heart pounded as he scrambled to find her. He retraced his steps to the alley he'd sent her down. He spotted a faint imprint of her shoe on a piece of discarded cardboard without any sign of struggle. Relief surged through him. He breathed a little easier. At least at this moment, she had been okay. He held on to that ray of hope as if his life depended on it because, in a way, it did.

He still didn't know how he'd managed to find her. It was as if some unseen force had drawn his attention to a yellow building with some kind of intricate detail. He couldn't explain why, but he couldn't shake the gut feeling that Mina would have been drawn to the building.

When he passed by an open door, he heard her laughter—a soft, lilting sound that made him freeze mid-step. For a moment, he thought he'd imagined it, a trick of his desperate mind. But as he spun on his heel, scanning the street, he realized it had come from inside the building.

A surge of something dark and primal took hold of him then. The need to see her, touch her, and confirm she was safe overwhelmed every other thought. It was more than just finding her—it was the desperate desire to feel her life, vibrant and real, pulsing beneath his hands. Driven by this fierce urgency, he moved toward the door, his heart pounding.

When his gaze finally landed on her, relief flooded through him, leaving his legs shaky. He couldn't take another scare like that, not now, not ever. It was by pure luck he had even managed to find her. He had been so sure Clint already had his hands on her. The thought made him break out in a cold sweat.

Looking down at her, relief surged through him again as if a piece of the puzzle had locked into place. Suddenly, the few inches between them seemed too large. He tugged her into his side, draping his arm over her shoulder.

Mina glanced up at him, her bright smile easing some of the tension gripping him. She slipped her arm around his waist, his skin rippling under her touch. The physical response was beyond his control, as natural and necessary as the air he breathed. He hadn't realized the hold she had on him until now.

"Are we going to the diner?" Mina asked, curiosity dancing in his eyes.

He shook his head. "It's too late for that. We need to get out of the area," Derrek said, pausing at a corner drugstore and nodding toward it. "Let's stop in here for a minute."

"Sure." She said, with an air of lightness.

That was one of the things he loved about her. It didn't matter what he said; she never hesitated to follow. As they stepped inside, Derrek cast a final glance over his shoulder. The street was clear, but he couldn't take chances. Pulling her in front of him, he wrapped his arms around her waist, keeping her close as they moved down the aisle.

Mina stood in his arms, her head tilted up as she scanned the shelves with wide-eyed curiosity. She reminded him of a playful kitten, always watching, curious about everyone and everything. He couldn't help but smile at her openness. Leaning closer, he nuzzled her ear and whispered, "I need to pick up a few things. Stay with me, all right?"

Her head tilted back, a bright smile gracing her lips as she met his gaze. "Okay."

He gave her a reassuring squeeze before moving toward a display of prepaid cell phones. Grabbing two, he shifted to the next aisle, scanning for essentials in the beauty section. He couldn't afford to waste time. With his cover blown and his usual resources out of reach, he had to make do with what was available. Tossing his phone earlier had been a calculated risk—AOD could trace it in seconds, and he knew better than to underestimate them. They could find anyone, anywhere. But that meant he'd need another way to reach Damian. He couldn't pull this off alone.

"You need a new phone?"

"Yeah," he said, keeping his voice casual. "I dropped mine."

Her brow furrowed with concern. Derrek wanted to trace the lines. "Oh no. That's terrible! That happened to me last year. Except I dropped mine in a bucket of water at Blossoms. I tried soaking it in rice, but it didn't work. It was toast."

Her grimace made him smile. For a moment, her lightness broke through the weight of the day.

He turned back to the hair products laid out before him and scowled. The options seemed endless. How many types of rubber bands did a woman need just to tie her hair up? His gaze dropped to the crown of Mina's chestnut waves, cascading down her back with a few strands draped over her shoulder. The soft waves made her look delicate—something he found himself drawn to. The last thing he wanted was to make her change her hair, but if it came down to it, he would. There wasn't a thing he wouldn't do to keep Mina alive and safe.

He frowned down at her hair. Lifting the ends between his fingers. "Can you do the knots in your hair?"

Mina scowled, twisting in his arms. "Knots? Are you talking about the hair ties?"

"No, my sisters would do this thing with their hair, and they would tie it up in knots when they played sports and stuff. You know, like twists and stuff?"

"I didn't know you had sisters," Mina said, full of delight.

"Yeah, I've got two of them," Derrek said. "Can you twist your hair that way?" He persisted.

"I wish I had a sister," Mina said wistfully. "I only have a brother, and we rarely talk. I don't even know where he is. I think he worked with my dad for a while, but then they had this falling out, and I don't know what he's doing. Not that I care. He was always so mean. He used to rip the heads off my dolls."

"I wouldn't hold that against him. I did my fair share of decapitations when I was young." Derrek admitted unabashedly.

"That's mean." Mina accused. "I hope your sisters made your army men suffer."

Derrek winked at her. "You know what they say, all is fair in love and war."

"I'm pretty sure that's something only men say," Mina argued. Folding her arms in front of her chest, she glared up at him.

"You may be right." He allowed just to get her back on topic. Trying to get Mina to stay on the subject was becoming more and more of an issue. His mouth twitched with a surprised grin. "About your hair..."

Mina lifted a hand, brushing the hair back from her face. "What's wrong with it?"

"Nothing. I just wanted to know if you can change up the style. "

"Of course I can. I've been doing my hair since I was ten. Braids, ponytails, you name it. I can do it."

Derrek snapped his fingers. "That's it. A braid. So, you can do a braid, then?"

"Yes, do you like them?"

He shrugged, snatching a brush, a comb, and some hair ties. "Not really. But if it keeps your hair tucked under the hat, then I'm happy."

"But I don't own any hats," Mina argued.

"That's okay, I'm going to get you one."

Derrek guided her toward the paper goods section but bypassed the usual items. Instead, he stopped at an end-cap display of wide-brimmed, floppy hats.

Grabbing a black one, he placed it on her head.

Mina peered up at him from under the brim. "It's a little big," she muttered.

He chuckled. "That's okay. I just need your face to not be as visible." He explained, selecting a soft gray to swap out with the black. He slipped a finger beneath her chin and lifted her face. "Which color do you prefer?"

"The gray, I guess. But why do you want to hide my face? Is there something wrong with the way I look?"

He chuckled at the disgruntled sound of her question. Leaving the gray one on her head, he pulled her to the next aisle, where he held up the ugliest sweater he'd ever seen. It was ugly purple, with the large face of a cat and a pun, and it happened to be at least two sizes too big for her.

Mina made a face at him. Looking from the sweater and then back to him. "I am not wearing that." She argued, already guessing where his thoughts were headed.

"Why not? It'll keep you warm." He offered.

"I'm not cold."

"You will be when the sun starts to set."

"By then, I'll have my coat, and I won't need this," she said with a subtle sneer.

Until now, Mina had gone along with everything he had asked of her. Evidently, ugly sweaters were where she drew the line. He didn't put the sweater back, instead, turning it inside out. Because he knew that she wouldn't be going back to Blossoms or her home for that matter. The clothes she had on and the ones in the bags were the only things she'd have to wear for a while at least. Eventually, he would need to take her to pick up some staples, but in the meantime, he needed to make sure she wasn't cold.

"What if we turned it inside out?" He offered. It did little to conceal the ugly color, but only so many options were available for him.

She shook her head, her mouth pressing into the mulish line of stubbornness. "I'm not wearing it."

He sighed, "All right." Without some kind of coat, they wouldn't be able to stay out on the streets as long. He'd have to make the next couple of hours count. His eyes fell to his watch. His mouth pressed into a frown. It'd be tight, but he could make it work as long as Mina continued to go with him willingly. Eventually, she would question him; he only hoped it didn't come until he had taken care of a few things. Because until he understood what was happening, he wasn't about to let Mina out of his sight.

He put the sweater back and pulled Mina toward the front of the store, where the cashier stood with his back to them. His eyes were down as he watched something behind the counter.

Derrek cleared his throat, and the man turned reluctantly. "You ready?

"Yeah. I don't suppose you have the cable car schedule?"

"No, that's all online. You can check your phone, "the man explained as he called up their items.

"Can you at least tell me when it'll be coming down this street?" Derrek asked. He'd already researched every transportation option and printed out a schedule—but like the rest of his supplies, it was at his place, now useless.

The cashier sighed, rolling his eyes. "Why don't you just call for a ride?" he whined.

Derrek's jaw flexed as he clamped down on his irritation, but before he could snap, Mina laid a hand on his arm and smiled sweetly at the cashier. "It's my fault," she said, batting her eyes. "I wanted to ride the cable car. I haven't had the chance yet. Is there any way you can help us?"

Derrek blinked down at her in surprise. Just like that, the man's belligerence melted away, and within seconds, he was rattling off the schedule. "Next one's in ten minutes," he said, far more helpful than before.

Mina thanked the man profusely, laying a hand on his arm, which Derrek didn't care for. He scowled at the contact but couldn't say why it bothered him so much. He had never been the jealous type, but he sure didn't like sharing any part of Mina with anyone.

"Come on," he muttered. "We have to go." After adding the bags to his growing collection, Derrek thanked the cashier for help, even though Mina had gotten the needed information.

He held the door open, letting Mina go in front of him. When she turned right, he caught the end of her blouse, gently tugging her to a stop. She turned, eyes wide with surprise, then smiled and gave him a quick kiss.

Derrek shook his head, his voice gruffer than usual. "What was that for?"

Mina tilted her head, "Isn't that why you stopped me? You wanted a thank you?"

"No," he said, nodding toward the other direction. "I was going to tell you you're going the wrong way. We need to head that way."

Mina's face flushed. "Oh. Right. Of course. Silly me."

He couldn't explain it, but he never wanted her to feel shy about showing him affection. So, as she moved past him, he caught her by the waist, spinning her back into his arms. His lips found hers—hard and fast. He wanted to linger over her, but the busy street wasn't the place to let himself go.

When he pulled back, satisfaction curled in his chest at the deepened flush on her cheeks—no longer embarrassment, but something else entirely. He winked at her bemused expression and tugged her forward.

"Come on," he said, smirking. "We don't want to miss our ride."

Chapter Twenty

Mina stood within the protective circle of Chris's arms, gripping the overhead bar. She wasn't sure why he kept pulling her close—maybe it was instinct, maybe something more—but she wasn't about to question it. Not when it felt so good. His warmth, the steady rise and fall of his chest against her back, grounded her in a way she hadn't expected. She'd never felt this at home with anyone.

It was ridiculous to think she was in love with a man she'd just met, but how else could she explain why her heart raced? The way she wanted to be near him, always? She laced her fingers through his, where they circled her waist. He didn't look down, his sharp gaze scanning their surroundings. Even without his full attention, he made her feel seen. Protected. He held her steady, his grip tightening with each sway of the streetcar.

She smiled to herself, a quiet swell of hope rising in her chest. Chris hadn't told her where they were headed. She assumed it was to the diner. She still hadn't eaten, and it was lunchtime. There'd be hell to pay when she got back to Blossoms after missing nearly two hours of work, but right now, none of that mattered. She was with Chris.

Mina leaned into his strong embrace as the crowded street blurred around them. "Where are we going?"

"I need to pick up a few things I have in storage," he said, his gaze constantly shifting from right to left.

"And then?" she prodded. She didn't need a detailed itinerary, but a general idea would be nice—especially if it included food. As if on cue, her stomach grumbled.

His arm loosened, and he stepped back. His hand remained on her waist, steadying her against the lurch as the cable car slowed. "This is our stop."

He held out his hand, helping her down before crossing the street, his eyes still watchful. He had beautiful eyes—the color of spring grass. She wished hers were more interesting. Brown felt so boring, while his could turn intense, concealing so much. She wondered what was going through his mind when that dark cast settled over his face.

"How close is the locker with your stuff?" she asked, trailing a step behind him as her energy dipped.

"Just a few blocks. We should be there in less than ten minutes."

Chris wove through the crowd, keeping her just behind him. There he was again, shielding her. It would almost be cute if it didn't feel so deliberate, as if there was something to protect her from.

"Chris?"

"Hmm?"

"Is something wrong?" The words seemed awkward, tripping over themselves as she spoke them. She wasn't sure why, but something about him felt...off.

He shot her a quick glance. "No. Why?"

She had to skip to keep up with him. Her breath came in little puffs. "You're practically dragging me down the street, for one thing."

Chris flashed her a sheepish grin and slowed his stride. "Why didn't you tell me sooner?"

Mina shrugged. She didn't want to be a burden. At some point, he was going to realize she wasn't worth the work. If that moment was coming, she wasn't going to rush it.

"I was okay at first." She said.

Chris squeezed her hand. "Next time, tell me before you're about to pass out. It's better to slow down than to have to carry you." His teasing tone softened the words.

They crossed the street and turned down another. The entire time, Mina looked all around; she hadn't ever been to this part of the city and found it as interesting as her little community.

A woman approached them with a beautiful yellow lab. The dog immediately jumped onto Mina and tried to lick her hand. Mina laughed, sinking to her knees. "Aren't you a big boy?" she crooned to the animal. He rolled onto his back, his tongue dangling out of his mouth, and his eyes closed in silent rapture.

"I am so sorry." The woman holding the lease said. "He doesn't usually jump on strangers. I don't know what got into him."

"It's quite all right," Mina said, waving off her concern. "He isn't the first dog to want to give me kisses, nor will he be the last." She scratched his sides. "He is a beauty. What's his name?"

"His name is Rainbow. My daughter named him." She rushed to explain at their incredulous expressions. "But my husband and I call him Red. You can see his face had a hint of red coloring."

Mina's chest constricted. "I see it now. What a good boy you are." She gave the dog one last pat before Chris helped her up. When she looked at him, she was surprised to find an irritated glint in his eye.

"You have a lovely day," Mina told the woman as she pulled Red away. The dog looked back at her, and she felt she had disappointed him for some reason. Which was ridiculous—except that he looked just like Red, the dog Elijah had been holding for her.

Despite the obvious harsh truth, her heart still sank. She couldn't take him. No matter how much she wanted to

Chris ran a hand down her arm. "What's wrong? Did the dog hurt you?"

"No, he was very sweet. He reminded me of a dog I was considering adopting at the pound."

Chris lifted a brow. "You were thinking of getting a golden lab? And keeping him at your apartment?"

Heat flooded her face at his incredulous tone. "I know, I know. It's crazy. I can't explain it. When I met him, I just *had* to keep him."

"Labs need a yard. He'd tear your place apart while you're at work."

"I know," she admitted, her shoulders sagging.

"Besides, dogs are a lot of work."

Mina bristled, squaring her shoulders. "You don't think I could do it?"

Chris shook his head. "It's not that. I just think it'd be tough with your job. You'd be working all day, then coming home and needing to walk, feed, and spend time with him."

"But it would be so nice to have someone waiting for me," Mina added, unable to conceal the longing in her voice.

Chris gave her a searching look before taking her hand again. "We need to keep moving."

"Why?" Mina prodded.

"Why?" he echoed.

"Yes, *why?* You know, as in—for what reason or purpose do we need to keep moving?" she snapped.

A look of surprise crossed Chris's face as he regarded her. Mina flushed and dipped her head. "Sorry, I didn't mean to be testy. I guess I am getting a little hangry."

"Hangry?" He mused, "Well then, I'd better feed you. Don't want you biting my head off."

"That isn't funny," she warned. "I just might."

He laughed, a rich, deep sound warming her from the inside out. "There's the storage facility." He nodded toward a white building up ahead. "We'll grab my things, then I'll buy you lunch."

"Deal." She said, brightening at the promise of food.

Chris hurried his step, forcing Mina to run to keep up. When she grumbled about it, he winked and told her a little jogging never hurt anyone. She glared at his back and growled in annoyance when he practically shoved her inside.

"Chris, what is the rush?" she demanded when his ground-eating strides didn't ease up.

"I thought you were hungry," he said over his shoulder. His customary devil-may-care smile was in place, but the roughish gleam in his eyes was missing.

"I *am,* but I didn't realize I had to *sprint* there," she grumbled.

Chris stopped in front of a small metal roller door and turned the lock until it clicked. With a flick of his wrist, the door rattled open, revealing a single black backpack in the otherwise empty space.

He set the bags on the floor and unzipped the backpack. Taking out the new clothes, he stuffed them into the black bag with little care. Mina winced at his rough handling.

"You can just leave my things in the shopping bag," she suggested, horrified as her new beautiful boots were removed from the box, roughly folded, and crammed into the backpack.

He left out the hat and sunglasses he'd bought for her but paused when he pulled out the cute bear socks she'd grabbed. He held them up, frowning. "Who are these for?" He asked, practically growling with irritation.

Mina flushed, heat creeping up her neck. She didn't want to lie, but she didn't want to admit they'd been an impulsive purchase for him. She sighed and dropped her head when he continued staring at her, clearly not letting it go.

"You," she muttered.

"What?"

Lifting her gaze to his confused one, she blurted, "I got them for you, okay? I thought they were cute, and I wanted to get them. Is that a crime?"

Something unreadable crossed his face, but he didn't argue. He just finished packing in silence. When he stood, the once pristine space was littered with empty shopping bags and torn packaging.

He pulled out two phones—slipping one into his pocket and holding the other up in front of her face. "If I give this to you, are you going to lose it?" His lips twitched with a suppressed grin.

"I *don't* lose things," Mina argued, crossing her arms. "I am always careful with things people give me. You can ask anyone."

"So, it's just *your* stuff you like to leave places."

Her face heated. She didn't love how quickly he'd picked up on that little problem. "Only when it's too much of a bother to deal with." She narrowed her eyes. "Why are you giving me a phone, anyway? I'll have mine back tonight."

Chris didn't answer. Instead, he tucked the phone into his other pocket as if deciding not to take the risk. She never *meant* to lose things—it just happened. And though she talked a big game, odds were she'd lose the thing in no time.

He led her through the maze of lockers, taking an exit different from the one they'd entered. She wasn't surprised when they stepped onto a street she didn't recognize. He'd been doing that all day, and she was coming to expect it. Instead of trying to get her bearings, she let him guide her, using the opportunity to admire all the beautiful buildings. There was so much history in the city. She loved the pulse of it. Something was thrilling about knowing she could reach out and touch a building that had stood since the turn of the century.

Chris wove them through an odd zigzagging route before stopping in front of an older diner tucked beneath a newly renovated high-rise. The contrast between the sleek modern architecture and the diner's retro facade was jarring but endearing. Mina read the sign and laughed at the pun.

When Chris held the door open for her, she stepped inside and smiled. The diner's name took on a whole new meaning. The booths, counters, and chairs looked like they had walked out of an old 1930s movie. *The place really was stuck in the past.*

A man in his fifties approached, offering a half-smile of welcome. Only the right side of his mouth moved when he spoke, the other side strangely motionless, as if time had frozen it in place—much like the diner itself.

He led them to a booth in the back corner. Chris guided her into the seat against the wall and slid in beside her. The space was tight; it forced them to sit close, with his thigh pressed intimately against hers. Mina's stomach fluttered. She wished they were beyond the awkward getting-to-know-each-other stage. She longed to rest her hand on his thigh, but she didn't want to push. She wasn't sure how *welcome* that would be.

As she skimmed the menu, her stomach rumbled.

Chris looked down at her and smiled. "Sounds like we got here just in time," he teased.

Wanting to change the subject, she asked the first thing that popped into her mind. "Is this the diner we were supposed to meet at earlier?"

Judging by Chris's flabbergasted expression, she assumed she'd been mistaken. "Is that not right?" She asked when he didn't say anything.

Instead of answering, he tilted his head. "Mina, which way is north?"

She frowned. "Why do you want to know where north is?"

"I don't. I want to know if *you* do." His arm stretched along the back of the booth, his fingers lightly grazing her shoulder.

"Oh." She hesitated, then pointed. "That way?"

Chris raised an eyebrow. "You sure?"

No. But she wasn't about to admit that. Instead, she gave a wary nod.

"Hmm." He sipped his water, his expression unreadable.

She resisted the urge to demand an answer. If she asked, she'd be admitting she wasn't confident in her answer. *Which she wasn't.* She had a twenty-five percent chance of getting it right. Not great odds.

Trying to focus on the menu, she found herself sneaking glances at him instead. He wasn't in a rush anymore.

She didn't know *what*, but her gut told her Chris was keeping something from her.

She studied his profile, her pulse skipping. He was gorgeous and made her burn, but she *hated* secrets. She'd had enough of them with her father.

Her fingers tightened around the menu.

"What's going on, Chris?"

Chapter Twenty-One

Derrek stilled under her questioning gaze. He knew she would eventually want answers. Sure, she was easily distracted and forgetful at times, but it wasn't from being stupid. Mina was a bright, educated woman with a career and a life full of people who cared about her. He witnessed this every day he watched her. He also knew she was naïve and sometimes too trusting, which was why she so willingly followed a stranger all across town.

It was only a matter of luck she hadn't pressed for answers sooner. He wiped the condensation from his glass as he considered his options.

He could lie to her. He'd done enough of that to let the lie build. But the problem with lies was that eventually, they would crumble, and when they did, he didn't know if she would stay with him. One of the beautiful things about Mina was her willingness to accept him as he was. He didn't want to risk driving her away, not when her life depended on staying with him.

On the other hand, if he told her the truth, a public place would be best to do so. She was conscious of others and wouldn't likely cause a scene. But he couldn't be sure she would stay with him, which was a problem because no matter which path he chose, Mina had to stay with him. She didn't stand a chance on her own. His stomach clenched at the thought.

She set her hand to rest on his thigh, concern burning bright in her eyes. "Are you all right?"

He studied her face. "Yes, why do you ask?"

"Because you looked like you were in pain a moment ago."

He laid his hand on top of hers, reveling in the feel of her so close to him. He couldn't get enough of her. And not just her physically. Her smell. Her smiles. Her innate goodness. Everything about her made him feel. Something he hadn't had in a long time.

He lifted her hand, kissing her fingertips. She blushed, which he loved watching, and gave him a shy smile.

"Tell me about your association with the Petrov family." He asked, studying her and was startled by the color washing from her face. Had she been lying to him? Did she work with them after all, and had this all been some sort of ruse? His stomach dropped.

"How do you know that name?" She whispered. Her voice was tight and strained.

"I think the better question is, how do you?"

She shook her head, her rich brown hair tumbling over her shoulders. "I don't know the name. Not really. The night after our date, a man, a stranger, grabbed me. I never had been more scared in my life."

Derrek tensed beside her, struggling to conceal the guilt turning his stomach. He wanted to forget the whole thing, but now he wouldn't only have to relive it, he'd have to hear it from the victim's mouth. He didn't think he was capable of feeling terrible about the things he did, but evidently, he was mistaken.

"Someone mugged you?" He asked, pressing her hand between his as if to offer an unspoken apology for what he did to her.

"No, he didn't try to take anything. He just asked me about that name. Aside from our date the other night, I had never heard it before. Why are you asking about Tommy? Is he in trouble?"

Derrek gave her a considering look. His brow knitting with conflict. "When you say Tommy, who exactly are you referring to?" He was tired of talking at cross purposes. It was about time they let all the dirty laundry air out.

Mina tilted her head, her confusion evident, but she didn't argue. "Tommy is a homeless man I met a couple of years ago. I don't know his last name, but you seem to."

"No. That man may be Tommy, but he isn't the Tommy Petrov I am referring to. Tommy Petrov is the second son of the elicit crime family centered out of Chicago. He's their go-to guy when they need to broker deals in guns, drugs, or women."

Mina's eyes were wide with horror and disgust. "Why would you think I would know someone like that?" She asked, the hurt evident in her voice.

"We'll get to that. What about the trip you took to the Middle East last year and the one you made to Russia in August?"

Water sputtered out of her mouth, covering the table and part of his shirt. "Oh, fiddlesticks." Mina grabbed a towel and dabbed at the water while choking on her laughter. She paused to look at him and laughed again. Derrek didn't care to be the butt of anyone's joke, and he couldn't help but feel as if Mina was getting a kick at his expense.

"Care to share what's so funny?" he asked with barely concealed ire.

"You," Mina admitted, snickering as she grabbed another napkin. "The farthest I've traveled is to Washington, DC, for a school field trip my senior year. Do I look like someone who would vacation in the Middle East? Trust me, if I am going to go anywhere, it will be on a boat where I won't have any risk of getting lost. Besides, unless there is a promise of golden beaches and lazy days sunbathing, I'm not interested."

Mina's description of her preferred vacation experience aligned more with his imagination than it did with her file, which he was becoming increasingly convinced was bogus. "You've never traveled outside of the country?"

"Never."

Derrek waited while the server slid two plates of hamburgers, fully loaded with a basket of steaming fries, in front of them. After agreeing to let her know if they needed anything, Derrek shifted in his seat, eyeing Mina as she dumped a load of ketchup on her bun.

"What would you say if I had a file saying you were a known supplier and contact for the Petrov family? If you were removed, this would considerably hinder their operations."

Without missing a beat, Mina lifted her hamburger. The contents barely stayed in place as she eyed the bun as if debating where it was best to take her first bite. "I would laugh and say that sounds like fantastic makings of a movie." Then she snorted, taking a big bite of her burger and moaning with delight.

"Is it good?" He asked with a half smile.

She nodded, taking another bite. Half of her toppings plopped onto the plate. "Oh darn." She used her fork to scoop up the precious loot and shoved it back inside. "Don't you hate when that happens? Why do the toppings always have to fall out? I wish I knew how to keep them in place." She muttered around another big bite.

"This is probably just a guess, but I would say it might have something to do with the amount of ketchup you use."

"How can anyone use too much ketchup? That's what the problem is, you know, someone is playing a nasty trick. It's the kind of thing my father used to do."

Derrek frowned in confusion. "Your father tricked you with ketchup?"

"What?" She gave him an incredulous look. "Why would my father trick me with ketchup?"

"I don't know. You're the one who said it, not me." Derrek argued.

Mina tilted her head, "What did I say?"

Derrek sighed, handing her another napkin, when the ketchup dripped onto the table. "You said that the problem was someone playing a trick, and your father used to do that sort of thing all the time."

"Oh, no. I was talking about the hypothetical folder. It's hilarious to think anyone would want a file on me. What would it even say? I wouldn't be surprised if my life could be summarized into a single page."

"Something tells me you are far more interesting than a single page," Derrek remarked.

"Did you know your southern accent disappears when you're upset?" Mina asked without much enthusiasm. Her focus was on salvaging what was left of her destroyed hamburger.

His stomach clenched, and instinct had his muscles coiling. "It does?"

"Yep. It's the kind of thing my father would find very interesting." She admitted, licking ketchup from her fingertip.

"Oh," he leaned back, watching her with the wariness of a hunter. "Why is that?"

"He likes that kind of mind stuff. He would probably want to dissect your brain after you died." Mina made a face before picking up a fry.

"I don't think you ever told me; who is your father?"

Mina shrugged. "He isn't exactly a first date conversation. He's more like the week before you walk me down the aisle kind of discussion." Her face reddened, looking up at him in alarm. "Not that I think that is where this is headed... I'm not that I would mind...if it were that is...I just..." She broke off in helpless horror.

Derrek lifted her hand, kissing its back. And licked a dab of ketchup from her knuckle. She shivered, and his eyes gleamed with interest. "Are you done eating?"

"Yes." She said with a sigh.

He tossed a few bills on the table and rose from his seat. He let Mina pass in front of him, watching her with fresh eyes. His mind replayed every twist and turn she had taken him down. Derrek smiled with wry humor. He needed to get in touch with Damian. It was the only way he'd know what was happening and why Mina was up to her pretty little neck in the middle of it all.

As far as dates went, this was far from conventional, but Mina was thrilled. Chris had bought her a present. Granted, it was an ugly hat that he shoved onto her head the minute they stepped outside, but still, it was sweet. He had also paid for the cute things she had found in that little shop—she'd have to remember that place. She wanted many things but couldn't afford to buy them all at once. And her boots. She almost forgot about them. Just thinking about them made her heart flip in delight. She couldn't wait to try them on.

Chris grabbed her hand, holding her close to his side. She didn't mind the contact, but the gesture felt more protective than romantic. It reminded her of how her mother used to clutch her wrist in the grocery store—making sure she didn't wander off.

"Chris," she started. His grip tightened almost like a flinch. She frowned at his back. "Chris, will you take me back to Blossoms?" She took a look around. "I honestly don't think I could find my back on my own."

"I need to find a library," he said over his shoulder, his head on a swivel as he led her across the street.

"Okay, but I need to get back to work. Kat is probably already mad that I've been gone this long. And I don't have my phone to call her." Mina thought to add.

"You can use the phone at the library." His pace quickened, forcing her to skip slightly to keep up.

"Why can't I use one of the phones you bought today?"

"I don't want the number linked to anywhere you go."

His tone was brisk, almost cold. Mina tried not to let it sting. Chris was like a pendulum, his mood swinging wildly from one moment to the next. She didn't understand why it mattered if his number was connected to her—unless...

A chilling thought struck her, sending a wave of cold through her veins.

"Are you married?" The words tumbled out, her voice barely above a whisper.

He barely spared her more than a quick look of disbelief. "No."

Still, unease settled in her stomach. Her steps slowed, but the abrupt tug on her hand yanked her forward again. She wanted to demand he stop, to explain himself. How could he be so caring one minute and then drag her through the streets the next without so much as an explanation?

"Chris, I don't like this," Mina admitted, her voice trembling despite her best efforts to keep it steady. "I want to go back to Blossoms."

He must have heard the fear in her voice because, without warning, he veered sharply, pulling her into the shadowed recess of a building. Before she could protest, he pushed her gently against the wall, shielding her from view.

His hands framed her face. His touch was uncharacteristically soft despite his grim expression.

"Don't be afraid," he whispered, running a finger down her cheek. "I can't explain it to you right now, but I need you to trust me. You can't go back to work, or you're your apartment. It's not safe." He spoke with an urgent, insistent tone. "I need to get to the library, and then I'll check us into a hotel. But for now, you have to trust me. Can you do that?"

She stared up at him, searching his face. There was no arrogance in his expression, no manipulation—just open, raw sincerity.

Could she trust him?

She knew she shouldn't, yet she did.

"Okay," she murmured. "I trust you."

Something in his eyes shifted. And then, before she could react, his lips were on hers.

This kiss wasn't soft or teasing—it was demanding. A test, a challenge, a claim. He wasn't just kissing her; he was *taking* something from her. Her trust, her desire—maybe even her heart.

A shiver ran through her as she clung to him, her fingers fisting into his shirt. She had never felt this way before. This raw, aching *need*. Her senses swirled in a sea of desire and pleasure. Chris lifted his head, his eyes dark and stormy, a stark contrast to the crooked smile that quirked his lips.

"We have to keep moving," he said, gripping her hand once more. "It isn't safe on the streets."

Mina followed, her heart still hammering.

Okay, so maybe she was playing with fire—following a man she barely knew, letting him pull her into something she didn't understand.

But suddenly, it didn't matter.

A smile played on her lips as she kept pace with Chris. Even as dark clouds gathered overhead, her heart felt lighter than it had in a long time.

Chapter Twenty-Two

The public library stood tall and inviting. As Mina and Chris passed by, a group of schoolchildren waited to board a bus, their laughter ringing over the hum of city traffic. Mina smiled as she watched them play, their joy momentarily drowning out the world around her. Chris held the door open, ushering her inside.

Mina stood at the threshold, mesmerized by the towering rows of books and vaulted ceilings. Dwarfed by the sheer size, Mina spoke in reverence. "This is beautiful."

"Yeah?" Chris flashed a curious smile. "You think so?"

"Don't you?" Mina wandered forward, overwhelmed by everything around her.

"I didn't realize you like books," Chris said, leading her past the shelves to a section filled with community computers.

"I love books but don't have much space, so I usually read on my phone or tablet. But if I ever have a home big enough, I want a library—one filled with the most colorful, cheerful books I can find."

"The story doesn't matter?"

"Of course it does, but that's why I'd only pick the bright colors. What kind of sad or scary story could hide behind a vibrant yellow?"

"Huh," Chris muttered, considering her words. Then he motioned toward the computers. "Look, I need to check something. You can sit with me or look around—but if you do, stay where I can see you."

"I'm going to look around." Mina grinned, already knowing her answer. But as she turned to go, Chris grabbed her hand and gently tugged her back into his protective embrace.

"You'll stay where I can see you?" He prodded.

She didn't care that he sounded gruff or his accent had disappeared again. He'd let her in, showing her what lay beneath his guarded exterior. If he needed reassurance, she'd give it to him gladly.

Rising onto her toes, she kissed his chin. "I promise."

His arm tightened around her waist, keeping her on her toes. "Why do you kiss my chin?"

"You don't like it?" Worry crept into her voice.

"Oh, I like it," he admitted. "But an inch higher, and I'd be a hell of a lot happier."

Before she could respond, he pressed a quick, firm kiss to her lips, sending her pulse through the roof. Then, just as swiftly, he let her go.

Mina walked away on wobbly legs, disappearing into the towering shelves of books.

True to her word, Mina stayed within the aisles, always keeping Chris in sight. She didn't know what had him on edge, but she trusted him—and that was enough for now. Soon, he'd explain everything, and then she could make an informed decision. Until then, she was content to wait and see.

By chance, she came across a book on plants, the colorful spine drawing her attention. She flipped through the pages, mesmerized by the vibrant images of flowers and greenery. One day, along with her dream library, she wanted a beautiful garden full of lush plants and fragrant flowers full of color. The thought made her smile, but it was short-lived. Then she realized she still hadn't told Kat where she was.

In the center of the room, an older woman with white hair and silver-framed glasses browsed a book. Mina approached with a soft smile. "Hi, I was wondering if there's a phone I could use. I left my cell at home."

"You can use the one at the checkout counter near the front entrance." The woman whispered back.

Mina thanked her and eyed the counter where Chris sat. It was in his line of sight, albeit a little further than the books, but he did know she wanted to call Kat. Mina weighed the decision until she pushed away her reservations. There was no harm in calling Kat, even if Chris was acting paranoid; there was no reason for her to do the same.

The phone rang twice before it was picked up on the third. "Blossoms, how can I help you?" Kat's cheerful voice rang in her ear.

"Kat, it's Mina."

"Mina." The warmth vanished from Kat's tone, replaced by urgency. "Where are you? Are you all right? I swear if that man hurt you—"

"Chris didn't hurt me! Why on earth would you ever think that?" Mina pushed down the wave of guilt. She should have called sooner. There had been no reason to worry Kat this way.

"After Chris took you to the back, some guy came in looking for you, but Chris seemed to know him. I thought they were going to fight right there in my shop. Luckily, Chris led him outside. We watched from the window—Mina, he threw a knife into the guy's shoulder."

Mina's stomach lurched. "Chris stabbed someone?"

"Is it a stabbing? If someone throws a knife, wouldn't it be called something else, like maybe slashing? Gouging?"

Mina pressed her fingers into her temple. "I—Kat, I don't even know what to say. Is the guy okay?"

"Oh yeah, he just pulled the knife out like it was nothing and walked off."

Mina felt sick. Her legs quavered, and she needed to sit. Her eyes flicked to Chris, still focused on the computer. Then she looked at the door, at freedom.

"Kat, can you come get me? Or Brad? I don't know how to get to Blossoms on my own."

"Of course we can. I'll come right now. Where are you?"

"I'm at the library, the one with the tall ceilings."

"Okay. I know where that is. I'll be there in ten minutes. Just wait out front for me."

"Okay, thanks, Kat."

Mina hung up, her hands trembling. She looked at Chris again, her chest tightening. She didn't want to leave him. But how could she stay? At best, he was a knife-wielding lunatic. At worst... she didn't even want to think about it.

Chris glanced up and smiled at her. She forced herself to wave. The second his attention returned to the screen, she moved toward the exit, her pulse pounding in her ears. She took the stairs two at a time, nearly stumbling in her rush.

A statue stood to her left, large enough to hide behind. She glanced at the plaque beneath it.

"Where trust dies, mistrust grows."

Mina swallowed hard and turned away. She told Chris she trusted him—was this how she proved it?

She hovered in uncertainty, torn between choices, until a hand settled on her shoulder.

The computer hummed as Derrek typed in his password. He hated using public computers for personal files, but necessity left him no choice. His only hope of reaching Damian was through his secure massaging program.

He glanced up, catching sight of Mina a few aisles away, hovering over a book. A smile tugged at his lips before he could stop it. She trusted him. Just like that—no questions, no hesitation. He hadn't lied to her. He *would* tell her the truth, all of it—just as soon as he had the information he needed. Until then, she had to hold on. She had to stay with him.

Derrek knew he was asking a lot, but Mina had already proven herself. Every time, she rose to the occasion. Soon, they'd be locked away in a hotel room, the world shut out. Then he'd tell her everything—his past, his real name. He already knew how he'd do it. Touch was powerful. He'd rub her feet while he told her the truth, let his hands soothe away her anger. And when words weren't enough, he'd kiss away her frustration, show her with his body what he couldn't with words.

The screen lit up with messages. He pulled out a pad of paper, jotting notes as he skimmed them. He wouldn't be able to call Damian now, but as soon as he and Mina were far from here, he could stop long enough to place a call.

The first message was from Alex. Derrek frowned as he read what Alex said. He wrote his number and a note to remind himself to ask Damian. Then he moved to his next message. It was from Clint. He scanned the words but deleted them. He didn't know how Clint got his number, but he wasn't going to get into a game with him and risk slipping up. Mina trusted him, and the thought made him warm inside. He wasn't going to let her down.

Finally, he had a message from Damian. His heart thrummed loudly in his ears as he wrote the information down. The air around him sizzled, putting him on alert. He looked up to find Mina on the phone. Her smile was genuine, though there was a hint of tension around her eyes. He knew she wanted to call her boss, and that was probably what was bothering her. Her boss was upset she wasn't coming to work.

Derrek turned his attention back to the screen, making a few more notes when every cell in his body screamed for him to move. He looked up.

Mina was gone.

His entire body went still. He scanned the room. Nowhere.

Forcing himself to remain seated. A hasty pursuit was pointless, leaving him exposed and achieving nothing. He typed in a virus to wipe any digital trace of his activity and shut the computer down. Slinging his backpack over his shoulder, he strode toward the exit. He didn't bother checking the aisles. She wasn't lost. She had *chosen* to leave.

Someone had gotten to her.

The thought sent a sharp spike of fury through him. Someone had whispered in her ear, poisoned her against him. And like any predator, he wasn't about to let someone else take what was his.

Mina *belonged* to him. She knew it, even if she was confused right now.

He pushed through the library doors, his eyes sweeping the crowd. He tried to ignore the sting of Mina's disappearance, but the ache was gnawing at him. Then—relief hit him like a punch.

She was near the steps, glancing over her shoulder, nervous.

Good. She *should* be nervous. She didn't know what was coming for her yet.

But she would soon enough.

A growl rumbled in his chest as he closed the distance between them. He reached out, gripping her shoulder and spinning her to face him.

"Going somewhere?" His voice was low, rough.

Mina's eyes widened in fear. She screamed, but the sound cut off as recognition sank in. For a heartbeat, he braced for her to fight, to struggle. Maybe he'd let her. Maybe he'd say to hell with it and let her go. But those thoughts were fleeting and completely vanished when she threw herself into his arms instead of running as he expected. Her arms wrapped around him; her body pressed tight against his.

"I'm so sorry." She whispered against his skin, her lips brushing his neck.

He shuddered. His arms locked around her, gripping her tightly. He let himself drown in the scent of her, the feel of her.

"What happened?" His voice was gruff, unsteady. "Why did you leave the library?"

She shook her head.

"You aren't going to tell me?" He asked in wry disbelief.

She shook her head again.

He exhaled sharply. "Will you at least tell me why you're shaking? Are you cold?"

"No," she breathed. "I'm afraid."

His chest tightened. "Of?" He prodded.

Her voice was barely a whisper. *"You."*

He took the hit like a quick jab to the stomach. His heart was tortured by her confession. He cupped her face, tilting it up to meet his gaze. "No, baby. Don't be afraid. I would never hurt you. Never."

She pulled away, putting a small but unbearable space between them. Worry clouded her features. "It's not that. It's this *feeling*. I don't know what to do with it."

Relief surged through him. He had her. She felt it, too. He wanted to move mountains, to change rivers, anything for her.

His fingers slid through her hair, brushing it from her face. He dipped his head, about to kiss her, when a movement caught his eye. His head snapped up, and he swore. He grabbed Mina's hand and yanked her toward the street.

"We need to go. *Now.*"

"What's wrong?" She gasped, trying to keep up with him.

He didn't want to make her run, but the need to get away was imperative. "They found us. Can you run?" He asked.

"Who's found us?"

"Grim reaper's minions." Derrek looked over his shoulder; he ran across the street, ignoring the blare of angry horns.

A car horn blared as he dragged her across the street, weaving between angry drivers. At the next corner, he pulled her into an alley, pressing a phone into her hand. His fingers gripped her shoulders hard enough to bruise. He *needed* her to listen.

"My number is the only one programmed in. You *only* call me. Understand?"

She nodded.

"I want you to run as fast and far as possible. Find somewhere to hide. Call me in one hour. If I don't answer, move and call again every ten minutes until I pick up."

Her lip trembled. "What if you never answer?"

A tear slipped down her cheek. He wiped it away with his thumb, swallowing the tightness in his throat. He searched her face for answers to questions he didn't know.

"I will."

She hesitated. He shoved her forward. "*Go. Now.*"

He watched as she vanished into the crowd, his heart a tangled mess of desperation and rage.

Then he turned.

A dark smile curved his lips.

Time to deal with Clint.

And this time—he'd make sure the bastard *stayed* down.

Chapter Twenty-Three

Derrek came around the corner just in time to meet Clint's fist. Pain exploded across his jaw, sending him back a step. His vision blurred, but he shut out the pain. He couldn't afford to slow down. If he did, he'd die.

Before Clint could press the advantage, Derrek drove a sharp kick into Clint's left side. The grunt that followed was satisfying, but Derrek wasn't fooled. He knew Clint could take a hit but needed to keep him off balance. If Clint recovered, Derrek would be in serious trouble.

While Clint was hunched over, followed up with a swift right hook aimed at Clint's face. Clint tried to deflect, but his reaction was sluggish, and the punch landed squarely enough to snap his head back. Clint grinned, smearing away a trickle of blood with his hand.

"Not bad." Clint sneered. His foot shot out, catching Derrek in the leg. Pain lanced through his thigh, his knee buckling. Derrek hit the concert, the pavement grinding into his skin. He swore, taking a breath. He couldn't stay down.

While Clint loomed above him, the people walking along the sidewalk scattered. Women startled screams. A man's voice cut through the commotion, yelling, "Someone call the police!"

Five minutes. Maybe less. He needed to end this now and get out before the cops arrived. Clint alone wasn't a problem. He was an idiot, and his attacks were powerful but clumsy. But Derrek's stomach clenched when Mitch and Stuart pushed through the throng.

Mitch, a bulkier clone of Clint, cracked his knuckles as he approached. His strikes were strong but sluggish. Derrek could outmaneuver him easily. Stuart, on the other hand, made Derrek wary. Stuart never fought fairly. He even sacrificed his teammates if it meant winning.

Clint grinned as Stuart and Mitch came into view. "Stuart, the girl went that way." He barked, jerking his chin in the direction Mina had fled.

"She has a name," Derrek growled.

"So? Soon, it won't matter much what you call her. Stuart."

Stuart smirked, sauntering off with a deliberate ease. Derrek watched him go, curling his fist. He hoped Mina ran the weasel in circles. If anyone could do it, she could.

Derrek tried one last time to end this before it started. "Clint, there's been a mistake. Mina is innocent. You can't do this?"

Clint hesitated, confusion flickering in his eyes. "Mina?"

"Dammit, man. Don't you even know the name of the woman you're supposed to kill?"

"I'm not here to kill a woman. That's Stuart's assignment."

"Oh, and what's yours then?" Derrek demanded.

"To kill you." Clint spat, his lip curling into a sneer.

"Don't let me stop you." Derrek taunted, motioning him forward.

Predictably, Clint and Mitch charged together, heads down like battering rams. Derrek waited, timing the moment, sidestepping at the last second. The two men collided in a tangle of limbs. Clint roared, struggling to his feet, and swung. Derrek ducked, the punch sailing past his ear, and countered with a quick right hook to Clint's ribs. The impact reverberated through his fist, and Clint doubled over, gasping.

Two minutes.

Dropping low, Derrek spun and drove his boot into Mitch's stomach. The force of the blow sent Mitch crashing into the wall behind him, crumpling to the ground.

One minute.

Clint lunged, and Derrek braced, taking the hit, white stars flashing in his vision. The punch left Clint open; Derrek took the chance and sent his elbow into her neck. Clint staggered back, choking, and tripped over Mitch's sprawled form.

The wail of sirens grew louder, piercing through the chaos. Derrek tipped his head, a faint smirk tugging at his lips. "That's my cue, boys." Without another glance, he melted into the crowd, his heart pounding as he moved in the direction Stuart had taken.

A cold fury burned in his gut as his feet struck the pavement. Stuart was only a few minutes ahead of him. If Derrek pushed harder, he could reach him before he got to Mina. Fear clawed at him, but he shoved it aside. He couldn't afford to panic—not now. Stuart was after Mina, but she was smart and resourceful. She'd find a way to stay ahead of him. She had to.

Mina ran until her lungs burned and the stitch in her side became unbearable. The trail of her hot tears stung her skin as the cool, salty sea breeze brushed her face. She wiped them away, but the tears persisted, blurring her vision.

She never imagined herself running for her life in a situation like this. And yet, here she was, trudging through unfamiliar streets, exhausted and afraid. She'd always thought she had more gumption than this. Was she really this weak? Crying like a child, for heaven's sake.

What was the matter with her? She'd faced scary situations before. Well, nothing quite like this.

Was anyone chasing her? She didn't see anyone. She'd operated solely on the sheer terror in Chris's voice when he told her to run. She might have posed a question or two and even argued if he'd calmly asked her to walk away. But the urgency in his tone had sent her into a blind panic, his fear igniting her own and driving her forward. Far away from Chris, doubt gnawed at her; had she overreacted?

Mina risked a glance over her shoulder, her nerves practically crawling out of her skin. No menacing figures. No footsteps pounding behind her. No one who resembled the stereotypical bad guy. Just a startled man who jumped in alarm when she turned. It probably wasn't nice to laugh, but his wide-eyed look had been memorable. A giggle bubbled up before she could stop it. What was the proper etiquette for scaring a random stranger? Should she apologize?

She snickered, her mood lifting. For a brief moment, she forgot the fear, the panic, and the uncertainty of the situation. Her cheerful disposition reasserted itself. Exploring the city wasn't so bad, especially during the day when the streets were crowded with people. She crossed the street impulsively, changing direction and heading toward the sun. It almost became a game, following the light as it peaked through buildings and trees. The warm rays kissed her skin, rejuvenating her spirit.

Mina stopped at a street corner, waiting for the light to change. A man stood nearby, separated by a woman with a small child. She turned to offer a polite smile, but the gesture froze on her lips. The way he looked at her made her skin crawl. Instinctively, she backed away, bumping into someone behind her.

"Hey, watch it!" the woman snapped.

"Sorry." Mina stammered, her eyes never leaving the man.

The light switched, signaling it was safe to walk with its insistent beeping. Mina raced across the street, daring a glimpse over her shoulder. The man followed with the crowd, his pace unhurried, but his gaze stayed locked on her. Ice flooded her veins. Mina couldn't explain it, but she knew. This was who Chris had warned her about.

She didn't wait. She ran. Her heart thundered as her shoes smacked against the pavement. Her breath came in shallow gasps, and the blood rushing in her ears drowned out the world around her. She wanted to scream, to cry out for help, but the words stuck in her throat. Desperation gave way to panic as her eyes searched the streets for a police officer, for anyone who could help her.

It might have been desperation or sheer blind luck, but Mina darted into a busy intersection, narrowly avoiding a car. The driver slammed on their brakes, shouting curses, but Mina didn't stop. She sprinted to the other side of the street and only then dared to look back.

The man stood at the far curb, his smile chilling as he licked his lips. Mina shuddered, stumbling backward into an older couple. She sobbed an apology, tears springing to her eyes. Without waiting for their response, she turned and fled.

She didn't know where she was going; all she knew was she couldn't stop. After a few random turns, Mina slowed, abandoning her frantic pace. Her only hope was he couldn't follow her trail. Only when she thought she was safe enough to rest did she look at the towering buildings surrounding her. None of them were familiar.

"Uh-oh," she whispered, turning in a circle, looking for something she recognized. Anything that could help her know where she was.

"Don't panic," she muttered, clutching the phone Chris had given her. She gripped it tightly, terrified she might drop it. It was her only lifeline. Without it, Chris would have no chance of finding her. There were too many places for a person to disappear.

Fear clawed at her throat, making it hard to breathe. She wanted to call him, beg him to come find her, and take her home. Tears welled up as the crushing reality of her situation settled over her. She didn't understand what was happening—or why. All she knew was she wasn't safe.

Mina wandered aimlessly, each step leading her further from the security of her familiar life. It felt like hours had passed, though a glance at the phone Chris had given her told her it had only been thirty minutes. She checked it compulsively, terrified she might miss his call or, worse, forget to call him. The almost laughable thought made her lips curl into a humorless smile. As if forgetting to call him was something she would do. Not when she was jumping at her own shadow.

Her eyes darted nervously from face to face, expecting the man to reappear at any moment. Her stomach churned as fear made her movements jerky. She couldn't understand how people moved around her going about their business while she was running for her life. She wanted to scream out her frustration. She wanted to call the police.

The phone in her hand taunted her. She could call Kat and Brad. They'd come to get her in a heartbeat. The temptation gnawed at her resolve despite Chris's warning. He wasn't there. She was on her own. He wouldn't know. Or maybe he would. Chris had an unsettling way of knowing things.

Lost in her spiraling thoughts, a flicker of movement at the edge of her vision caught her eye. Her heart seized, panic clawing its way through her chest as she whipped her head around. Her eyes widened as she gasped for air. She turned to run and collided with someone, the impact hard jarring her momentarily out of her frightened state.

"Oh! Easy there, sweetheart," said a woman with an inviting smile, her blonde hair piled high in a nest of curls and stiff bangs. The warmth in her voice barely registered through Mina's terror as she looked back over her shoulder. Only the man she swore she'd seen wasn't there. The crowd shifted and parted, leaving a space where her nightmare had stood.

The woman's smile didn't waver, though her expression grew more concerned. "You all right? You dang near ran me over just now."

Mina flushed, her face burning as she tried to steady her breathing. "Sorry," she mumbled, glancing over her shoulder again. "I thought I saw someone..." Her voice trailed off. What could she even say? *I saw a man who was trying to kill me.* Not exactly the kind of thing you told a stranger in the middle of a busy street.

The woman tilted her head, her curiosity mingled with a motherly warmth. "Honey, we're all seeing folks. Who do you think you saw? And why do you look like you've seen a ghost?"

Mina blinked, her vision swimming as the woman seemed to blur and multiply before her eyes. One moment, there was one; the next, there were three—each with the same perfectly coiffed hair and sincere smile, their expressions an uncanny mirror of concern and curiosity.

"Look at the poor lamb, Tami. She's shakin' like a leaf," said the woman to Mina's left, stepping closer. The other two followed suit, cocooning Mina in a wall of motherly warmth.

"What happened to scare you so?" asked the tallest of the trio, her dark skin crinkling around eyes that shimmered with concern.

"Phyllis, feel her fingers. She's cold through to the bone," declared the shortest of the three, her wide frame taking up what little space remained.

Mina glanced helplessly from face to face, unsure whether she wanted to laugh or cry. Every time she opened her mouth to speak, one of them would cut her off with another exclamation of concern.

The blonde woman Mina had bumped into seemed to be the group's leader. Seizing Mina's hand, she smiled warmly and declared, "You're coming with us. We're just headin' to a quaint little restaurant. I'm goin' to buy you lunch, and you're goin' to tell us all about it."

Chapter Twenty-Four

Mina's mind raced, first in dread, then in amused delight. She could no more stop the tide of the three women surrounding her than she could halt a rolling wave. Instead of resisting, she let herself be pulled along, the three women clucking over her protective as hens.

From their chatter, Mina gathered they were best friends celebrating Gabby's birthday. They had spent days exploring the city and were due to fly home tomorrow.

The restaurant they chose was on the roof of an older building rich in the city's history. The outdoor dining area offered breathtaking views, and tall space heaters were spread throughout to combat the evening chill.

The women ordered enough drinks and appetizers to break the table. Gabby chuckled when Mina asked why. "Because we're celebratin'."

"Oh, right," Mina said, blushing. "Happy Birthday."

"No, not that," Gabby said with a grin. "We're celebratin' *you*."

Mina's eyes widened. "Me. Why?"

"Because if anybody needs a little pick me up, it's you," Tami explained, sipping her drink. She leaned forward, eagerness gleaming in her eyes. "Now spill. Who are you runnin' from?"

Gabby leaned forward, too. "And why?"

"Yes, what happened?" Phyllis asked.

Mina bit her lip, glancing at the phone in her hand. Her resolve crumbled under their curious gazes.

"Oh, it's been a nightmare. I met this man..." she began.

"I *knew* it!" Phyllis proclaimed, raising a finger. "All messes start with a man."

"Amen," Tami and Gabby chorused, laughing.

"I'm sorry," Phyllis patted Mina's hand. "I interrupted. You were saying."

Mina fought back a smile. "Yes, well, this man took me to dinner a few nights ago, and then I didn't hear from him."

"Typical," Tami muttered. "I raised my son to be better than that. Not that he's ready to settle down just yet, but he knows how to treat a woman right. Not leave her hangin' in the breeze."

"Yes, you did, Tami," Gabby agreed. "He's a good boy."

"Handsome, too," Phyllis added.

Mina cleared her throat. "Anyway, I had practically given up hope, then he showed up at my work and asked me to lunch this morning. I was excited, but it was only ten. He didn't care and insisted we go right then. I thought it was a little strange, but honestly, it was kind of exciting, too." She paused, leaning forward. "As we were about to go out the front door, he shoved me back inside. A little roughly, I might add."

The women all nodded with understanding.

"The next thing I know, he's rushing me out the back door, telling me how to get to some diner. But I only remember half of it, which I forgot the moment I stepped into the alley. It was disgusting." Mina admitted with a grimace.

"I don't believe he'd do something so dangerous. Imagine sendin' a delicate flower like you into a scary alley." Tami complained, her mouth set in a sour line.

"This young man doesn't sound like a keeper," Gabby said.

"Well, now, ladies, let's not jump to conclusions," Phyllis said, turning to Mina. "Was *this* the man you were running from?"

"Oh, no," Mina said quickly. "Chris would never try to kill me. I admit he scared me when he caught me trying to leave the library, but only because he was trying to protect me."

The women gasped, startling the waitress who arrived with their food. "I'm sorry, were ready for the plates?"

"Yes, of course." The women bustled with the skills of years of mothering, making space for the ten dishes.

They waited a beat for the waitress to leave, and then all eyes turned to Mina.

"Someone is trying to kill you?"

"Are you sure?"

"I can't believe this."

Mina couldn't decide which question to tackle, her mind flitting between them. "At first, I didn't believe Chris when he told me. But when I was walking alone, a man appeared... and the way he looked at me—I knew he wanted to hurt me." She shuddered. The image of the man's face seared into her memory.

"Oh, you poor thing. "Tami crooned. "Why don't you call the police?"

"I don't know. Chris gave me a phone and told me to only call him," Mina explained. "I can't thank you enough. I was so scared." Her eyes clouded with tears. Gabby clucked and put an arm around her.

"There is nothin' to thank," Gabby said, sliding a plate in front of Mina. "Now, let's put this mess aside and eat. We'll mull this over and help you come up with a plan."

For the first time since Chris told her to run, Mina smiled with hope. Perhaps things weren't as terrible as they seemed.

Derrek was hot on Stuart's trail. He'd lost him for a minute, panic clawing at his chest until he'd caught sight of him.

And then, Mina.

His breath hitched, and his thoughts scattered. A roar of rage erupted inside him, propelling him forward.

Then, as if Mina had sensed danger, she darted across the street.

Derrek hated to see the fear on her face as she glanced back, her wide eyes frantic. His stomach twisted as Mina fled into oncoming traffic, horns blaring, burnt rubber searing the air. By only sheer luck, a car swerved, narrowly missing her. His legs nearly gave way. He roared in fury, the sound tearing through the surrounding turmoil.

Startled faces turned to him, the crowd scattering to clear his path. Stuart's gaze left Mina to lock on him.

"You bastard," Derrek growled, the words raw in his throat.

His fist shot out, driven by anger. He missed, grazing off Stuart's shoulder as he sidestepped. Stuart spun on his heel. A fist came out of nowhere, slamming into his gut. Pain exploded through him as the air rushed from his lungs. He doubled over, clutching his middle.

Derrek glared at him through narrowed eyes. His teeth bared as he reevaluated. He deserved to be knocked on his ass. Charging in without a plan, drunk on emotion, was never a good idea. Stuart was a calculating bastard. Nothing ever ruffled his feathers. If he continued to allow his anger to make the decisions, he was going to have his ass handed to him. He couldn't let that happen. Mina needed him.

"When are you going to learn? You make it too easy." Stuart taunted. Then he tilted his head as if studying him. "What are you getting involved with a job for? Not that I haven't done so myself a time or two, but it never stopped me from finishing the mission. I never pegged you for the type to mix business with pleasure. Although…" he paused, a cruel smile curving his lips. "after seeing her for myself, I can see why you wanted to play a little first. I might do the same. It'd be a shame to waste such a tasty piece of ass."

"If you touch her, I'll kill you. The oath be damned." Derrek growled. The thought of Stuart anywhere near Mina made him break out in a cold sweat, but now it was worse. He'd shown his hand, and Stuart was too astute to have missed it. Now, if Stuart caught Mina, he wouldn't kill her and be done with it. No, Stuart would want to play with her first, and no one wanted to play like that.

Stuart lifted the line of his brow. "Still adhering to the code, are you?"

"I didn't think it was an option."

"For some," Stuart admitted with a shrug. Then his gaze locked on Derrek, sinister and dark. "Others…"

He let the words trail off, and the meaning was clear. There were operatives within the AOD who were not bound by the code of conduct. The idea was too appalling to give any weight to. But if it were true…Derrek shuddered.

Then he realized what the odd gleam in Stuart's eye was. He was going to kill him. Derrek's mind searched for an out. A way to delay. He'd already given Mina time to get away, to get lost, but he needed to lose him too. Unlike Stuart, Derrek wasn't prepared to break any of the codes, even if it was tempting.

From the corner of his eye, a cable car was approaching. The light would change any minute, giving way to a surge of people crossing the street. If he timed it right, he might manage to slip away, but he would go in a different direction than Mina. As much as he wanted to go after her, to make sure she was safe, for now, she was safer on her own.

The bell of the cable car rang as it drew close. Derrek smiled, taking a step back. "As fun as it's been talking with an asshole like you, I hear my music calling."

He stepped off the sidewalk into the street. Stuart sneered, lunging forward, but Derrek was faster. His heart hammered as he blended into the crowd, losing Stuart in the crush of bodies. On the other side, he hesitated as his body turned to follow Mina. It took all his willpower to force his body to go the other way. With each step, his heart sank. She'd be okay. Maybe if he kept telling himself that, it'd be true.

In the meantime, he needed a place to lay low and call Damian. An hour had been long to tell Mina to wait before calling him. They didn't need that time, but *he* did. Without having to worry about Mina overhearing his conversation, he could call Damina and hopefully get some answers.

He didn't find his opening for another fifteen minutes. When he came across a coffee shop with a nice little outdoor dining area. Going inside, he ordered a drink, smiled at the barista, and got a free muffin for his efforts. Once outside, Derrek found a table far removed from everyone else. He sat with his back to the wall, his left side shielded by a pillar holding up the patio roof.

With his back covered and his stomach full, he shifted his focus. Pulling his phone from his pocket, Derrek looked around, his eyes searching. He knew it would be impossible to relax. Not now, not when everything was tenuous at best.

Derrek let the phone ring until Damian's voice asked for him to leave a message. Derrek swore, rattling off the new number, and demanded a call back ASAP. He ended the call, but what he wanted to do was throw the damn thing.

Patience had never been a strength, and now it was being tested to its limits. He had time. He reminded himself. Mina wouldn't call for a while yet. He had a good view of the street and anyone who might pass by. He might as well take a break.

Derrek settled into his chair, his eyes, concealed by the dark lenses of his sunglasses, allowed him to watch without anyone being aware. He watched people all the time, so much so he could often tell the shady characters from the virtuous ones. It was probably why he struggled with the assignment from the beginning. Mina never betrayed that darker side he so often saw in people. He wanted to know what Damian had found, and the waiting was killing him. When Damian called early, he'd wanted to know more, to know everything, so he wouldn't be forced into a dangerous situation blind.

No such luck. Not only had he gone into it blind, but he'd also handled it terribly. Mina had almost gotten caught twice. He frowned, staring at the name written on the cup. His brow puckered as he focused. How had they found them at the library? He supposed it could have been a routine check, and they spotted Mina. It wasn't like she was easily missed or forgotten.

Unless she'd told someone where they were when she'd called her boss, he should have warned her against giving anything away, which reminded him. Why had Mina been outside? He wanted to shake some sense into her when he realized she'd gone. Didn't she realize the danger she was in? His hands curled into fists. She was driving him crazy. The only other woman who drove him nuts but whom he would do anything for was his mother—and by some stroke of luck, he hadn't run into her yet.

Chapter Twenty-Five

Mina sputtered on her drink, water spraying out over the table. "I'm sorry," she gasped, laughing so hard her sides hurt. She couldn't remember when she'd had such a fine time. Tami had been relaying stories of her children, especially her son. Although Tami didn't say, Mina suspected the woman had a special spot for him.

"Gabby and I had hoped he'd take a shine to Glisten, Gabby's oldest daughter. But they grew up together, and I think they consider each other more like siblings. It worked out right and tight for Glisten, though. She married a nice young man a few years back. How many kids do they have now, Gabby?"

"Two. Little angels. She just told me they got another on the way. Six months out, yet." Gabby said with a note of pride.

"Now, Phyllis has boys. They are just as wild and reckless as my son, but at least they have settled down now." Tami turned to Phyllis. "She got one grandbaby coming soon. Don't you, Phyllis."

"Bobby and his wife. Just heard last week, it looks like two." Phyllis said, looking like a cat who just ate a canary.

Excited squeals erupted from the women at the table. Mina smiled in delight. It was nice to be wrapped up in the woman's chatter. Their bright, carefree laughter lifted her burdens. For a moment, she almost forgot what troubled her.

Then, like a splash of icy water, the stark reality hit her, a cold shock that stole the warmth from her thoughts.

What time was it?

Her hands scrambled for the phone Chris had given her. She was supposed to call him. How could she have forgotten to call him? Relief washed over her when she lifted her napkin and found the phone waiting underneath. The screen lit up with four missed calls. Each one was placed a minute apart.

Her pulse spiked. She grabbed the phone, intending to call him back, when it vibrated violently in her hand. Mina jumped, heart hammering, nearly dropping it. Her fingers trembled as she swiped to answer.

"Hello?" she said, trying to keep her voice steady.

"You were supposed to call me fifteen minutes ago. Are you all right?" Chris roared in her ear.

She winced and pulled the phone away, shooting a pained look at the women at the table.

"Is that your man?" Phyllis whispered loud enough for everyone to hear.

Mina nodded, though she wasn't sure how to categorize what Chris was to her. Meanwhile, Chris was still talking—fast, frantic, demanding. She barely caught a word of it. She seized onto his last question and cut in. "I haven't seen anyone. I ran into some lovely ladies on the street, and we're having lunch."

Chris went silent for half a second. Then, a low growl. "Lunch?"

"Yes, *lunch*," Mina said primly, bristling at his challenging tone.

"Where are you...*exactly*?"

She shifted in her seat, acutely aware of three pairs of eyes locked on her. "I don't know, *exactly*," she replied, mirroring his impatient tone. What did he have to be so cranky about? She was the one who was running for her life. It only seemed fair to indulge in some good, clean fun. Mina covered the phone's mic and leaned forward. "Where are we again?" she asked the group. Tami told her the restaurant's name, which she repeated to Chris.

"I'll be there in fifteen minutes," Chris said, his voice dropping into something almost pleading. "Don't move until I get there, all right?"

"Sure," Mina said with a smile. Then, before he could hang up, she added sweetly, "Oh, and Chris..."

"Yeah?"

"Take your time."

The entire table burst into laughter.

"He's on his way," she told the group, grinning.

"I see." Tami looked thoughtfully at the table. "I suppose now is as good a time as any to figure out this mess. I'll not have her out on the streets again without a firm plan in place."

Gabby was the first to come up with an idea, and the others nodded in agreement. Each woman offered Mina a piece of clothing. If Mina looked different enough, she could pass by unnoticed.

Mina agreed as long as they each left her an address to return their things. Mina had Phyllis's scarf wrapped around her hair and half of her face, with the hat Chris had bought her perched on top of her head. Gabby contributed a knitted poncho in vibrant pink, and Tami gave her a sweater to stuff under her shirt to make her look pregnant. Mina giggled as she maneuvered the fabric under her shirt, trying to smooth away any awkward lumps.

"Stand up, let's have a look at the overall effect." Gabby insisted.

Mina rose from her chair and did a slow spin. Her arms held out wide.

"Not bad." Phyllis mused, sitting back in her chair. "Just make sure you keep the scarf covering your mouth. It's a dead giveaway."

Mina touched her lower lip, frowning. "It is?"

"Yep, it is." Gabby agreed. "It's too wide and full. Men will look at your mouth and instantly know it's you. Maybe she could try bitin' her lip." She suggested.

"That's not bad. But Gabby, you can hardly expect her to do it all the time." Tami complained.

"I'm not askin' her to do it all the time, just until she gets wherever it's safe," Gabby argued.

"As long as she keeps the scarf up, she'll be fine," Phyllis said with a nod.

"I can't wait to meet this Chris character." Tami mused. "It seems to me he could use a firm talkin' to. To think of what you've gone through because of him." Tami huffed, working herself into a lather.

Mina's eyes widened as the women bristled like hens, ready to peck Chris apart. She winced, nibbling her lip. "Perhaps I should wait for him downstairs."

"What did he ask you to do?" Tami inquired.

"To wait right here," Mina sighed, sinking in her chair. She'd grown very fond of these women in the short time she'd spent with them, but that didn't mean she was prepared to have them corner Chris, bombarding him with questions. She shuddered at the thought.

Unfortunately, she didn't have a chance to come up with any kind of plan. Chris was there. A sharp wave of relief hit her at the sight of him. She wanted to run to him. To throw her arms around his neck. He was the one solid reality in the sea of chaos the day had become.

With the focused energy of a predator, he advanced towards her. His eyes were hidden behind sunglasses, but she could see the worry around his mouth. She knew that look.

She smiled at him, waving him over. The ladies at her table turned to look. Her smile faltered when his steps did. He stood frozen in the middle of the dining area, tension stiffening his frame. "Chris?" she called, confusion tightening her chest.

Then, as if coming to face the gallows, Chris approached the table with a wariness that startled her. He stopped by Tami. His hands tucked into his back pockets as he rocked back on his heels.

Mina opened her mouth to ask him if something was wrong, but the words were lost in a chorus of startled laughs and joyous reunions.

"Derrek! I can't believe it. What are you doing here?" Tami exclaimed. Rising from her seat, she hugged Chris. Or perhaps it was Derrek. Mina watched the scene unfold in confusion.

Phyllis pushed back her chair and circled Chris in a hug. Proclaiming he seemed bigger than the last time she saw him. Gabby hopped from foot to foot as she pranced around the three. She giggled and laughed. "Did you decide to surprise your Mama, or did your father put you up to this?" Gabby wanted to know.

Mama? The word struck like a slap. Mina's stomach coiled. The heat of humiliation crawled up her neck. Not Chris. Not Simon. She couldn't believe she had been so gullible. Questions flooded her mind, one after another, until only one beat at her struggle against tears. Who was he?

Mina rose from her chair. Although Chris...no Derrek!...was answering the many questions being thrown at him, his focus remained locked on her. She cursed his sunglasses. She wanted to see his eyes to read the carefully concealed lies hidden there.

A fool. Again. She couldn't breathe past the crushing shame. Unable to even offer the most basic goodbye, Mina fled. The world blurred, but she ran, pushing through tables, ignoring the stunned voices behind her. She only needed to get away.

Her heart hammered as she raced to the elevator. She didn't look behind her; she didn't want to see if he tried to come after her.

She heard Derrek call her name, but she ignored him. The elevator door slid open in time for her to slip inside. She hit the close button. The doors shut on Derrek's angry face. She jumped when his temper pounded at the metal separating them. Mina sagged backward. Her legs trembling, she rubbed her arms, tears slipping down her cheeks.

She didn't know what to do now. Chris had been her next step, no Derrek! Not this stranger who lied so easily.

The elevator ride was slow, stopping at what seemed like every floor on the way down. The people who joined her cast curious glances her way, but no one commented on her distressed state. When the final chime of the bottom floor sounded, Mina sagged. She didn't know where she was supposed to go now. Nor did she know where she was. She could always call Kat, but that scary man was still after her, and she didn't want anyone to get hurt because of her.

Mina stepped into the lobby of the building, her head down. She moved with the crowd from the elevator toward the door, letting flow make the decisions for her. She barely made it two steps before colliding with a solid chest. Strong, firm hands gripped her arms. She looked up—straight into Derrek's furious gaze. He half dragged, half pushed her to a hallway she hadn't noticed before.

Her heart pounded, confusion and something dangerously close to anticipation colliding inside her. She didn't know who Derrek was, but his touch sent an electric charge through her body, sharp and undeniable.

Derrek stopped at a door labeled family restroom and shoved the door open. He ushered Mina in and locked the door behind them. In a flurry of movement, Mina found herself pinned against the wall, Derrek looming over her. His finger threaded through her hair as he tilted her face up.

She wanted to shove him away and demand answers. But the warmth of his body, his familiar scent, made her falter. When his lips claimed hers, she forgot—just for a moment—the lies. Her fingers tangled in his shirt as she clung to him, relieved to see he was all right and he'd found her.

When he ended the kiss, he only pulled back enough to peer into her face, his gaze searching. "Are you okay?" he asked, his voice husky with desire.

Mina trembled; she wanted to press her hand over his heart to feel the steady rhythm of it beating. Instead, she let her head rest there. The tears that threatened suddenly let go. She clung to him as her body wretched in deep-seated sobs. He gathered her into his arms, rubbing her back, cradling her neck as she cried.

When her tears dried and she quieted in his arms, Derrek still held her. He reached for a paper towel, handing it to her. Mina blew her nose, mortified to have to do something like that in front of him. "I'm sorry," Mina said, her breath catching. "I don't know what came over me."

"It's been a long day," Derrek whispered into her hair. He kissed the top of her head and gave her a gentle squeeze, then forced her to release him so he could step back. His eyes searched her. "Are you all right?" he asked again.

Mina sniffled, nodding miserably. "I'm okay."

"Good. Now, we need to get out of here." He said, handing her a phone. She looked at it, puzzled.

His mouth twitched. "It's the one I gave you earlier. You left it on the table upstairs."

Mina blushed. "I did." She took the phone. She needed to do better. She couldn't risk losing this connection to Derrek. Not when she was so lost without him. "Thank you."

Derrek slid an arm around her waist, pulling her in for a quick hug. He kissed her temple and nuzzled her ear. "It will be okay. I promise. As long as you listen to me, we'll make it through."

Mina dipped her head back, looking into his face. The same face she had come to trust with her life. Yet she didn't know him at all. "Who are you?"

Chapter Twenty-Six

Derrek could think of hundreds of places he would rather be. Ten of which were within walking distance. Thirteen years on the job and none of it had prepared him for this.

Under different circumstances, he might have considered making a run for it. But instead, here he was: stuck in a hotel room with the woman he desperately wanted and his mother.

He glanced from his mother to Mina, then back again. He sat in stunned disbelief, caught between the urge to laugh and to bury his head under a pillow. A deep sigh escaped his lips, instantly met with his mother's sharp, disapproving glare. Dropping his gaze, he retraced every decision that had led him here, but none of them had pointed to *this*. It was too bizarre to have predicted, even in his wildest imagination.

At least while Gabby and Phyllis had been around, there was lightness. Now that they had gone downstairs, the room held a notable chill. Derrek appreciated their willingness to try to secure a room for him under Gabby's name. It made things cleaner, and this way, they would be less likely to trace him. It wouldn't hold forever, but it would give him time to make a plan.

His gaze shifted to Mina, sitting stiffly on the edge of one of the beds. Her hands were clasped in her lap, her eyes glued to the floor. She hadn't said a word since they'd run into his mother. He wished they could be alone for a moment so he could explain. His mother, however, had different plans.

Derrek recognized a losing battle when he saw one. When his mother told him they were going back to the hotel, he had meekly trailed them. The women encircled Mina, whisking her out of his reach and leaving him to follow in their wake.

His mother paced the hotel room, stopping to glare at him now and then. Derrek resisted the urge to roll his eyes. He could practically feel the accusations boiling under her silence. She hadn't spoken to him yet, not beyond the sharp command to follow her earlier. He sighed, running a hand through his hair. He'd tried to explain, but she'd cut him off with a withering look.

"In all of my days," his mother finally spoke. Derrek started to stand, but she stopped him. "Sit down, young man. I've got an ear full for you, and that is only the beginnin'. Just wait until I tell your father. How could I have raised a boy so thoughtless? It makes me want to cry. When I think what you put this poor child through."

"Mina is hardly a child—" Derrek added, thinking of sticking up for Mina, but was greeted with a glare from his mother and an irritated look from Mina. So he clamped his mouth shut.

"Mina is a dear, sweet girl, and I have grown quite fond of her. I feel it is my responsibility to make sure you are doing right by her. Now I have heard her side of things and know how she feels, which leaves me with you. How do you feel about her Derrek?"

Derrek's eyes jerked to Mina. She has feelings for him? He wanted to ask her what they were if she still had them and if he could convince her to give him another try, but he wasn't about to have *that* conversation with his mother in the room.

"Well, son. Do you have feelings for Mina?" Tami demanded.

"Mama, I don't think I should discuss it with you before I talk things over with Mina. Do you?" He hoped she agreed. The idea of having to say what needed to be said with his mother watching made his stomach churn.

Tami glared at him. Her green eyes narrowed with disapproval. "Fine. Would you care to explain all this nonsense about Chris? Did you have your name changed and didn't tell me? I can't understand why. Derrek is a fine name, nice and strong. It suits you perfectly, not to mention it was my brother's name. You remember my older brother, your dear uncle, who died from a snake bite when he was only ten."

"Yes, Mom. I remember Uncle Derrek. No, I didn't change my name. I'm working, Mother, and I need you to give me and Mina a little privacy so I can explain it to her."

Tami wagged a finger in his face. "Don't forget I know you, Derrek. There is no way I am letting you out of my sight until I am satisfied that this girl will be taken care of."

Feeling a little insulted, Derrek stood, his hands braced on his hips. "Do you honestly think I would do anything to jeopardize Mina's safety?"

"I'm not talkin' about her safety. I'm talkin' about her heart." Tami pointed a red manicured nail at Mina, whose eyes were wide with surprise. "That girl loves you, son. I don't want you breaking her heart."

Mina gasped, her hand pressed over her lips. The color drained from her face as she stared in horror at Tami. Derrek whipped his head around, his gaze fixed on Mina. "I appreciate your concern, but Mina and I need to talk. Alone."

Just then, the hotel room burst open. Gabby and Phyllis strode in, demanding an update. Derrek tried to get an answer from either of them about the room, but neither seemed able to focus.

Gabby danced around the room, singing a song about love. Meanwhile, Phyllis collapsed on the other bed, her feet lifted into the air. She asked

Derrek to remove her shoes, as she had done countless times. It wasn't surprising to him, and he didn't mind helping her. "Phyllis, did Gabby get a room for me and Mina?"

"She got a room for you," Phyllis said with a hearty chuckle.

Derrek's brow knitted together. "What's that supposed to mean?"

Gabby poked him in the chest. Her inch-long spiked nail dug a hole in his skin. "It means that if we don't like your explanation, you're going to the room alone, and Mina is stayin' with us. We all talked and decided to take her home with us. She can't keep runnin', and if you aren't goin' to fix it, then we will."

Mina looked like she might argue, so he stopped her before she said something that might ruffle well-meaning feathers. He seized the opportunity provided by the sudden chaos to lift Mina into his arms. She put her arms around his neck, and he was so happy he couldn't resist kissing her full lips.

"Phyllis, Gabby, Mom," Derrek gave them each a firm look. "I appreciate your concern and help, but this is between Mina and me. Now, I'm going to take Mina to *our* room, and we will talk. You are going to finish your vacation and not think a moment longer about any of this. All right."

"But, I—" Tami protested.

Derrek cut her off. "Mom, I am putting my foot down. Do you remember what I told you when I started my job?"

Tami stared at him for a moment, then nodded. She held out her hand. "Key, Gabby."

Gabby handed her the room key, which Tami slipped into Mina's hand. She gave them both one big hug and stepped back. "I expect to hear from you, young lady, even if it's only to say you're okay."

Mina's eyes filled with tears. He figured he had a minute, tops to get her out of there before she started crying again. "Room number?" He called out as he headed toward the door.

"Four-twenty-two. Sorry, they didn't have any open on this floor." Gabby called out at the door clicked shut behind him.

Derrek let out a long, slow breath, the tension easing from his shoulders. Three floors between them. Finally, he could be alone with Mina. Something he had been chasing since he first laid eyes on her. He had her now, and everything inside him shifted and settled into place. Glancing down at her in his arms, the first hint of a smile curled his lips.

"I can walk." She grumbled, squirming in his arms, making a half-hearted attempt to escape.

"But I like carrying you," he replied, unable to keep the dopey grin off his face.

Mina let out a soft huff but didn't protest further.

In the elevator, Derrek set her on her feet, her body sliding against his. Too warm. Too soft. His pulse hammered. He meant to let her stand on her own but couldn't. Instead, he pulled her back, locking her in his arms.

Her head fit perfectly against his chest. His hand slid up, cradling the back of her skull, fingers threading through her hair. He just held her, eyes shut, breathing her in.

She's here. She's safe.

If he repeated it to himself enough, he could regain his ability to breathe. A shaky breath escaped his lips. Relief crashed over him, so intense it left him unsteady. His hands wouldn't stop moving—stroking her back, tracing her face, flexing around her hips. He'd come too damn close to losing her. The fear was still there, raw and unspoken. His arms tightened. Closer. He needed her closer. He buried his face in her neck.

Mina hesitated. Then her arms wrapped around his waist, holding him just as fiercely.

Not as long as I'm alive and breathing. The thought burned in his mind. Mina was his to protect, and there was no way he'd let anything—or anyone—take her away from him.

When the elevator doors slid open, Derrek released her, even though his heart screamed in protest. He wanted to scoop her back up and run to the room. To hide her away until he knew what to do next. But he held himself back. There had been enough drama for one day.

Their assigned room was at the end of the hall, the last door on the right. Perfect. No one would come this far unless they had a reason. He opened the door, holding it for Mina to enter before following her inside.

As soon as she stepped in, Mina flipped on every switch, flooding the room with light. She moved to the large windows and spread the curtains, opening to the outside world.

Then she turned to face him, stark terror plain on her face. Derrek winced, the look hitting him in the gut. She was afraid of him. It was a horrifying realization.

He wanted to say something, anything, to ease her fear. He wanted to tell her she never had to be afraid of him; all he wanted was to protect her. The words stuck in his throat, tangled in the knot of emotions coiling inside him.

Mina rubbed her arms, her gaze unwavering. "I want you to tell me who you are, why you lied to me, and who that man was chasing me."

Derrek exhaled, running a hand through his hair. "I will. As much as I can. But there are things I can never tell you—not because I don't want to, but for your safety."

Mina scoffed and stormed toward the small chair in the corner, collapsing into it with a huff. "Yeah, likely story. Why even bother telling me anything at all?"

She had every right to be angry. If their positions were reversed, he'd be livid, too. But throwing a fit wasn't going to change anything.

Derrek clenched his jaw. This wasn't going well. Mina had a hard day; her whole world was knocked upside down. "I understand you're upset," he said in a calm and soothing tone. "You have every right to feel this way. However, you have to realize the things happening have nothing to do with you," then thought to add, "With us."

Mina's head snapped up, her eyes flashing. "Us?" She fairly screamed, causing Derrek to wince. "You think there is an us?"

He inhaled sharply, forcing himself to stay calm. "Yes," he said, his voice steady, sure. "There is. Whether you want to admit it or not. Now, will you let me try to explain things? I promise it will seem better after I do."

Mina glared at him but nodded.

He might have pushed back harder if he hadn't caught the shimmer of unshed tears in her eyes. It wasn't her fault. None of this was. If anything, it was his. But casting blame wasn't going to change anything.

Derrek sat on the bed, facing her. He reached out and pulled the chair close so she sat between his thighs. He took her hands in his, scowling at their icy coldness. He focused on warming her hands as he spoke.

"My job gives me assignments," he said finally. "I can't explain the details, and I can't tell you who I work for. It's classified."

Mina's brows furrowed. "What, like government stuff?"

He hesitated. "Yes, you could say that. Anyway, my assignments take me all over. This last one brought me here." He glanced up at her face, gauging how well she was taking things so far. She was frowning but seemed to be listening, so he continued. "I was given a file on you."

Her breath hitched. "Me?"

He nodded. "It said you worked with the Petrov crime family."

Mina's lips parted, shock flickering across her face. "That name…"

"Yeah." He watched her closely. "I was ordered to keep an eye on you. At first, I thought the file had to be wrong. So, I made a few calls. That was my mistake. I should have been more careful because the people I work for sent someone else."

"To do what?"

His jaw tightened. "To finish what I started."

Mina's expression clouded. "And what is that? To arrest me."

"No. We don't deal with the judicial system."

Silence hung between them.

Mina's face paled. "You mean, you were supposed to…"

"Kill you," Derrek admitted. The hurt in her eyes made his stomach clench.

"And that man who chased me?"

"Was sent to do the same thing."

Mina swallowed hard. "So, you're an assassin."

It was a statement, not a question, but he felt compelled to clarify. "Yes, you could say that." His voice was low, reluctant. "But I don't kill innocent people. Every job is an order, not a choice."

Mina let out a hollow laugh, pressing a hand to her chest. "But *I'm* innocent." She shook her head. "Would you have killed me?"

The answer should have been simple. He'd done it before—eliminated people with dark pasts, people deemed a threat. But Mina… Mina had never been that.

He'd wanted to protect her even before he knew she was innocent. Wanted her.

"No," he admitted. "Not even if you were everything the file said you were." He didn't like the look on her face. "What are you thinking?" He asked, fear tightening in his gut.

She shook her head, standing, her eyes darting around the room. "I need to get out of here."

Derrek stood, too. "You can't. I need to make a plan to get you out of here. Until then, we have to stay here. They won't be able to track us here—not for a while, at least. But if you leave and they find you on the street, there is nothing that I can do to stop them."

She stared at him, then suddenly turned toward the door.

"Mina." Derrek stepped in front of her. "You can't leave."

Her fists clenched at her sides. "Watch me."

His hands came up to stop her, resting on her shoulders. "Please don't make me tie you up."

Mina gasped. "You wouldn't."

"I would," he said evenly. "If it meant keeping you alive. Please. Stay." He was asking, but it wasn't a request. If she tried to leave, he would stop her and contain her by any means necessary.

He hadn't expected her to fight, so he doubled over when she spun around, her elbow catching in his middle. Pain lancing through his side. Mina tore out of his grasp and sprinted to the door. He was on her before she got the bolt turned. Derrek tossed her over his shoulder.

"Put me down!" She beat her fists against his back.

Ignoring her feeble attempts to hit his back. He stalked to the bed, tossing her onto the mattress.

She glared at him and tried to roll over to the opposite side. He caught her ankle and flipped her back. She fought like hell. Her fingers curled into claws as she scratched at him. He grabbed her wrists, pinning them above her head. She thrashed under him, using her body to buck him off. He settled his weight more firmly over her, locking her legs between his.

"Mina," he ground out. "Stop. What in the hell is wrong with you?" He hissed. His eyes narrowed as he glared at her flushed face. His cheek stung from the place where her nails had caught his flesh.

She panted beneath him, her chest rising and falling. A tear slipped free, trailing into the dark curtain of her hair.

"You!" She screamed in his face. "Who are you? What kind of man are you?" Her words were harsh, holding all her frustration and hurt. "I don't even know your name?" She finished with a sob.

His expression softened. He wiped the tears from her eyes with his mouth, trailing feather-light kisses from her eyes to her nose and then her mouth. He brushed his lips over hers, coaxing her to open for him, to trust him.

"You know me." He murmured against her parted lips. "Names mean nothing; they change with the seasons. Who I am, you know that. I lied about my name, but everything else was real."

"How am I supposed to believe you?" She asked her eyes pools of hurt and hope.

He pressed his lips over her heart. Her skin was soft under his mouth. "Because you can feel it here." She trembled under him. The doubt faded by degrees from her eyes.

Chapter Twenty-Seven

Mina sat on the bed, tucking her legs under her. She studied Derrek, trying to reconcile the man in front of her with what she now knew. A killer.

He sat on the other bed, his bag emptied as he sorted through its contents. His expression shifted subtly—small flickers of thought crossing his face like a silent film playing just for her.

She hugged a pillow to her chest, her heart raw from the day's chaos. It still didn't make sense. He did it so naturally. The way he moved, the intensity in his gaze —how could she have missed it?

"How long have you been this, a killer?" She asked, choking on the word.

Derrek looked up, one brow lifting. "Thirteen years."

Mina's eyes widened. She shook her head. "I don't understand. How do you become something like that?" She asked, refusing to use that word again. "It's not like you had... experience before, right?"

She hadn't considered how little she knew about him, not even his real name, until today. The thought churned her stomach. What if he wasn't just an assassin? What if he was something worse? A serial killer who murdered anyone he deemed worthy of death?

Derrek's mouth twitched, the faintest hint of a sardonic smile. "No, I didn't have 'experience,'" he said dryly. "I took some tests and wound up in a study." His expression darkened. "I can't go into detail. Remember?"

"Right." Mina hugged the pillow tighter. She watched him for a little longer. Her mind continued to bounce from here to there. The silence stretched between them, heavy and suffocating, until she thought she would go crazy.

She hesitated, then admitted, "I know all about tests. My father used to have me take all kinds of assessments. He said he was collecting data. I don't know what he was using the information for. He never told me."

Derrek paused, looking up at her. "How old were you?"

She frowned, plucking at the pillow in her arms. "The earliest I can remember was nine. But it could have been all my life." She added with a shrug. "My dad was funny that way."

"He doesn't do it anymore?"

"No. We don't talk much now. He missed our last weekly call…" Derrek looked up when she let the words trail off.

"Is something wrong?"

"He's supposed to call tomorrow night."

"Sorry. It looks like you'll miss two calls."

Mina sighed. "Yeah, that's what I figured."

He was quiet for a moment, then said, "I promise. When I get you somewhere safe, I'll find a way for you to contact your dad. Okay?"

"Okay." Mina agreed with a feeble smile.

She wanted to believe him, to believe her thoughts and feelings mattered, but her mind kept circling back to the fact that Derrek was a killer. She couldn't wrap her head around it. She'd noticed something different in him from the beginning, but she never figured it was this.

"How do you do it?" Mina blurted out.

Derrek lifted his head, his expression unreadable. "Do what?"

Mina rolled her eyes, her voice heavy with impatience. "Kill people."

His expression hardened, his mouth thinned as he replied, "*We are what we repeatedly do,*" he said finally. "I do what I was trained to do."

Mina stiffened, unease prickling the back of her neck. Something about those words tugged at a memory she couldn't quite grasp. "Where did you hear that?"

Derrek's gaze sharpened. Slowly, he set the file in his hands aside and turned to face her fully.

"It's a quote drilled into us during training. I think it's from Aristotle. The full version is: '*We are what we repeatedly do. Excellence, then, is not an act but a habit.*' Why? Does it mean something to you?" He asked, starting to climb off the bed.

Mina waved him back. Rubbing her fingers into her temples. "I don't know. It's nothing. Probably something I learned in school." She tried to smile, hoping it didn't look as brittle as it felt. "I think I'll take a shower." Mina looked down at her clothes and grimaced. "I suppose I'll just wear this to sleep in."

Derrek tossed her a bundle of black fabric. She shook the material out and realized it was one of his shirts. Her face heated. "Thanks," she mumbled, clutching the material to her chest as she struggled to meet his eyes.

Locking herself in the bathroom, Mina leaned against the door. She closed her eyes and took a breath. Derrek's words had stirred something in her, a memory. She could almost take hold of it, but not quite.

She set his shirt on the counter and stared at her reflection in the mirror. Her hair was a mess, her face pale and drawn. She turned on the shower to hot, steam filling the bathroom. Mina drew on the mirror, a wave across her face. *We are what we repeatedly do.* She couldn't explain it, but she knew this was important.

She stood under the spray, her mind turning the words over.

Mina let the hot water cascade over her. She lathered her hair, trying to focus, to work the memory loose. *We are what we repeatedly do.* She knew those words. She knew them from something important. And then, it hit her. The memory rushed back through a thrown-open door.

It had been a warm summer day, the sand hot beneath her feet. She'd wandered along the beach with her pail and shovel, searching for treasure. Her brother Braxton suggested if she looked near the rocks, she would have more luck.

She had made her way to a cove where the rocks formed a cave along the rocky shore. Armed with a pail and shovel, Mina searched the whole area. She was determined to bring home the gold of some long-lost pirate.

She'd been so focused on her search she hadn't noticed the tide creeping in. By the time the water had reached her, the cave she'd ventured into was nearly submerged. She should have left her pail and shovel behind, but her father had warned her not to lose them.

The rocks at the mouth of the cave were slick. Mina tried to scale the wall, but her grip slipped as she scrambled for a hold. Her food slid, and she plunged into the icy water. The undertow caught her, dragging her down and pulling her farther out to sea.

She kicked and thrashed, her lungs burning as she fought her way to the surface. When her head broke free, she gasped for air, only to be sucked under again. Every time she clawed her way to the top, the ocean would slam her down again. The saltwater stung her eyes and filled her nose, choking her. She couldn't scream, couldn't call for help.

Fear made her whimper as the tide pulled her under again. Her muscles ached, and exhaustion made her unable to stay above water. She'd thought she would die and no one would know she was gone. Her tears were washed away in the waves of a turbulent sea. Then, as if by a miracle, two arms circled her, pulling her out of the water and dropping her on the shore.

It had been fate, her mother proclaimed. A young surfer, catching one last wave, had seen her struggle and saved her.

Her father's response had been cold. "Mina, *we are what we repeatedly do,*" he'd said, his frown deepening as he lectured her. "You will never be anything if you continue to let your emotions govern your actions."

"But it was an accident," she argued. Her father refused to listen.

"Accidents are nothing but mistakes made avoidable by rational thought." Her father frowned, his brow forming a disapproving line.

"Braxton told me to look there," Mina said, hoping to prove it wasn't her fault, that she hadn't been impulsive and foolish.

Her father's mouth pressed into a firm line. "Your brother seems to understand better than you. *We are what we repeatedly do.* When will you learn your brother always has ulterior motives.

She hadn't understood what he meant by that. Not until years later when her brother intentionally led her into a dangerous situation. That time on the beach hadn't been her only near miss; the last time had almost cost her life and forced her parents to send him away for college. She hadn't seen Braxton in years, nor would she.

Mina opened her eyes, the memory fading. Here she was again, in perilous circumstances. But this time, she wouldn't let herself fall victim. *This time, I'll learn faster.*

Derrek frowned at the closed door. He didn't like the way Mina's face had gone deathly white, her eyes wide and staring. He didn't know what had spooked her, but she was scared. She didn't trust him yet, but he hoped her innate goodness would overrule her reluctance. He knew she wanted to trust him, and he was good with that for now. If he could only figure a way out of this mess.

He glanced down at the supplies he'd laid out on the bed. Cash—thankfully, since her shopping spree had nearly wiped him out. His mouth twitched at the memory. There was his passport, a secondary ID, and an assortment of weapons: two serrated knives, a Beretta with an extra clip, a container of mace, and a couple of percussion grenades. He also had two changes of clothes for himself, basic toiletries, and survival essentials—a fully stocked first-aid kit, flashlight, water, and energy bars. Enough to last him 24 hours if he needed to run.

He had nothing specific for Mina except the extra clothes he bought her today. She could reuse her underwear or go without it. The thought of her improvising tugged at the corners of his lips for a moment. It would be better if she were ready for anything, which meant he might need to risk leaving to get her something unless he could call in his mother. She would be more than happy to help. Besides, she liked Mina, which made him happy.

Just as he reached for his phone, it vibrated in his hand, Damian's name flashing on the screen. Derrek answered on the first ring.

"Oh, man, am I glad to hear from you. Tell me you know what is going on."

"I wish I did," Damian replied, his voice grim. "The few people willing to talk are only giving me bits and pieces, nothing that connects the dots."

Derrek pinched the bridge of his nose, swearing. "Okay, so fill me in on what you *do* know."

"Mina Turner, aka Mina Rose LeSeur," Damian began. "Daughter of Lyla Turner and Dr. Charles Ellis LeSeur. She changed her last name to her mother's maiden name when she turned eighteen. Her mother lives in Florida with an orthodontist."

"Go on," Derrek urged, his gaze flicking to the bathroom door.

"Here's where it gets interesting. Her father has degrees in behavioral science and psychology. He's an expert in identifying personality traits and has developed tests used across the educational system."

"Yeah, that tracks," Derrek said. "Mina mentioned he liked to test her as a kid."

Damian's tone turned colder. "What you might not guess is that while working on a classified government project, he used a pseudonym to keep his personal life separate. Care to guess what name he went by?"

Derrek's stomach tightened, his eyes darting to the bathroom door again. "Tell me."

"Mr. Green," Damian said, his voice like a blade. "AOD is his damn brainchild, and we are his puppets."

Derrek closed his eyes, a bleakness washing over him. Mr. Green, the man behind the curtain, had manipulated the AOD participants from the beginning. He had been instrumental in the selection process and in creating the conditions in which they could take a life on command. Mr. Green might not have put the gun in their hands, but he was a big part of why they pulled the trigger.

This wasn't good for Mina. If her dad was behind the AOD project, something must be happening behind the scenes. If Mr. Green wasn't cooperating, then someone within the AOD was using Mina to get to him.

"Does your girl know what her daddy's been up to?" Damian asked. Jerking Derrek out of his head.

"I doubt it. They aren't close." Derrek said. He shoved his hand through his heart. His mind scrambled for an option. "I guess what's missing from your full picture is the one behind this?"

"You've got it. The best I can find is there may be a shift in command. I'd heard rumors and was debating about the position I would take, but this has pretty much set my course." Damian stated in a tone so matter of fact it sent chills down Derrek's spine.

"Does that mean I can count on you?" Derrek asked, holding his breath.

"Yeah. Ransom could be called in, too, if we need him. I want to wait, though, if we can. If too many AOD agents show up within twenty miles of each other, someone is bound to notice. I don't know about you, but that is the kind of thing I am hoping to avoid. At least for now."

"What about Alex? Did you learn why he was trying to find me?"

"Not yet. I haven't been able to find him. I think he might be with Calista."

Derrek whistled. "And how do you feel about that?"

"There's nothing to feel." Damian snapped.

"Right." Derrek agreed, his mouth twitching. "I don't suppose you have any idea of how I can get out of this mess alive?"

His gaze was drawn to the bathroom door as it opened. Mina walked into the room, her hair wrapped in a towel, his shirt hitting her mid-thigh. She sat on the bed, her amber eyes wide.

"Kill the girl," Damian muttered.

Not a chance in hell. Mina sat as she had earlier, a pillow cradled in her arms. She looked fragile, sitting there all alone. He wanted to go to her, hold her, tell her everything would be okay.

"Listen, if you learn anything else, you know how to reach me. I'll be in touch." Derrek said, ending the call. He dropped the phone on the bed and went to Mina. He lifted the comforter and slid under the cover. He put an arm around her waist, frowning at the tremble in her body, and pulled her into his side. Tucking the blanket over her legs, he turned on the television and leaned against the headboard. Mina snuggled into his side. She unwrapped her hair, dropped the damp towel on the floor, and laid her head on his chest.

There were things to discuss and plans to be made, all of which could wait. Right now, all he wanted to do was hold her, even if it was only for this one night.

Chapter Twenty-Eight

Mina was running.

But she wasn't getting anywhere. All around, she could feel fingers clawing at her skin. She screamed for help, calling for her father to save her, but he stood off to the side watching her. The same notepad he used when she was a child lay in his hands. Forever taking notes. She cried to him. Pleaded for him to look at her, to see her. Nothing helped. Nothing changed. Then, she was dropped into the office in her grandfather's beach house and was eleven years old again.

Her father sat behind the desk, his hands stacked as he looked at her. He'd been lecturing her for hours. She couldn't remember all that he said. Her mind had wandered to far-away beaches and buried treasure.

Then, he slammed his hand against the desk. The loud crack made her jump. Her eyes jerked back to him, and that's when he told her about the men who would come for her.

"Mina, you must listen to me. There is a darkness that lies within all of us. Most don't ever allow this side of them to see the light of day, but some, those who can walk both sides, are the ones you must watch for. I have figured out how to see the darkness within, but it comes at a price. I fear that you may be the one to pay it."

Tears blurred her eyes; she swiped them away quickly, not wanting her father to see her weakness.

He kneeled in front of her, holding her hands in his. His behavior scared her. She wanted to pull away from him. He wasn't acting as himself.

"Don't cry. Don't be afraid. Just remember, *we are what we repeatedly do*. If I say these words to you, come to the beach house and wait for me. Do you understand?" He clasped her shoulders, squeezing enough to make her wince. "Promise you will remember. What are you to do if I ever say to you: *we are what we repeatedly do*."

"Come to Grandpa's house."

Her father smiled, squeezing her arms again. "That's right. Come to the beach house." He pulled her close, hugging her tight against his chest. The fabric of his shirt smothered her face, and she couldn't breathe. She tried to move her face to breathe, but she couldn't. Then she wasn't in her father's arms but back in the sea, the waves like fingers pulling her down. She clawed at the water, fighting to be free; she gasped, sobbing.

Then she was awake, Derrek leaning over her in the soft glow of the bedside lamp. His hand brushed the hair away from her face. His eyes glittered with concern. "Shhh." He soothed, brushing away the tears. "You were only dreaming."

Mina took a shuddering breath. "I'm sorry. I didn't mean to wake you."

Derrek grinned, his hand resting on her waist, his finger tapping her hip bone in a restless movement. "Do you want to tell me about it?"

She gnawed on her bottom lip, her eyes searching his. "It was about my father."

He lifted a brow, "Do you have nightmares about your dad often?"

Mina shook her head. "This was the first one. But it was more like a memory than a dream."

"What happened?"

"I remembered why that phrase made me react the way I did. It was something my dad told me a long time ago. He wanted me to remember it as some kind of code so I would know to go to my grandpa's beach house if he ever told it to me."

Derrek frowned, his brow puckered as he focused on her. "What exactly did your father tell you?"

Mina shuddered. Her mouth went dry. "He said there is darkness within all of us, but only a few can walk on both sides. There may come a day when those who can will come for me, and I would need to leave to find him at my grandpa's house."

Suddenly cold, her body trembling. Derrek pulled her closer, his heat warming her. His hands rubbed her back. She arched into his touch, desperate to wipe those scary memories from her mind. Her finger dug into his back, his skin so alive and pulsing beneath her hands.

He seemed to understand what she needed, holding her against him, his hands stroking over her body in smooth, soothing strokes. Her racing pulse slowed until her eyelids could hardly stay open. Mina struggled to stay awake. There was more she needed to tell him; something important flashed in her mind the minute she opened her eyes, but it faded until sleep claimed her.

Derrek felt the minute sleep overcame her once more. He held her a little longer, indulging for a minute in the joy of having her snuggled so trustingly in his arms. He pressed a kiss to her brow, making her wrinkle her nose. Then, in slow increments, he eased out of bed. Tucking the covers around her, he looked down at her sleeping form and wished he could crawl back under the covers with her.

It hadn't been his plan to get up early, but Mina's nightmare had activated his brain, and he knew there wasn't any hope for sleep now. His talk with Damian left him restless, feeling he was missing something obvious.

Slipping into his pants, Derrek went to the window, peering into the dark, cloud-covered sky. He watched Mina's reflection in the glass. His mind ran over Damian's words. After she had showered, they hadn't talked about anything important. He could see the strain in her eyes, the pinched look about her mouth. She didn't need him prodding her. It could wait. He planned to order room service, and he had some questions he needed answered while they ate. However, the more important ones were those which he knew Mina wouldn't have.

Someone within the AOD had sent Clint, Mitch, and Stuart. They were the cruelest of the recruits and didn't work well with anyone. They weren't particularly good at executing a job with precision. They had a louder approach, which often didn't work for most jobs. They tended to be sent in when casualties were considered a reasonable loss.

To have them here meant AOD had marked him for death. Clint had said as much. Damian was right. He was out. There would be no going back for him. If he survived this, he'd have to disappear. His mother wouldn't be happy, but she'd understand. But what would he do with Mina? His gaze landed on her sleeping form. She looked so young, fresh, as if nothing dark ever touched her. He wanted to bask in her glow. But just because that's what he wanted didn't mean she would too. She'd already suggested their relationship was no longer a relationship. He hoped that wasn't true and she was just reacting to the confusing situation. When he disappeared, he desperately wanted her to come with him.

Before he slipped into the darkness, he needed to figure out who wanted Mina dead and why. Even though he would love for Mina to go with him, she might not want to. He couldn't leave her behind if there was a risk to her. For him to walk away from her, she had to be safe, which meant he had to remove the threat.

He stalked across the room, his silent, lethal grace not disturbing Mina. Picking up his phone, he shut himself in the bathroom, turning on the fan to muffle any noise he might make. It was time he started gathering his information, starting with Alex.

He didn't know what Alex wanted from him, but if he went through the hoops Derrek had set up to reach him, then it must be worth hearing. Since he didn't know where Alex was, he didn't worry about the time. It could be the middle of the day for him for all he knew. He dialed the number Alex had given him and waited. A knot twisting in his gut.

"Hello."

Despite the grogginess of his voice, Derrek recognized Alex. A flare of irritation had him snapping. "What the hell are you calling me for?"

"Well, hello to you too." Alex's voice brightened. "What happened? You wake on the wrong side of the bed? Or perhaps with the wrong woman?"

Alex, forever the joker, always had to poke and prod until he got a reaction. Not in the mood for his games, Derrek jumped to the point. "What do you want, Alex?"

Alex chuckled. "I remember you being more fun."

Derrek ground his teeth. "I'm kind of busy. Can you quit with all the bullshit already?"

"All right. No need to bite my head off. I heard you were working in San Francisco."

"Yeah? Who told you that?"

"I have my sources." After a beat, he asked. "Is all well?"

The code phrase triggered Derrek, his muscle coiling as he clenched the bathroom sink. "No, not yet."

"I see. Is there any reason why?" Alex prodded.

The last thing he needed was for Alex to know of the mess he'd gotten himself mixed up in. The Alex he knew back in their training days was a friend. But this man, Derrek, didn't know. A lot happened in thirteen years. He wasn't about to risk Mina's life by trusting someone who might not deserve it. "Nothing I'm willing to share."

"Hmm. And what if I told you I might have information you would find interesting."

"I would demand to know what it is?"

Alex clucked his tongue. "That isn't how this works. You want the information; you have to give me something in return."

With a snort, Derrek said, "Only if you tell me where you came by your information."

"Same rules apply."

Derrek swore, shoving a hand through his hair tousled hair. "Fine. What do you want to know?"

"Why are you holding back? Too complicated?" Alex asked.

"No, raw deal, " Derrek said. The code was something they had been forced to use in the beginning. Derrek only used it when communicating directly with the AOD. He didn't know why Alex was using it now, but it made him restless.

"Thought or feeling?"

"Un-uh. I gave you the first part. If you want to know more, then you need to give me something."

Alex chuckled, "You always were a shrewd handler. Fine, you're right. My source is Abigail Weaver."

"Bullshit." There was no way the ice queen would ever freely give anyone information that might give them the upper hand. That woman had ice in her veins. Nothing bothered her.

Alex barked with laughter. "I swear, but she doesn't know she's helping me."

"How is that possible?" Derrek asked, frowning into the mirror.

"Simple, I break into her house every few months and raid her safe."

"The hell you say! Are you crazy? She'll have you killed before you even know it's coming."

"Where's the fun without the thrill?" Alex asked. "Besides, it keeps my skills honed."

Early on, Alex showed a remarkable talent for picking locks, cracking safes, and getting into tightly secured places. From what Derrek had heard over the years, Alex was rarely sent on a kill mission but instead used for gathering information.

"All right, so you broke into her safe. What does this have to do with San Fransisco?"

"She's got two files on your girl. It made me curious to see how they were so different. So I looked into her, only her information was buried so deep it took me a few weeks to crack through. Turns out she's got secrets."

Derrek's hand tightened around the phone, his gut twisting. "What do you mean she has secrets?"

"That's where it's interesting. That information has been scrubbed. It's gone. From everything. Even the file in Weaver's safe didn't reveal it."

"So what makes you think she's got anything to hide?"

"Because that's why you got her file. Someone wants whatever it is to disappear. If your girl dies, then the truth dies with her."

"And if she doesn't know anything?"

"Doesn't matter because someone thinks she does, and as long as she's living, she's a liability. You better know what you're doing because you are ass deep in this shit, and there isn't any way out."

"If you're jerking me around…" Derrek warned between bared teeth.

"Not likely, besides I don't want Damian on my ass, which is what would happen if I sold you out."

"Ha, shows what you know," Derrek said, unable to resist the jab.

"What's that supposed to mean?"

Derrek smiled, his lips curling into a sardonic grin. "Being shacked up with Calista wasn't the best move."

"Hey, I'm not shacked up with anyone. If I were, it sure wouldn't be Calista. I'd have to be out of my mind to get mixed up with her. Besides, if I ever was going to try with someone from the team, it would be Kate. I haven't seen her in several years, but before, she sure had one dynamite ass."

"That and a killer right hook. Kate would knock you on your ass before you got the question out."

"It's probably why I never asked. Listen, I can feel the heat breathing on the back of my neck. I'll be out for a while. Don't do anything stupid."

"Right." Derrek's mouth pressed into a grim line. "Why did you call me? Why the heads up?"

"Because I think a shift is coming, and only those prepared will weather the storm."

Derrek hung up, turning the nob to the bathroom door as quietly as possible. He slipped back into the room, his eyes falling on Mina, who still lay sound asleep. It didn't look like she had moved at all since he'd left the bed. He took off his pants and slid in next to her, needing to hold her. He didn't understand the urge, but it was riding him hard. Mina turned to him, her head resting on his shoulder. He pulled her close, wrapping his arm around her waist and holding her against him. Her heart beat in time with his. He left his mind shut off, finding peace for the few hours remaining until the sun would rise and he would be forced to face what lay ahead.

Mina had a secret. And Derrek wasn't sure if it was one he wanted to uncover.

Chapter Twenty-Nine

Mina jolted awake, her heart hammering against her ribs. The room was dark, unfamiliar for the half-second it took her to remember where she was. Someone was at the door.

She pushed up on one elbow, breath caught in her throat. Before she could move, Derrek was already there, his silhouette cutting through the dim light as he reached for the handle.

She let out a slow breath, pulse still racing. Her still-sleepy brain didn't register what was happening until she saw a tray laden with food pass through the doorway. Her stomach rumbled, and she threw the covers off, climbing out of bed.

"Mmm. This smells delicious." Mina said over Derrek's shoulder. Her mouth salivated as he revealed two plates overflowing with food, but the bacon stole her attention.

Derrek smiled, pressing a warm kiss to her throat. "I didn't know what you liked, so I ordered a variety of things."

Mina snatched a crispy slice of bacon and took a bite. "I'm not picky. This is perfect." Derrek held out a chair for her, and Mina slid into the seat. He set one plate in front of her and a glass of juice. Then he took the other chair.

"How did you sleep?" Derrek asked, his green eyes sharp with interest.

Mina let out a dry laugh. "You mean after I woke you up screaming?"

His mouth twitched as he took a bite of eggs. "You weren't screaming." He tilted his head slightly, studying her. "Do you remember your dream?"

Mina shifted, images flashing in her mind in a disjointed blur. "Yes and no. I remember bits and pieces, but nothing that makes sense. But this... this yuckiness—" she shuddered "—I get this awful feeling every time I think about it."

Derrek arched a golden eyebrow. "What kind of feeling?"

"It's hard to explain." Mina pressed a fist to her stomach. "It makes me feel sick. Almost a restlessness, like my skin doesn't fit my body. Does that make sense?"

His gaze sharpened. "Have you had dreams like this before?"

Mina shook her head. "Never." She hesitated, tilting her head as a thought surfaced. "But it is weird... I've been thinking about that family trip a lot lately. More in the last few days than I have in years."

She wasn't sure, but it felt like Derrek tensed beside her. His muscles coiled—subtle but unmistakable.

"What's wrong?" she asked, watching him carefully.

"Did you go there often?" His tone was casual, but his body was anything but.

"No. Just the one time. My grandpa died the next year, and as far as I know, the place has just been sitting there."

"You never went back?"

"No." She frowned. "It was a great trip, but... I don't know. Something about that place makes me uncomfortable. Like the boogeyman is waiting in the dark."

Derrek grunted. His eyes were on his plate, but Mina knew he was aware of every move she made. The feeling might have been almost romantic if there hadn't been an air of uncertainty. She kept getting the impression he knew something and wasn't telling her.

Mina laid her fork down, shoving her plate away. She looked at Derrek and asked, "What now? Where do we go from here?"

He leaned back, his arms folded over his chest as he studied her. "Why don't you tell me?"

"How am I supposed to know? This isn't my world. If I had a choice, I would go home."

"You always have a choice."

She let out a sharp laugh, disbelief curling in her gut. "Really? That's funny because last I checked, going home *wasn't* one of the options. You made it pretty damn clear that I can't contact anyone in my life. So tell me, how exactly is this a choice?"

"It's simple; you have three options. That is a choice, is it not?"

Mina's patience snapped. Whether it was exhaustion, frustration, or the overwhelming loss of control, she didn't know. She pushed away from the table and stormed to the bed, throwing herself onto the pillows. Pulling the comforter over her shoulder, she stared out the window, watching people go about their lives—free, unburdened.

She envied them.

The bed dipped as Derrek sat next to her; she ignored him. She was probably being childish, but she didn't care.

Derrek put his arm around her shoulders. She wanted to shrug him off and tell him to get lost, but she didn't. She couldn't, not when part of her wasn't sure if he would stay if she told him to leave. She hated to admit it, but she needed him.

Leaning against the headboard, Derrek patted the bed by his side. Maybe if she didn't feel so utterly alone, she could have resisted his silent invitation to lean on him. But she didn't. Instead, she rested her head on his shoulder, her mind circling everything again.

The puzzle wouldn't let go. Every time she thought of the beach—or her house—her mind slammed into a wall she couldn't see beyond. A dull, persistent pain throbbed behind her eyes. She rubbed at her forehead.

Then, she stiffened. A light flickered on in her mind.

"What is it?" Derrek asked, alerted by the change in her body language.

Mina sat up. "I need to go to my apartment."

Derrek's expression darkened as he shook his head. "I already told you they're watching your place. If you go anywhere near your place, you'll be dead before you reach the door."

"But there has to be a way in." She turned to him, determined. "You could figure it out for me, couldn't you?"

Derrek narrowed his eyes. "Even if I got you inside, then what?"

Mina scowled at him. "I don't want to stay. I just need to grab something."

Derrek eyed her suspiciously. "What?"

"A letter."

"A letter?" Derrek said in a state of stunned disbelief.

"Yes, a letter. The one my dad sent me the night we went to dinner.."

Derrek's fingers tightened on Mina's arm. "What letter? I don't remember you mentioning a letter."

"I did, but it wasn't significant until now. I need to read it again.

"Why? What's so damn important about a letter that you might not survive getting?"

"I think my father gave me instructions on what to do. Can you get me in or not?" Mina asked an obvious challenge in her voice.

"It doesn't sound like I have much choice," Derrek muttered, cursing under his breath.

Derrek grimly checked his gun, sliding it into the holster at the small of his back. His jaw tightened as he strapped a knife under his arm. He glanced at Mina. She'd slipped into the jeans he bought her but had kept his shirt—the one she'd slept in. She tied the end into a knot at her hip. And now she was running her fingers through her hair as if she wasn't about to walk into a damn war zone.

He should have expected her stubbornness. He just hadn't realized how deep it ran until now. Every argument, every plea to keep her here, had been met with a soft smile and that maddening little hum, like he wasn't telling her how easily she could die.

Even though Stuart preferred the up-close kill, he was proficient with a rifle and could end her life before Derrek had a chance to do anything about it. The thought sent his teeth grinding together.

"I can't guarantee you won't be hurt." He tried again. But he couldn't bring himself to say *killed*. Injuries could heal. Death was final. His stomach twisted, dread sitting heavy in his chest.

Mina smiled at him in the mirror. "I have faith in you."

He wanted to tell her—*don't*. He didn't deserve it. Only good people should be allowed to hold starlight in their arms.

"What about the two old guard dogs?" he asked, changing the subject.

Mina arched a brow. "Edgar and Abel? What about them?"

"They could get hurt?"

"I don't see how." She said, seemingly unbothered by the possibility.

"That's because you don't know how the darker side of the world operates."

"And you do?" Her mouth curled with amusement."

"Yes." He growled, shoving a hand through his hair. "Will you just listen to me?" He begged in raw desperation, making his voice sound tight.

Mina came to him. She laid a hand on his chest and rose onto her toes, brushing her mouth over his. "I am listening. It will be fine. You won't let anything happen."

His chest tightened, his muscles coiling with the need to break something. The inner beast gnashing its teeth, snarling at the thought of all the things that could happen.

He wanted to reach out to her, touch her, to keep the connection between them tangible, but his hands dangled uselessly at his side. "If you come with me, you have to do exactly what I say. Not arguments."

She practically danced in front of him. Her eagerness was palpable in the air. "Of course. Anything you say. I'll do it."

Resignation had never tasted so bitter. He pulled her close, his mouth lowering to hers. She turned her face eagerly, awaiting his kiss. Her acceptance of him, of what he was, rocked him. He wanted to put her away, where nothing bad could touch her. He gloried in her sweetness, his burning light of hope.

"Come on, let's get this over with."

He opened the door leading to the hallway and came to an abrupt halt, his brain refusing to accept what his eyes were seeing. Instead of leaving, he took a step back, then another, allowing space for his mother, Gabby, and Phyllis to pile in.

His mother closed the door, her eyes narrowed, and she watched him with an air of disapproval. "Derrek," she said with a bite of irritation. Then she turned her gaze, her face brightening into a radiant smile. "Mina, darlin', how are you? Did my son treat you well?"

Mina giggled, hugging his mother, something he never would have imagined happening. "I am just fine. We were on our way out." Then Mina frowned. "I thought you were leaving this morning."

"We were, but then last night, we decided we were needed here, so we canceled our flight," Tami told her, her eyes on Derrek.

"We did." Gabby agreed. "Why, I knew the minute Derrek showed up this was a mess of a situation. Tami assured us you weren't playing some horrid game. Which is what I thought."

"No, that's what I said it was," Phyllis said. "But then you suggested it was just a simple misunderstanding and that they would figure it out. You were set to leave this morning, remember?"

"Only because Derrek is a capable young man, and I had every faith he would make things right. And look, all seems well here. Are you sure we can't fly out today?"

"No," Tami and Phyllis stated. However, Phyllis did so with a wide grin. She looked to be enjoying herself immensely.

Derrek didn't know what he was supposed to do. His plan fell apart merely because his mother had shown up with her friends. This was a complication he didn't want or need. At the rate the conversation was going, he realized any hope of controlling the situation had slipped through his fingers.

"Don't slouch, son. It's bad for your back." Tami said, walking further into the room. Her eyes moved around, pausing at the unmade bed. His face darkened, but he refused to comment. His and Mina's sleeping arrangements were no one's business but their own.

"I see you ordered breakfast. Did you eat enough?" She asked, eyeing him in the way she had when he was a child as if she could assess his internal health by staring at him.

Derrek pinched his nose and counted to three. "Yes, Mom. I'm full. Mina's full. If you don't mind, we were just heading out." He said, attempting to usher everyone to the door.

"Perfect. We just need to bring our luggage inside."

Derrek blanched. "What?"

"Well, what did you expect us to do with our things? We lost our room this morning. You'll recall we were supposed to check out today. While we decide what's what, I thought we would stay with you."

He groaned, his eye beginning to twitch. "Mom, you can't mean to?" He looked around, his little sanctuary filling with his mother and her friends' things.

"I most certainly can. I'll remind you, Gabby paid for this room."

"I am paying her back," Derrek grumbled.

"Be that as it may," She said with a searing edge to her tone. "I'm not leaving until I am sure this young lady is in good hands. I never thought I would say those words. Never in all my days did I think I would be worried about a person in my son's care. We talked a long time about all this," Tami nodded, "Phyllis, Gabby and I. We just knew you had gotten into some mess and dragged this sweet girl into it with you."

"Oh, no. Tami, it isn't like that at all. You see –" Mina argued for him, which surprised him.

"Nonsense. I see everythin' quite well." Tami cut in. "I know where this is goin', and I am not leavin' until I make sure it gets there."

Derrek eyed his mother warily. "Where do you think this is going?" His gut twisted as he considered what his mother might say.

Tami gave him her most motherly expression, "Marriage. Of course."

Chapter Thirty

He had no idea how things had escalated so quickly. One moment, he was heading out the door with Mina on his heels; the next, he was sneaking around to the back entrance of her apartment building while his mother and her friends created a distraction out front.

Derrek shook his head, a smile playing on his lips. Mina kept surprising him. When he realized his mother was dead set on staying until she was satisfied, he'd braced himself for an argument. But Mina hadn't even tried to talk her out of it. Instead, she'd embraced the chaos, rallying them into her plan as a seasoned commander. And to his utter disbelief, his mother, Phyllis, and Gabby had jumped at the chance to cause a little chaos.

The plan was simple: while his mother and her friends occupied Edgar and Abel, he and Mina would slip in from the other side. Getting in wasn't the problem—avoiding a trap was. He had no doubt his mother could handle herself, but if they failed to hold Stuart's attention, he'd be in trouble.

Stuart was still out there. Derrek did not doubt that. The man had never been one to leave a job unfinished. The only question was where he was hiding. He was like a spider, lurking in some dark corner, waiting for the perfect moment to strike.

Derrek just hoped they didn't do anything to shake his web.

"Have you done this before?" Mina whispered the question in his ear.

Derrek paused, glancing at her. His face remained carefully blank. "Pick locks? Sure."

"No. Pick *this* lock."

He hesitated, his fingers stilling on the tools. "Why do you ask?" He hedged. He didn't like where this conversation was heading.

Mina studied him, her tone more curious than accusing. "I don't know, you just seem familiar with this door."

His grip faltered, and the pick slipped. He swore under his breath and tried again, but Mina's presence was impossible to ignore. The damn pick slipped again. A sharp curse escaped him, a string of words that would have sent his mother reaching for a bar of soap.

Mina's mouth twitched. His eyes narrowed in warning. "Never mind," she murmured, biting her bottom lip.

"Will you give me a little space?" He growled. Mina took a step back. "No, not backward. Stay against the building. Just stand over there." He pointed to the wall a couple of feet from him.

She smiled and moved to where he indicated. "Is this better?"

He grunted and tried again. It took him three times longer than usual to get the lock open. Derrek shoved the door open and pulled Mina, who was laughing like a loon, inside. "Will you be quiet? We're trying to remain unnoticed."

Mina failed to stifle a giggle. "Sorry. You're right." She said, sobering. Then she added. "I thought you would be a little more fun."

"Fun?"

"Well, yeah. It's kind of exciting, breaking into my apartment. I thought you would have been more playful about the whole thing."

Derrek stopped, turning to face her on the stairs. He gripped her arms and set her on the step ahead of them, bringing them nose to nose. His jaw clenched as his temper flared. "This isn't a game. Stuart is trying to kill you.

Don't think for one minute that he can't do it. You may have wanted this to be some kind of adventure, but I assure you, if Stuart gets his hands on you, there won't be anything bright and happy waiting for you."

Mina's face crumbled. Fear washed the color from her face. He could feel her trembling beneath his hands and hated himself for doing it to her, for extinguishing the light in her eyes. But she had to understand this wasn't a game. This was real. The danger was real, and he wasn't some prince charming. He was as dark and twisted as Stuart. They all were. The minute they joined the AOD, he had sealed his fate.

Frustration boiled his blood, guilt eating away his resolve. He wrapped his hand around her head and pulled her toward him, kissing her trembling lips. She melted against him. He gathered her close, using his mouth and hands to show her he cared and was sorry for scaring her. He ended the kiss, pressing his forehead to hers, rolling it side to side. "Stay with me." Looking her in the eyes, "Right with me. Don't move unless I move. Don't speak unless I say it's okay to." His hands flexed on her arms. "Promise me."

She lifted her hand to his face, cradling his cheek in her palm. "It'll be okay."

Derrek closed his eyes, taking in the moment. Then he pulled away, taking the lead. "Let's go."

On the fourth-floor landing, Derrek held up his hand, signaling Mina to wait. He cracked the door, wincing at the betraying squeak. He peered down the hallway; it looked okay—empty as far as he could see. He took a steadied breath. Over his shoulder, he gave Mina a warning look.

He took her hand and led her down the hallway, stopping at her door; he checked for any threats and went to work on her lock. This one he had open in less than five seconds. Mina made to go in, but he grabbed her arm, holding her back. When she moved to speak, he pressed his finger to her lips and shook his head. With his gun in hand, he moved through the apartment, clearing the room. He slipped his weapon back into the holster and turned to find Mina right behind him. He swore.

"I told you to wait."

Mina shook her head. "No, you told me to stay with you."

He signed, "Fine. Let's get the letter and get out of here." His skin was crawling. He didn't know where the threat was coming from, but it was coming.

Mina practically danced around her apartment. There was a giddiness about her that pulled a reluctant smile from him. She fluttered around the living room talking to her plant and then crowed in delight when she found her phone lying on the couch.

"You can't take it." He told her, already anticipating what she was going to ask.

A frown creased her brow. "Why not?"

"They can track you. Put it down and get your letter." He reminded her.

""Right." Mina turned, hesitation flickering across her face as if she wasn't sure which way to go.

With a sigh, Derrek helped her look. He was going through a stack of mail she had on the coffee table when he realized the room had gone too quiet.

His heart seized. Surging to his feet, he hissed her name. No response. A cold dread seeped into his bones, weighing down his legs as he stalked toward her bedroom.

"Mina?" He shoved the door open wider.

She stepped out of the bathroom, holding a flat iron in one hand and a can of hairspray in the other.

Derrek scowled at her, taking the can out of her hand. "What are you doing?"

"I thought I could pack a bag since I was here." Mina smiled at him as if they didn't have a care in the world.

She had a point. She was going to need some things, but they didn't have time to mess around with this. "Okay, fine. Grab a few changes of clothes. Necessities only." He couldn't believe he had to make that distinction for her. After all, he just got done telling her in graphic detail the risk they were running just by coming here.

Derrek went back to the living room and shifted through another pile of papers. Mina came from the bedroom, her arms laden with clothes. "What do you think I should bring?" She asked, holding up two different shirts.

His skin vibrated, practically singing at him to hurry. He shoved a hand through his hair. "It doesn't matter. Anything. Just hurry."

When Mina turned to go back to her room, he saw her phone peeking out of her pocket. He approached her, slipping out and holding it in front of her widened eyes.

"Why are you carrying this?" He demanded.

Mina blushed, her eyes falling away. The warning bells sounded in his head. His heart was hammering even as his hand went to his back, where his gun was tucked away.

"I didn't want Kat to worry." Mina began.

Derrek shoved her to the floor. "Get down!"

The window shattered in a hail of bullets, showering them with shards of glass. Her door burst open, slamming against the wall. Stuart poked his head in as Derrek fired. Wood splintered the door-frame inches from Stuart's face, forcing him back.

On the floor next to him, Mina huddled into a tight ball, her small body shaking as silent tears streamed down her face. He put his hand around her waist and hauled her up to her knees. "Get to your room," he whispered in her ear and gave her a little shove to get her moving. As she scrambled away, Stuart lunged through the opening, gun blazing. Bullets shredded the couch. Derrek's expression darkened as he looked at the damage. If Mina had still been hiding there, she'd have been riddled.

Blood surged through Derrek's veins, hot with rage. He pushed off the pillar, raised his gun, and fired. Stuart dashed toward the kitchen, almost making it. Derrek's last bullet hit him in the shoulder, jerking him backward.

Derrek approached, his gun raised, his blood pounding in his ears. Stuart slumped against the counter, pressing Mina's kitchen towel to his injured shoulder.

"Who's on the roof?" Derrek demanded. His gun was trained on Stuart.

Stuart sneered. "Mitch."

"What are his orders?"

"Open fire if I don't report in."

"How long?"

Stuart spit on the tile. "Five minutes."

Derrek's lip curled in disgust. He lifted his weapon, prepared to kill—

Click.

Empty.

Stuart's eyes gleamed with madness. He launched away from the counter, a knife in his hand. Derrek jumped back, sucking in against the cold rush of air. The knife flashed. Derrek dodged right. The blade hissed past, a mere whisper of steel missing him by inches. He stumbled back, reaching inside his coat. His fingers found his knife. Derrek flipped the handle in his palm, the cool steel sliding along his forearm. He lunged, slicing through Stuart's shirt, just shy of flesh.

Stuart spun. His blade sliced Derrek from wrist to elbow. Not deep, but enough to bleed. Derrek ground his teeth, ignoring the white-hot pain searing through his arm. He swung his blade around, following with a hard jab to the gunshot wound on Stuart's arm. Stuart grunted, swearing, falling back against the kitchen cabinets. His bloody hand holding onto the counter, he panted, his eyes dark with rage.

"What about the code?" Stuart panted.

Derrek gave a hollow laugh. "I think the code is shot to hell, don't you?"

Stuart moved from the counter, his confident smirk slipping. "You kill me, you sign your death warrant."

Derrek stepped forward, eyes cold. "It was signed the minute I failed to complete my objective." The harsh reality rested on his shoulders, a bitter weight for his choices.

Stuart sneered. "Too bad. I would have preferred to finish you off with the others, but I suppose dead is dead."

The hairs on Derrek's neck rose. His instincts hummed a warning. "What is that supposed to mean?"

"Nothing that concerns you." Stuart let out a chilling laugh, sounding like that of a madman.

Derrek's temper flared. He lunged. The knife clattered to the floor, knocked from Stuart's blood-soaked. Derrek kicked it away and slammed Stuart into the wall. His elbow wedged in Stuart's throat, he lifted him off the ground. Stuart gasped, clawing at Derrek's arm.

"What do you know?" Derrek asked, pressing down on Stuart's windpipe, making his eyes bulge as he struggled to breathe.

A soft exclamation from behind pulled Derrek's attention. He turned to find Mina standing across the room, her face pale and drawn. "Mina, go back to your room." He snapped. But his attention had been off Stuart too long. As cunning and conniving as ever, Stuart drove his knee into Derrek's ribs. The jab lacked some of the power but packed enough punch that he lost his grip. Stuart crumpled to the tile with a dull thud.

Stuart's leg shot out, catching Derrek in the knee. He swore, pain lacing up his leg. Derrek tried to recover, but he was already on his way down when Stuart kicked out again, catching him in the ribs. Derrek grunted, his eyes watering. He rolled to the side, narrowly missing the boot headed for his face.

Derrek shot out with his knife. Stuart kicked the blade away, sending it skidding across the tile floor. Derrek wrapped his leg around Stuart's chest, locking his arm above his head, and pulled. A sickening pop echoed as Stuart's shoulder dislocated. Stuart howled. Pain glazed his eyes, fear of death making him wild. He rolled away, crawling to Derrek's discarded knife.

Panting, Derrek hobbled behind him. He reached down, his hands on Stuart's head. With a sharp twist, Stuart convulsed and then went still.

Derrek looked down at the body. A coworker. Someone he had a history with. He waited for something—guilt, regret—but there was nothing. Just the same hollow numbness as every kill before it.

Empty.

Cold.

He stood up, turning to find Mina there. Derrek took a step toward her. She flinched, her wide eyes locked on Stuart's body. She took a step back. Then another. And for the first time, he felt something.

Fear.

Chapter Thirty-One

Mina stood frozen. Her eyes fixed on the body lying across her kitchen floor.

She should have stayed in her room but couldn't take the sounds anymore.

When Derrek told her to hide, she'd done so gladly. Her skin felt raw and burning where the jagged shards of glass had sliced into her. She crawled to her room, silent tears slipping down her cheeks. Her body trembled, whether from shock or fear; she couldn't tell.

She curled up near the closet, hands clamped over her ears. The gunfire rattled her bones, each deafening shot a violent percussion that echoed in her ears. The coppery taste of blood filled her mouth as she bit her lip, trying to stifle the screams that threatened to escape. She rocked herself, willing it all to stop.

As if in answer to her prayer, the shooting ceased.

Hesitantly, Mina peeled her fingers from her ears. She tilted her head to listen. The sharp scrap of a scuffle made her cringe. A breath hitched in her throat as Derrek's voice broke through the chaos. Relief flooded her, leaving her lightheaded. She couldn't make out their words, but hearing his voice was enough.

Mina inched forward, pressing herself against the wall before daring to peek around the doorframe. She winced as the dull thud of flesh meeting flesh echoed through the room. Then she saw him.

Derrek.

The sight of him almost sent her knees buckling. A strangled sound caught in her throat as she stumbled forward.

Derrek moved in a blur of motion. The man grunted. Followed by the horrifying thud of a body against the wall. Mina took a step closer and gasped. Blood, thick and red, trailing down Derrek's arm.

A soft moan escaped her lips before she could stifle it. Every part of her screamed to run to him.

But then he turned. His face was cold, unreadable. She took a step back.

Then he snapped at her. The sharp edge of his voice cut through her. She recoiled, the sting of rejection as sharp as fear's icy grip on her heart. She ran back to her room, crumbling to the floor. With her arms around her waist, she wept. Through blurred vision, she spotted the edge of her father's letter peeking out from beneath the bed. She grabbed it, fingers shaking, and stuffed it into her pocket.

She couldn't stay there.

Mina stood unsteady. The urgency to leave at war with the desire to hide. Uncertain what to do. She wanted Derrek. She covered her ears against the sound of fists hitting flesh echoing from the other room. Her stomach lurched. She forced herself to move.

She stepped out of her room and toward the kitchen.

Silence.

Her skin rippled. A thick, suffocating silence stretched across the room.

Derrek stood stiff, his breath coming hard and fast. His gaze was locked on the floor.

Mina crept toward him, her heart hammering against her ribs. She followed his gaze. The man was dead.

She looked at the lifeless figure, expecting to feel something. Shock. Horror. But there was nothing. She'd never seen a dead body before. She thought she might feel sick or terrified. Instead, there was only an eerie, weightless calm. Her head tilted to the side.

Across from her, Derrek's hands fisted at his side. Tension rolled off him in waves. She wanted to say something but didn't know what.

She parted her lips to speak, but they withered on her tongue as his head snapped around. Sharp, unrelenting green eyes held hers. She froze. A chilling awareness crawled down her spine. The blood in her veins pounded, alive with something she couldn't name. Her reaction—to him to the situation—felt strange. Unfamiliar. She stepped back. Not willing to look at what it meant. Not brave enough to ask herself why it worried her so.

"We have to leave," Derrek said. His voice curt as he picked up his knife.

Mina nodded, backing up another step. Could she go with him? What was wrong with her that she thought it would be okay to do this?

"Where's your bag?" Derrek asked, moving toward her as a large cat might approach its prey. His eyes held hers as his hand reached out, grasping her wrist in a firm yet gentle grip.

"In my room. On the bed." She said, her lips trembling.

"Go on and get it. We've got less than a minute."

Confused, Mina looked at him. He ignored her questioning gaze and gave her a gentle shove toward her room. She ran the last few steps, slinging her bag over her shoulder. She grabbed an extra pair of shoes and went to Derrek. "Ready," she said with an abundance of cheeriness.

His eyes watched her with a wariness that made her stomach flip. He went to the door, looking out into the hallway, and signaled for her to follow.

The hallway vibrated with hysteria. Doors opened and closed with shuddering force. Mina's gaze locked with a neighbor she had seen in passing but didn't know. The fear in the woman's eyes made her look away. This was her fault. All these people could have been hurt because of her.

Mina quickened her step until she was no more than an inch or two behind Derrek. She ducked behind his solid frame, using his size to hide her face. She released an unsteady breath when the stairwell door closed behind them.

She noticed the slight limp in his gait. "Are you okay?" She asked, barely about a whisper.

He grunted, taking the stairs ahead of her, this solid wall in front of her. Even injured and clearly in pain, he still placed her safety above her own. Only he was a killer. Surely, a man who held human life with so little reverence wouldn't be bothered with seeing to her protection. Mina had a hard time merging the two men.

She frowned at him as he led her silently down the empty staircase. Her gaze slid down his body, and her mind turned away from the uncomfortable thoughts to something far more pleasing. Mina grinned in appreciation, watching his muscles move beneath his shirt. She trembled with delight.

Derrek held her hand, pausing every so often before taking a few more steps down. She eyed his blood-smeared arm. In a way, he hardly seemed human. The cut had to be painful, but he didn't even pause long enough to tend his wound.

At the bottom, the stairs led to the back door they had used to come inside, but to the right was a long hallway. Mina knew it would take them into the lobby area. She hadn't anticipated Derrek taking that route instead.

He held the door open a crack but kept her firmly tucked behind him.

"What are you waiting for?" Mina whispered.

Tami, Phyllis, and Gabby came tearing around the corner, and Derrek stepped back, pressing the door wider. "Mom, how'd it go?"

"How'd it go? Son, have you lost your mind? It's crazier than a hornet's nest in the middle of June." Tami said, pausing to kiss Mina's cheek. "How are you, honey? Did you get what you needed?"

Gabby shoved her way through them, hightailing it to the rear door. "I hear sirens; talk later, Tami."

"I thought Abel was going to throw us out on our ears," Phyllis admitted with a chuckle. "The gunfire exploded, and then he wouldn't let us leave. Kept insisting it wasn't safe for gentlewomen like ourselves to be out in such a dangerous situation."

"Later." Gabby hissed, waving everyone forward. "If I get arrested on my birthday, I'll never forgive you."

"Your birthday was four days ago." Tami reminded.

"Doesn't matter. The whole month is off-limits. Only good things are allowed. You know that." Gabby muttered. Her wide girth moved with surprising speed.

Mina watched Derrek move to the front of their group. His expression was carved into stony silence. He didn't smile or speak. He wasn't acting as she was used to. She couldn't put her finger on what had changed, but something had shifted.

"Where are we going now? Back to the hotel?" Mina whispered. The need to be quiet seemed ridiculous, considering the bedlam of the streets.

"Lunch," Tami said. Phyllis and Gabby both readily agreed.

"No. We have to get out of here." Derrek said. His eyes swung in restless sweeps.

"No," Tami said with just as much impatience as Derrek. "You are taking us to lunch. We can hide in a restaurant." There was steel in her words. Her back straightened as she stared down the hard glint in Derrek's eye.

Mina was impressed. She looked from mother to son in wide-eyed appreciation. She didn't know who would win, but she was sure interested to find out. They stood toe to toe, Derrek glaring down at his mother, then relented, his endearing smile returning. "Only if you agree to get on a plane and go home afterward."

Tami gave her son a hard look and then nodded. "All right."

"Great." He slipped Tami's arm through his. "Let's find a place with a nice bathroom."

Tami gave him a perplexed look. "Why?"

Derrek held up his arm. His mother blanched. "Ladies, we are going back to the hotel."

"What? No food?" Phyllis whined.

"We'll have to order in," Tami said with a firm nod. "Derrek, take Mina back to the room. The girls and I will stop at a pharmacy and pick up lunch."

Before Mina knew what was happening, she and Derrek were once more alone. He took an odd way back to the hotel, turning down alleys and back streets until Mina was thoroughly lost. She thought she knew where they were at one point, but Derrek grabbed her hand and turned her around, leading her in the other direction.

He'd shaken his head, a smile pulling at the corner of his mouth. She didn't care if he laughed at her. If it erased the blank expression from his face, it was worth it to her.

"What happens now?" She asked. Unable to hold the silence a second longer.

He looked down at her for a moment, his expression an unreadable mask. "We're going to the hotel."

Mina pushed down her impatience. "After that. What happens next with this whole mess? Are we safe at the hotel? Will they find us there?" She couldn't keep the worry out of her voice. If those people came at them again, someone would inevitably get hurt. Some innocent bystanders would fall in the line of fire. She shuddered at the thought. What if Derrek's mother or her friends were hurt? Blood fell from her face, leaving her lightheaded. Her hand tightened in his. Derrek looked down at her, question in his eyes.

"I don't want anyone to die." She confessed in a hollow voice.

"Let's get my mother on a plane, and then we'll decide what's next."

Mina found comfort in his steady voice. He was right, one thing at a time. If she danced too far ahead, she would inevitably fall.

Four hours later, Mina sat alone in the hotel room, her father's letter resting in her lap. She'd read it a dozen times. Still, nothing.

Frustration simmered under her skin. There was always a reason behind everything her father did, yet the words refused to make sense.

She tried everything. She did a handstand, feet braced against the wall, reading the letter upside down. She soaked in the bathtub for fifteen minutes. She lay on the bed, her head dangling over the edge. Most of her strategies involved being upside down. None of them worked.

The words reminded just that—words. A message from a man she barely knew.

Tap, tap, tap. Mina drummed her nails against the wooden table, the rhythmic beat sending a strange pulse through her thoughts. Her vision blurred, the room shrinking until everything looked minuscule and distant.

Just as Alice tumbled down the rabbit hole, her mind spun, the letters twisting and shifting until a single phrase glowed like a beacon.

We are what we repeatedly do.

Whoosh.

Mina was back in her grandfather's study.

Her father stood over her.

"Come to the beach house. If I ever tell you this phrase, you come home to me."

The memory struck like lightning. The day of the near-drowning.

She could still feel the waves pulling her under, the panic in her chest. The surfer had hauled her to shore, his hands steady against her shaking frame. When she had stumbled home, her mother had wept in the kitchen. But her father? He had taken her into his study, his voice calm, measured.

Come home.

Mina sucked in a breath. The beach house.

That's where she needed to go.

Chapter Thirty-Two

"Derrek, I've never asked you about your work. I figured you knew what you were about and let you go about your business. But now I think you need to tell me." Tami said, her honeyed tone taking on the sterner edge of a mother. "Are you a criminal?"

"What? No, Mom. I'm not a criminal." Derrek said, swerving to miss a car that broke hard in front of him.

The last thing he needed was an accident, especially because he was already on borrowed time. Clint was bound to track down the car eventually.

Still, the problem remained—he needed a car. More importantly, Mina needed to disappear. The easiest solution was to drive to another city and catch a flight from there. But first, she needed a new ID. Luckily, he knew a guy who was quick and thorough. Once his mother was safely on her plane, he'd take Mina to get what they needed and vanish.

"Honestly, I'm relieved," his mother said, pulling him back to the conversation.

"I can't believe you thought I would break the law," he muttered.

Tami shrugged. "You always had a funny way of looking at things, even as a child. Not a lot of black and white with you. You saw the world in gray, and I think you still do."

"You'd be right." He grinned, his back teeth grinding together. "A person can't do what I do if everything has to fall into a nice little compartment."

"Be that as it may, I am worried. I know the girls joked and laughed all through lunch, but what happened at Mina's apartment was real. Those were shots we heard. Bullets tore apart the wall of Mina's apartment. You could've died." Tami said and shuddered. Her usual cheery face was washed with fear.

"Mom, anyone can die at any time. You could die crossing the street. Dad could die of a heart attack. We can't live our lives as if we are doomed to die."

"True, but your father and I aren't flirtin' with the Grim Reaper."

Derrek stopped at the red light and turned to his mother, the bitter truth settling in—this might be the last time he ever saw her. Mitch and Clint were still hunting him. He'd gotten lucky with Stuart, but luck wouldn't save him twice. He wouldn't sugarcoat the situation. Facing two AOD operatives at once was a death sentence. They were trained just like him. They knew how to kill.

"Are you excited to get home?" he asked.

His mother smiled. "I guess we're through discussing this?" Tami asked, a sparkle of humor shimmering in her green eyes.

The airport was busy—no surprise there—but he didn't want to be away from Mina any longer than necessary. They had managed to stay off AOD's radar thus far, but eventually, they would find them at the hotel, and if they hadn't moved on by that point, it would be too late.

He wished he could find a way to right everything so that Mina could be free. A life on the run wouldn't be contusive to someone like her. She couldn't be able to live somewhere without making connections. He'd never met a woman quite like her. She was a soul who needed others.

He pulled to the curb once a minivan pulled away. He unloaded the six luggage bags and hugged Phyllis and Gabby. When he turned to his mother, tears shimmered in her eyes. "I love you; you know that, don't you?"

"I love you too," Derrek said. He tried to memorize every line on his mother's face. Tomorrow, he could be gone. The reality made him shudder. He wrapped his mother's slight frame in a big hug. If this was his last moment with his mother, he wanted it to be memorable for her.

"Listen, Mom, things are going to be a little hectic. I'll call you when it calms again in a few weeks. All right?"

Tami nodded, pressing a tissue to her nose. "Be careful."

Derrek grinned. "Always."

He stood at the curb and watched her walk away, his heart aching. He hoped he was wrong and that he would be able to defeat both Mitch and Clint, but he knew the odds, and unfortunately, they were not in his favor.

Derrek let himself into the hotel room an hour later. Mina danced around, excitement radiating from her. She ran to him, jumping up to wrap her legs around his waist and her arms around his neck. She kissed him—quick, closed-lipped, nothing dramatic—yet his pulse was still racing.

He stood holding her, waiting to see what she'd do next. To his disappointment, she unhooked her legs and slid to the ground.

"What have you been up to?" He saw the bathroom empty of the few small things he'd bought her. "What's this?" He asked when he spotted her bag packed and sitting by the door.

Mina clasped her hands, her excitement palpable. "I remembered! You know what was so important in my father's letter. Can you believe it? You should have seen me. I tried all these crazy things in hopes of triggering a memory, and then bang. There it was, clear and unmistakable. We need to go to my grandfather's beach house."

"Whoa," Derrek said. "Slow down." He steered Mina to the bed, having her sit. She bubbled with a humming energy he struggled to understand. Her words came as a flurry of incoherent sentences. He sat across from her, clasping her hands between his. "Start from the beginning."

Mina continued to squirm, but she remained seated. Her eyes danced with victory. "I remembered," she squealed. "Can you believe it? I almost gave up, but then I just knew." She waved the letter in his face. "I didn't see it at first, but then I did. See, it's right here." She pointed to the page. "The phrase my father told me. The one you quoted to me. It was here all along. It's like my eyes couldn't see it, but my mind could."

Derrek took the letter from her hand, smoothing out the page. He scanned the words and looked at her. "Where? I don't see it."

The corner of Mina's mouth quirked as she leaned forward. "I didn't either. But see here?" She pointed to a word written in block letters—except for the 'w,' which curled into a looping script. "And here." She tapped another word where the 'p' swirled the same way.

Derrek scanned the letter again, this time following the curling script until the hidden words took shape. His eyebrows shot up in disbelief. He turned to Mina. "How'd you know to do that?"

She shrugged, dropping her gaze to her lap. "My father liked to do puzzles."

When she didn't elaborate, he wanted to press her for more, but the grim set of her jaw stopped him. Instead, he said, "So, all this means we're going to the beach house?"

Her smile returned, the shadow in her eyes lifting. "Yes. My father will be there. And maybe he can explain what's going on."

Derrek studied her. He still hadn't told her that he knew about her father and his tie to the AOD. Part of him held back. Trust never came easily, and even though Mina was starting to matter to him, there were pieces of himself he wasn't ready to share. Secrets he would never tell.

"All right, let's go, but we need to make a stop first."

The two-story red brick building had been painted so many times the original color was lost. It looked run-down; time had shown it little mercy. Derrek led Mina inside, guiding her by a hand at her waist. The glass on the inner door was broken and covered with dirt. Derrek laughed at Mina's expression. "Not everyone can live in luxury," he teased.

"Properly tended would be nice," Mina said, sidestepping a pile of rotting wood. "Who are we supposed to be meeting again?"

Derrek took her hand, leading her toward the stairs, which looked like they'd seen better days. He nudged her away from the banister. Several screws were missing, and he knew it was about as structurally sound as a house of cards.

"His name is Spitz," he said, keeping a wary eye on where he stepped. "He's got papers for me."

At the top of the stairs, the threadbare carpet ended abruptly at a wall stretching from one side of the building to the other. In the center was a pair of rusted metal doors, solid and forbearing. Derrek knocked twice, then stepped in front of a thin slit on the right side.

"Spitz, open up."

A low buzz sounded, and Derrek pushed the door open, ushering Mina inside. Her mouth fell open, and he smiled.

The loft opened into a surprisingly modern space. A large leather couch faced an array of high-end electronics. Along one wall, an elaborate set up of computers hummed softly, multiple monitors flashing static images.

Spitz emerged from around the corner—a thin man with perpetually hunched shoulders. His tank top only emphasized his wiry frame. A thick gold chain dangled from his neck, and when he grinned, a wide gap between his front teeth stood out.

"Eric, how are you, my man." Spitz came forward to shake Derrek's hand.

"I'm good. Do you have what I need?" He asked, shooting Mina a wary glance. Sure enough, her face flushed, and her eyes narrowed.

"Yeah, man," Spitz said, his eyes locked on Mina. "Introductions first. Who is this delightful package?"

"Mina, this is Spritz. Spritz, Mina." Mina turned a bright smile to Spritz. "It's nice to meet you, Spitz." She tilted her head. "Spitz is an unusual name. Is it your last name?"

"No, baby. It's a nickname I picked up years ago." He said, licking his top lip.

Mina tugged her hand free, her smile faltering. "How do you know, Eric, was it?" She turned to Derrek, her left eye twitching.

"Oh, Eric and I go way back," Spitz chuckled. "But he's never brought me a delectable piece like you."

Derrek pulled Mina into his side, his arm draping over her shoulders. "And I'm not today either," he growled, steering her toward a makeshift photo setup consisting of nothing more than a sheet hanging on the wall with a camera positioned across from it. "Let's get this over with."

Mina lagged, casting Derrek an uncertain glance.

"He needs your picture to finish the ID," he explained.

"Oh. I see." She relaxed visibly, turning to Spitz. "Where do I stand?"

"Right here, baby. X marks the spot. Hooo." Spitz adjusted the camera, snapped a shot, then told her to smile and took another. "Okay. Have a seat, and make yourself at home. I'll be back in no time."

As Spitz disappeared into the back, Derrek sat next to Mina. Her gaze stayed fixed ahead.

"This won't take long," he assured her. "Then we're out of here."

Mina turned to face him, accusation in her eyes. "Eric? It's a little on the nose, don't you think? What, you couldn't think of a better name, so you just started saying rhymes?"

"Shhh." He hissed. Looking past Mina's shoulder. He leaned forward, pulling Mina into his arms. His nose nudged her ear as he whispered, "Spitz has this place wired. We can talk about anything you like once we're gone, but until then, don't say anything you wouldn't want the world to know in the five seconds it would take him to upload it."

Mina pushed away from him. He frowned down at her. He didn't know what she was so upset about. It wasn't like he could tell Spitz his real name. He hadn't been kidding. Spitz collected information. Sometimes, he used it to blackmail; other times, he just held on to it for another day.

Spitz was a contact he'd picked up years ago but wasn't the only one. Several AOD operatives used the same resources. The truth was, there just weren't that many people out there capable of creating convincing papers.

Derrek looked at the monitors, his skin tingling with an eerie edge. He glanced at his watch and then down the hall, where Spitz disappeared. His foot tapped the floor, his hands tensing in his lap.

"What's the matter?" Mina asked, her brow furrowed.

He looked at the monitors again. His agitation made it almost impossible to stay still. He surged to his feet, stalking down the hallway where he'd seen Spitz go. As if on cue, Spitz emerged. His eyes widened in alarm. "Hey, hey. What's this? You need the john?"

"No." Derrek snapped, his eyes narrowing. "I need my order. Where's my papers?"

"Right here." Spitz waved them in the air. "Just need your lady love's signature."

"Let's get this done." Derrek stalked to the living area, unable to shake the feeling that something was off with Spritz. He was too cheerful, too accommodating. Spritz was a weasel. He wined and wheedled until he got what he wanted. He never did a job without complaining about at least one step of the process. Spitz was never one to be obliging.

Derrek's gaze landed on the empty couch, his pulse spiking. Then he spotted Mina at the window, silhouetted against the city skyline. When he looked at Spitz, irritation flared—there was a gleam in the man's eye, a predatory entitlement aimed at Mina. Derrek's hands curled into fists.

"Mina, come sign this," Derrek barked, his patience fraying as he fought the urge to put himself between her and Spitz.

Mina spun around, her eyes wide with fear. Hugging herself, she took slow steps toward them.

Derrek kept his gaze on Spitz, watching as Spitz watched her. Mina forced a hesitant grin, but it lacked her usual light.

Spitz laid a passport on the table. Derrek barely caught a glimpse of the image before Spitz slapped his palm over it.

"What the hell?" Derrek snapped, shoving Spitz back. He snatched up the passport, swore, and hurled it at Spitz's head.

Spitz pulled a gun.

Derrek had already anticipated the move. His knife was out. With a quick jab, the blade sliced along Spitz's right arm.

The gun clattered to the floor as Spritz crumbled, clutching his wound and wailing.

He cradled his injured arm, crying.

Derrek crouched, pressing the cold steel of his knife to Spitz's cheek. "Who paid you?"

Spitz babbled nonsense, swearing it was no one. Spittle flew from his mouth.

Derrek pressed the blade harder. A bead of red pooled around the tip. Spitz whimpered.

"Clint," he gasped. "He's on his way."

Cursing, Derrek grabbed Mina's hand and bolted for the door. His heart pounded. Clint could arrive any second. They had to move.

Weighing his options, his gaze landed on a window at the far end of the room. He yanked it open and pushed Mina through.

"Go!" he ordered.

She hesitated only for a second before climbing onto the fire escape. He followed, taking the stairs two at a time, Mina close behind. She panted but didn't ask questions.

At another time, he might stop to consider what it meant—her quiet, unshakable trust in him.

But right now, all that mattered was running.

Chapter Thirty-Three

"**K**eep moving." Derrek urged.

Mina held onto his voice, the single thing keeping her moving. She ran behind him, her feet aching, but she didn't complain. She didn't know what happened but knew it wasn't good.

Derrek led her down an alley. She tried to keep up with his longer stride. When he came to a pothole, Mina didn't have the reach he did. Her foot caught the edge, but not enough to hold her place. She tried to stay upright, but gravity pulled her down. She fell to her knees, her hand slipping from his as she hit the ground. Her teeth rattled, snapping together. The sound of rent clothes made her wince. She didn't know what tore, but she felt the battering her body had taken.

She got to her knees. Her palms throbbed from the deep gashes. A grimace twisted her face as she looked at the injury, wincing at the black gunk covering them. Derrek was at her side. His warm, reassuring grip enveloped her elbow. Concern shimmered in his vibrant green eyes. "Are you okay?"

"I think so." She panted, pain vibrating through her body.

"Can you stand?"

Mina gave him an impatient look. "Yes. I'll be fine. I just needed a minute."

Derrek's eyes left her to look beyond her. "We don't have a minute. We've got to get to the car."

Mina nodded. She knew he was right, but it didn't make the task any easier. "How close are we?" She asked in short, gasping breaths.

A smile curved his adorable mouth. She couldn't image what he found to be so funny. Mina certainly didn't feel like laughing. "The car's just around the corner," he said.

"What's so funny?" She asked, glaring at his back. Here, she was wounded, and he was laughing. Oh, he was making an effort not to, but she could hear the humor in his voice and the betraying motion of his shoulders. The man had the sensitivity of a lizard.

Derrek shot a quick look over his shoulder, his mouth twitching as he tried—and failed—to hide his laughter. "You don't know where we are?"

"Duh. I wouldn't be asking if I did." She knew she sounded petty, but she was hurt and scared and didn't like being laughed at.

He paused at the end of the alley, holding out a hand to stop her from getting too close. Peeking around the building, he scanned the area before turning back to her. "The car is about twenty feet that way," he said. "Stay behind me. Hold onto my pants, okay?"

Mina slipped her hand into the back pocket of his jeans. The stiff material made her wince, but she pushed the pain aside and held on. He didn't ask much from her, but she would do what she could. He had already fought two men for her, and she knew at least two more coming. Clint seemed to make Derrek genuinely uneasy. The last thing she wanted was to add to his worries.

After one final glance at their surroundings, Derrek turned to her. "We go on three."

Her heart jumped with each number he counted off. One. Two. When he whispered "Three," her breath caught—and then she ran.

Derrek unlocked the door and slid into the driver's seat, the car already in reverse before she even had her seatbelt buckled. He pulled into traffic, weaving through the streets with practiced precision. Only after several turns, putting distance between them and the city, did she notice the tension in his body finally start to ease.

They drove for almost half an hour before Derrek pulled into a gas station. He parked in front and told her to wait for him. When he came back, he tossed a bag into the back seat and pulled back onto the road without a word.

They drove for another ten minutes and stopped when they came to a park. Laughter rang through the air—children playing, mothers chatting. Mina found herself smiling faintly, momentarily caught in the normalcy of it all.

Derrek led her to an empty picnic table. He straddled the bench and pulled her leg into his lap. Silently, he unpacked the bag, meticulously arranging the supplies. He tore open a gauze pad with his teeth, then grabbed a bottle of peroxide.

Mina barely had time to brace before the sting hit. "Owe!" she hissed, jerking away from him.

Derrek's grip tightened. "Hold still."

She gasped as he pressed gauze to the wound and smacked his hand when he dumped a clear liquid that burned like the devil.

He ignored her, swiping the pad over raw skin. The pain was immediate, searing. Mina shot up, shoving him. "What are you doing?" she snapped. "That hurts!"

"It'll hurt worse if it gets infected," he pointed out. His tone was calm, and his focus never shifted.

She scowled but stayed put, her breathing ragged gasps. Once he seemed satisfied, he taped a bandage over her knee and let her leg go—only to take her hand next.

Mina tensed. He turned her palm over, inspecting it in silence. The first scrape wasn't too bad, and she exhaled in relief when the cleaning barely stung. But then he picked up her other hand.

Her stomach dropped.

Her appreciation was short-lived because the palm of her other hand had faired far worse. Pain shot up her arm as he worked, tweezers pulling out bits of gravel embedded in the raw flesh. Tears sprang to her eyes.

She nearly crawled out of her skin when he poured the clear liquid again. Her body jerked with each spark of agony, but his grip was firm.

"Derrek," she ground out, tugging against his hold.

He put a bandage on her palm, rubbing the corners flat with his thumbs. Then, he brought her hand to his mouth, pressing a tender kiss to her sensitive skin. The touch sent something sharp and unexpected through her. The tears in her eyes burned for an entirely different reason now.

"What happens with Spitz?" She asked, needing to ease the tension surrounding her heart. "Did he do the passport wrong?" She asked.

Derrek sorted through the items, discarding the unnecessary ones. "He didn't do anything. The passport was someone else's. He was just stalling us until AOD could show up."

"What's AOD?"

Derrek's eyes flickered her way before resuming his task. "It's a program I belong to."

"And Spitz?"

Derrek grinned, his eyes crinkling at the corners. "No. Spitz belongs to no one. His loyalty goes to the highest bidder."

"I take it you weren't the highest bidder this time?"

"You got it." Derrek stood and held out his hand to her. "Are you ready?"

Mina hesitated, his hand and what he offered looming in front of her in a way that scared her. He represented a world full of uncertainty. Part of her longed for the adventure that awaited, and another part wanted to recoil and pull away.

He smiled, and she yielded. The warning ringing inside quieted as her heart sang.

The beach house was exactly as she remembered it. That one summer she'd spent there had been one of her happiest memories. She never did know why her father never took them back.

Rather than using the front steps leading to the porch, Mina circled to the rear. She could see her father sitting in one of the wicker chairs on the back porch facing the sea. Derrek followed behind her. He didn't speak; he just let her lead.

She went to the door and rose to her toes, searching around an ornate seashell hanging on the wall. Her hand came away with a small black box. Sliding the lid off, the house key was exactly as she remembered it.

Mina took the key and slipped it into the lock. When it clicked, she turned the key and went inside. The air was thick with a heavy silence. "Dad?" Mina called out, but there was no answer.

Derrek stepped forward, reaching for the gun she'd seen him tuck at his back. "Stay behind me until I've cleared this place," he said over his shoulder, his attention already locked on the empty rooms ahead.

Mina followed, her mind swirling with memories of a long-ago summer. Her fingers trailed over the counter, disturbing a thick layer of dust that dulled its once-pristine surface. She wandered into the living room, where the piano her mother used to play sat untouched, its keys blanketed in neglect. She tapped a key and winced. It needed to be tuned.

Brushing dust from her hands, she moved toward the foyer. Her fingers rested lightly against the grandfather clock—

Pain lanced through her skull.

Mina gasped, stumbling back. Her breath came fast and shallow as she pressed a palm to her forehead, squeezing her eyes shut. The sharp agony dulled to a relentless ringing in her ears. She inhaled once, twice until the worst of it passed.

Shaking it off, her gaze drifted past her grandfather's study to the hallway that led to her childhood room. The upstairs had belonged to her parents and Braxton. But she... she had slept on the bottom floor, in a tiny room tucked in the back of the house.

Mina moved down the dark hallway, the silence ringing in her ears. Her heart was pounding inside her chest as she drew closer.

Her old door was just as she'd left it. The sign she'd hung there—a rainbow with bold letters reading "Smiles Welcome"—was miraculously still intact. Warmth flickered in her chest. She wrapped her fingers around the handle and pushed inside.

The air was stale, heavier than anywhere else in the house. She wrinkled her nose and stepped toward the bed, running a hand over the faded covers. A memory surfaced—slipping a journal under the mattress, hiding her thoughts where no one could find them. She reached beneath the mattress, fingers searching. They brushed something—

Agony exploded behind her eyes.

She collapsed.

A strangled gasp escaped her as she curled into herself, bile rising in her throat. She bit down on a cry, muffling it with her fist, but her body writhed against the pain.

Mina rolled to her back. Her feet pushed against the floor, away from her room and back toward the door. Derrek ran into the room, almost stumbling over her. He fell to his knees, pulling her into his arms even as she cried.

His arms convulsed around her, "What happened? Where are you hurt?"

Her head thrashed, tears seeping from her closed eyes.

"Talk to me," Derrek demanded. His voice was harsh with concern.

She whimpered, burrowing into his arms as if she could burrow under his skin. Her mind couldn't form words, couldn't grasp what was happening.

Derrek, cursing under his breath, scooped her up. The moment he turned toward the bed, her body seized violently.

He pivoted, racing back down the hall.

By the time they reached the front door, Mina managed a breathless whisper. "I'm okay."

He pressed his mouth to her forehead, his exhale unsteady. "What was that? You scared the life out of me."

She shook her head, trying to force coherence into her thoughts. "I don't know. I was just... reaching for my journal under the—"

A scream ripped from her throat.

Derrek barely had time to brace before her body convulsed again, her hands clutching her head. He swore and carried her to the couch, forcing her to look at him as she trembled.

"Mina, has this ever happened to you before?" His voice was tight, urgent.

She forced herself to focus on his face, her own contorted in pain. "Never."

Just like the other time, the pain almost receded immediately. She gasped at the last vibration of pain. "I don't know what's happening to me."

Derrek brushed her hair away from her face, studying her with worry etched into his brow. Then, without a word, he stood and left her on the couch.

Mina glared at the ceiling. It rippled before her eyes—shifting, distorting—before settling back into place. She pushed herself upright, a strange stillness creeping over her. Slowly, she rolled her head in a circle, an odd sense of déjà vu washing over her.

Something was wrong.

She leaned back. The war inside her head tore her raw. Her mind felt like a battlefield, her thoughts clashing in a war she couldn't understand. She gripped the couch fabric, her knuckles whitening, grounding herself in the present. Across the room, an abstract painting of the beach hung on the wall. The chaotic swirls of sky and water had always blurred together, energy coiling in a restless dance. How many years had she stared at that painting, unable to tell where one ended and the other began?

Her breath caught.

Derrek returned, a pink spiral-bound book in his hands. The moment she saw it, recognition flared. Her chest tightened. She knew that book. Knew it the way she knew her heartbeat. And yet... she couldn't remember the last time she'd held it. One moment, it had been a fixture in her life. The next, it vanished—gone, as if it had never existed.

"Is this what you were looking for?" Derrek asked, holding it out to her.

She wanted to take it. To read the thoughts of the child she had been. But when she willed her body to move, nothing happened.

Derrek arched a brow. "Don't you want it?"

"Yes," she said firmly. But her arms remained frozen, unresponsive. "I can't move my arms."

Derrek's expression darkened. He set the book beside her and knelt, running his hands along her arms, applying gentle pressure. "Can you feel this?"

She nodded. Tried again to lift her arm—and this time, it obeyed. A shaky laugh escaped her. "That was weird."

"Yeah, it was." He stood and helped her up. "Pick up the book."

Mina looked down at it. Her arms dangled uselessly at her sides, a strange weight settling over her. Derrek grabbed the book and placed it in her hands.

She collapsed.

Derrek caught her before she hit the floor, his arms locking around her as she gasped in pain. Pressure swelled inside her skull, unbearable, suffocating. A strangled cry tore from her lips.

He tossed the book away.

The pain vanished.

For a moment, silence filled the space between them. Derrek said nothing, just watched her, his gaze sharp, assessing. Mina panted, her body aching, her hands trembling. Her eyes flicked toward the study door—then back to him.

She didn't want to open that door.

She didn't want to step into that room.

Her heart pounded, each beat a painful drum inside her chest. Every instinct screamed at her to run. To turn away and never return. She moved forward, her hand outstretched. As she turned the knob, the door creaked open.

Unlike the rest of the house, the study smelled fresh, as if someone still used it regularly. That didn't make sense. But she had no time to dwell on it—

Mina crossed the threshold, and with it, her memories came crashing over her in a tidal wave of sensations. She gasped, gripping the doorknob for support as the truth shattered through her.

"It's a lie."

Derrek's hand found her waist, steadying her as she sagged against him. "What is?" His breath was warm against her forehead.

Mina squeezed her eyes shut.

"My life. Everything. It's all a lie."

Chapter Thirty-Four

Mina wandered the small confines of the office, trying and failing to untangle what she remembered from what was real.

Across the room, Derrek watched her. He stood silent and unmoving, waiting for her to crack.

The joke was on him. She had already cracked wide open.

Every memory she cherished, every happy moment, felt fragile, false, and wrong. Was any of it real? She didn't know.

There were things she knew were true. Braxton, her brother. He was real. Photos of them growing up together covered the office walls.

She'd looked over them, searching for some kind of certainty. Those were real. How else would they exist? She remembered some of what had happened in them. But what bothered her most wasn't the pictures—it was the clashing memories inside her head. Competing, twisting, and fighting to overwrite one another.

Everything about this room was ingrained in her; it was as if she had stepped into a half-forgotten dream.

The sharp and familiar scent of furniture polish and leather tugged at something buried deep. She took another breath, her stomach clenched, nausea rolling inside. Something was beating at the door of her subconscious, but it wouldn't come.

Her fingers trailed along the desk's smooth, worn surface. She knew how the leather chairs would feel beneath her, how they would sink under her weight, swallowing her whole. She knew the paintings on the wall, the way their eyes followed her, judging, always watching.

There were secrets in this room.

The knowledge tiptoed toward her consciousness, only to vanish as quickly as a receding wave. The harder she tried to grasp it, the more it eluded her.

Something was wrong.

Something was *missing*.

Her pulse hammered against her ribs as she squeezed her eyes shut, willing the memory to surface.

Nothing.

Only an empty void where something important used to be.

It didn't make sense.

One summer. That was all she should remember.

And yet... it felt like she had been here her whole life.

Derrek stood at the bookcase, fingers trailing along the thick spines. He pulled one out, slid it back, then chose another.

Mina's vision tunneled. Her mind spun back to her father, standing at the bookcase, speaking to her as he moved the bronze-winged statue.

Mina surged forward, shoving Derrek aside. He shot her a questioning look, which she ignored. Her hands found the cold metal, gripping the wings, and pulled. A soft click sounded as the room vibrated. The wall to the right of the bookcase shifted, revealing a door.

Derrek's brow lifted. "Stay here," he ordered, blocking her when she moved toward the opening.

Mina bristled. "Wait, I'm not staying here. I'm coming with you." She followed close on his heels.

Derek spun on his heel, stepping forward. Mina stepped back. Again. Until the wood of the bookcase pressed against her spine. His hands flattened against the shelves, caging her in. His nose was an inch from hers. "You stay where I tell you." His voice was low, firm. Dangerous. "I'm not going to let you run into a room I haven't checked."

She stared at him, pulse hammering. Something wild and unfamiliar stirred inside her. The charming facade he presented to the world was gone, replaced by the predator she was beginning to think was more to who he was.

"No," she said, her mouth set into a firm line. Talk about poking a bear, but she couldn't help it. The day had left her raw, exposed. This moment was something she could control, and she refused to let him take it from her.

Even as he narrowed his eyes and puffed out his chest, she stood her ground. "I'm coming with you. This is my life. My past. I have a right."

His hand moved to her side. His fingers tightened around her waist. He pressed into her, the hard plains of his body molding to her soft ones. "You promised me you would listen to what I said."

His touch steadied her jittering nerves. She sighed, meeting his intense gaze. He was right; she had. But that didn't seem to matter now. Not here. Not in this place, where everything felt like an integral part of her.

She kissed him, just a whisper of contact, a fleeting reassurance. Over before it had truly begun. "It'll be okay. Let me do this. I need to."

He wavered, doubt flickering in his eyes, but after a beat, he nodded and let her go. She took his hand, needing the connection as she stepped into the darkness. There was a light switch somewhere; she remembered that much, but she couldn't remember where. Leaving them to move forward, guided only by her memories.

A coldness settled deep in her bones, making her shiver. Derrek wrapped an arm around her waist, pulling her against his chest. His warmth chased away only the chill on her skin, leaving the deeper cold untouched. She tried to force the memories, to fill in the blanks ahead, but nothing came. The unknown made this so much harder.

The hallway gave way to a vast, open space, far larger than she expected. It stretched beneath the house, the full size of the structure above. No one looking from the outside would ever suspect a hidden chamber like this existed.

Derrek released her and moved ahead. The next moment, the room was flooded with harsh, sterile light.

A stainless-steel counter with a sink lined the wall. Medical equipment was scattered all around them. Her heart pounded. A flash of memory struck an image of her as a child sitting on the cold metal examination table, wires trailing from her head.

She swallowed hard, shaking the memory away. Not wanting to remember that or any of the other images clawing at the edges of her mind.

"What is this place?" Derrek asked.

"This," the response came from the far corner, where a shadow revealed an opening to another room. "Is my lab."

Mina gasped, whirling around to see her father. Her stomach tightened, nausea rearing up until she was forced to run to the sink. Her mind twisted, flipping inside out, pain searing through her skull. One arm clutched her convulsing stomach; the other hand pressed against her temple, her fingers digging into her hair.

"What's wrong with me?" She gasped.

"You've come home, Mina. I always knew you would." Her father smiled. It was cold and practical without any love or warmth.

Derrek was at her side, his hand supporting her as she leaned against the counter. She couldn't stop the memories from coming. The floodgates had opened. She wanted to curl into a ball, surrendering to the pull of oblivion.

Mina turned accusing eyes to her father. "What did you do to me?"

Dr. Charles Ellis LeSeur stepped forward, his gaze sharp, clinical. "It isn't so much what I did to you, Mina, but what I helped you become."

Mina's breath hitched. A chill raced over her arms, sinking into her chest.

Her father went on, his voice unnervingly calm. "I've always been fascinated by nature versus nurture, but theories mean nothing without proof. Unfortunately, no parent would willingly offer up their child for such an experiment."

A cold, detached smile curved his lips. "So, the next logical step was to find children whose parents wouldn't care." He paused as if allowing the words to sink in. "That left me with only one option – my own."

Mina's stomach twisted violently. "What are you saying?"

"It's simple." LeSeur clasped his hands behind his back, delivering his words with the measured tone of a conference presentation. "I needed two children. One from a violent, unstable background. The first was easy. A baby girl was born to a heroin addict who overdosed weeks after giving birth. Her father, a man serving life in prison for killing a man in a bar fight. When authorities found her, she was barely six weeks old, starving, forgotten." He shot Mina a pointed look.

Her throat went dry.

"For the second, I needed the opposite: morals, values, and an upbringing steeped in structure. That opportunity presented in a preacher's teenage daughter who found herself pregnant. She wanted to give her baby up for adoption. Her father and I agreed the child could serve a greater purpose."

Derrek muttered a low, angry oath. Mina barely heard him past the ringing in her ears. Horror filled her gaze as she looked at the man she called her father.

"What about Mom?" she whispered. "She was okay with this?"

LeSeur chuckled, shaking his head. "Lyla?" He waved a dismissive hand. "She was a nurse. Nothing more."

"Nurse?" she echoed, her world crumbling beneath her feet.

"What did you expect?" His tone was almost amused. "The state wouldn't allow a single man to adopt two babies in a matter of months. I needed a wife on paper. She agreed to a fifteen-year arrangement. It worked out well, far better than I ever anticipated."

He studied her in the way that she remembered, the way that made her skin crawl. "But you see, Mina, I realized early on that you weren't quite what I needed." A thin, almost cruel smile stretched his lips. "Still, I never waste perfectly good test subjects."

"Gene therapy targeting specific neurons is another area where I've invested many hours of study." He took another step forward. His eyes gleamed with something dark. "And you have no idea how much promise you hold."

Derrek's grip on Mina's waist tightened, tension radiating off him in waves. "You used your own daughter as a lab rat." he spat.

LeSeur's eyebrow lifted. "And you? What was she to you—a toy to play with until it was time to complete your mission?" His gaze flicked to Mina. "Did he tell you he's part of my program? The *Administers of Death* project is my creation. *I* chose who advanced. *I* designed the final stage, ensuring each recruit was given a dossier that would push them to kill. Don't let him fool you. He is what I made him—a weapon. Nothing more than a killing machine. I point, and he fires."

Derrek took a threatening step forward. Mina pressed a hand to his chest, stopping him—not by force, but giving him the chance to come to terms on his own.

"It doesn't matter," she whispered against his ear.

Derrek's eyes dropped to hers, and he shuddered.

"None of this explains why AOD put a kill out on her," Derrek growled, muscles coiled beneath her palm.

LeSeur's gaze shifted between them. "I'm afraid it's tied to my neurological research."

Derrek's jaw clenched. "Are you telling me you've been messing with some other person's life?"

Despite the tension, LeSeur's face remained neutral. "Not at all. All my research was completed with Mina. What I have is proof of how it works. And some will do whatever is necessary to get their hands on it. To create the perfect soldier. One who never questions. One who *always* follows orders."

"But I'm not like that. That isn't me," Mina argued. The man she called father, the monster standing before her—was spouting nonsense. She didn't know how to fight, let alone kill. "I don't understand what any of this has to do with me."

LeSeur offered a patronizing smile. "It doesn't. Not really. You were always just a means to an end. But, I must say she played her hand masterfully."

Derrek's muscles went rigid. Mina caught the sharp shift in his posture, the way his jaw clenched. His eyes locked onto her father, dark and unreadable.

A prickle of unease ran down her spine. A puzzled frown creased her brow as she reviewed her father's words, searching for the trigger she'd missed. Something had primed Derrek to pounce.

"You see, I disappeared, taking all the data with me. Once I knew what they were intended to do with my research, I had to leave. This is *my* project, *my* vision, and they wanted to corrupt it." His lip curled in disgust.

A scream of frustration clawed at her chest. She squeezed her hand only to realize it was cradled in Derrek's. Had he taken her hand, or perhaps she had taken his? It didn't matter. Nothing did, not now when she was faced with this...mess.

Her father—she wouldn't call him that anymore—kept talking in circles. She needed the truth. He had changed her, altered her in some unseen way, and she needed to know how. Better yet, why?

"I don't care about any of that!" she screamed. "Tell me what you did to me?" Mina thumped her chest.

LeSeur exhaled as if speaking to a slow-witted child. "I already told you. I redirected my focus when you didn't respond to my earlier tests. Instead of breaking your spirit, I explored what I could do with your mind—specifically, your memory." His eyes gleamed with sick fascination.

"The brain is a marvel of intricate pathways." His voice turned almost giddy. "All you need is the right key, and you can erase an entire sequence of memories. Imagine it, Mina! The power to erase an embarrassing moment, a painful failure... a heartbreak. We could wipe away history's darkest stains."

Mina looked at him as if seeing him for the first time. How had she ever missed it?

He was a monster. No heart. No soul.

Her voice shook, but she forced the words out. "You can't do that," she said, unable to stay quiet a moment longer. "Our past shapes who we are. Without it, we're nothing but empty shells destined to repeat the same mistakes. Erasing pain doesn't heal us—it destroys us."

Silence stretched between them. For the first time, Mina hoped her father would listen to something beyond the cold logic that ruled his mind.

Chapter Thirty-Five

D errek kept Mina close to his side. Nothing LeSeur said eased the tightening in his gut. If anything happened, if LeSeur made a move, he needed to be ready. Getting Mina out of harm's way was his only priority, no matter the cost.

Even now, she faced her father with fragile, wavering courage. She deserved better than the life LeSeur had forced on her.

Frowning, he looked over the lab equipment scattered around the room. It made a frightening blueprint of Mina's childhood. She'd grown up as nothing more than a glorified lab rat. He could almost see her—sweet little Mina, desperate for love, doing whatever LeSeur asked just to earn his approval.

Mina trembled beside him. He tightened his grip around her waist, pulling her into his side, silently urging her to lean on him. Whatever she needed—his strength, his protection—he'd gladly give it.

Then his eyes locked on the wall behind LeSeur. Unlike the pristine office upstairs, the photos here were unframed and tacked haphazardly to the wall. They were a chaotic collage of glossy images, sticky notes, and scraps of paper with bold, scrawled messages. One photo in particular made his pulse hammer.

Lies. Deceit. Manipulation. He'd played his fair share of games over the years, never giving it much thought. But seeing the truth laid out like this, being on the receiving end of it, unleashed a rage so hot it burned through him.

He turned to Mina, his voice dangerously calm, a stark contrast to the storm brewing inside him. His fingers curled around his gun, lifting it with deadly precision. He refused to give in to the anguish crushing his chest.

"Derrek?" Mina's eyes darted around, wide with confusion. "What is it? What's wrong?"

"You didn't tell me you knew Clint." His voice was sharp. Each word was a knife twisting in his back. He scowled, waiting for her to deny it. But she couldn't. It wasn't a question—it was a fact. The evidence hung right there on the wall.

Mina tilted her head. Her stare was a mirror of confusion as she approached the wall. She was good. She didn't give anything away. If he didn't know better, he might have believed her show of innocence. Frustration tightened his jaw, baring his teeth.

Mina studied the photos. She looked at him, her amber eyes reflecting her bewilderment. He growled in frustration, tapping the picture of Clint standing next to LeSeur.

She laughed, even as she faced him. "Oh, you mean Braxton. I told you about him. Don't you remember? He's my brother."

Derrek's stomach twisted. His gaze snapped to LeSeur. "This man," he ground out, "is your brother?"

Mina nodded. "Why? Do you know Braxton?"

Derrek let out a harsh laugh. "Oh, you could say that. We go way back. Except I know him as Clint. He's one of the AOD operatives sent to kill me."

She gasped, spinning around to cast an accusing glare at her father. "Is this why you and Braxton stopped talking?"

LeSeur arched a brow, amusement flickering in his gaze. "Who said we stopped talking?"

"You," Mina shouted. "Years ago. I remember asking where Braxton was, and you told me you sent him away."

LeSeur's lips curled in satisfaction. "Did I?"

Derrek stepped forward, gun raised and pulse thudding. "You sent your son to kill your daughter?"

"Oh no, you give me too much credit. I never wanted harm to come to Mina. Why do you think I called her home?"

LeSeur's gaze locked onto her, unreadable. "You did come home, didn't you. From the beginning, I put a few fail-safes in place."

A chill slithered down Derrek's spine. His eyes flicked around the room. "What sort of fail-safes?"

LeSeur's smile sharpened. "Nothing as crude as a bomb, I assure you." He extended a hand. "Come, child."

Derrek's stomach dropped as Mina stepped toward her father.

A harsh "No!" escaped his lips as he lunged. His fingers wrapped around her arm, the touch both urgent and rough. She turned to him with a radiant, vacant smile.

Panic tore through him as she tried to pull away.

"Don't." His hand tightened on her arm.

"She can't help herself," LeSeur explained. "It's all in the tone and words, you see."

"What do you mean?" Derrek demanded. He kept a firm grip on Mina, unsettled by the strange pull LeSeur had over her. It didn't make sense, but he wasn't about to let her get anywhere near him.

LeSeur let out a weary sigh. "As I was explaining before, Mina wasn't an ideal candidate for my other experiment. No matter what I did, nothing would alter that innate goodness in her. Vexing, really. I was tempted to sell her and recoup some of my financial losses, but inspiration struck.

As you can see, Mina has always been so eager to please. With the right...persuasive suggestions and a bit of chemical assistance, well—." He spread his hands, smiling coldly. "Success."

Derrek's pulse pounded in his ears. "What did you do to her?"

LeSeur smiled, cruel and menacing. "No need to get upset. Mina is perfectly fine, and she will stay that way. As long as you don't do anything violent, shall we say."

Panic clawed at Derrek's chest, threatening to unravel his last shred of control. He wanted to tear LeSeur apart, but he held back. Until he understood what had been done to Mina, he couldn't risk hurting her. She continued to pull against his grip, caught in a silent battle. Her face remained eerily blank, doll-like. Her movements were stiff and mechanical—like an animation without thought or feeling.

LeSeur's expression flickered, a muscle twitching in his jaw before he masked it. He pulled open a cabinet door above the counter, rummaging through its contents. Glass clinked together, breaking the tense silence.

Derrek kept his weapon up, his gaze hardened. "What are you doing?"

"You can let her go. I won't hurt her," LeSeur said offhandedly.

Derrek let out a sharp laugh. "Yeah, you've done a bang-up job so far."

Anger flared in LeSeur's eyes, betraying his composure. He shrugged and turned back to the cabinet. Derrek tracked him with his gun, but the gesture didn't seem to bother the man. He wasn't sure how he felt about that.

"Relax, Mr. Borup. Nothing dangerous. Ah—" LeSeur turned, a syringe glinting in his hand.

Derrek's breath seized. His focus slipped—just for a second, drawn by the threatening syringe. His grip slackened. Mina slipped free.

He dove for her, but she slipped around the exam table, just out of reach. His heart pounded, desperation clawing at his control. "Mina, baby, come to me." His voice wavered, raw with panic. His stomach twisted—he was begging. His fingers twitched, aching to pull her behind him, to shield her.

Mina hesitated, her steps faltering.

Hope flared. "Mina, come back to me," he pleaded, voice cracking.

He saw her muscles twitch, a subtle movement under her golden skin, a flicker of defiance against LeSeur's control.

LeSeur lifted his brow, his head tilting to the side. His eyes watched in a way that set Derrek's teeth on edge. He almost seemed amused. "I never thought you'd be the one to fall for a woman. The notorious ladies' man." A mocking gleam curved LeSeur's lips.

Derrek ignored him. His attention focused on Mina. He stepped in front of Mina, gripping her shoulders. He gave her a little shake. "Mina, can you hear me?"

Nothing. Not even a flicker of recognition. Snarling, he lifted his gun, leveling it at LeSeur. "What did you do to her?"

"Tsk, tsk. Don't forget who is in charge here. You will do what I want when I want. Do you understand?"

"Yeah, and what exactly do you want me to do?"

"It seems I have caught the attention of some who wish me harm. I want you to kill them for me. After the job is completed, then I will release Mina, and you two can be on your way."

Derrek shook his head. "Fat chance. There is no way I am leaving her here, alone, defenseless, with you."

LeSeur shrugged. "I'm sorry to hear that. I had hoped you would be more receptive."

"I thought you were supposed to be some kind of genius. You should have known I wouldn't bend to your will, so why this elaborate charade? Seems like a pretty big gamble."

"Who said you were the plan?"

Cold dread ran through his veins. His gaze darted to Mina.

"That's right. Mina might not have the killer instinct, but she is very susceptible to suggestion. I've gotten her to do quite a few interesting things outside of her personality parameter." LeSeur confided in his damn clinical droll.

"For instance?" Derrek growled.

LeSeur watched him with cold amusement. "You want details, don't you?" He turned to a nearby filing cabinet, flipping through folders with unnerving ease. The quiet rustle of paper only elevates the tension in the room.

"Ah, here we are." He pulled a file, laying it open on the counter with an air of casual delight. "When she was sixteen, I sent her on a little shopping spree. Four stores. Over a thousand dollars in stolen merchandise. Not bad for a first attempt."

Derrek barely heard him. His gaze snapped to Mina. She stood still, eerily vacant, her expression a blank canvas wiped of all emotion. His stomach clenched. *Fight it, baby. Please.*

LeSeur continued, flipping another page. "Ah, but my favorite test? A convenience store robbery. She was instructed to steal ten dollars and shoot the cashier." He sighed, shaking his head as if recalling an amusing antic from Mina's childhood, not the dangerous experiment that could have killed her. "Clever girl. Even under my control, she found a loophole. Instead of killing the man, she barely grazed his arm."

LeSeur clicked his tongue. "She was more compliant the second time."

Derrek's pulse pounded. He wanted to tear this man apart. His fingers itched to rip the smug satisfaction right off LeSeur's face. A sickening weight settled in Derrek's stomach, twisting his gut. "You made Mina kill someone?"

LeSeur chuckled, a slow, satisfied sound that set Derrek's teeth on edge. "Of course. It took several tries, but I finally managed a successful experiment. It's too bad," he mused. "She would have made a fine operative if not for her unfortunate habit of throwing up when I release her."

The word *experiment* ignited Derrek's temper. His grip on his gun tightened, his mind reeling. The image of Mina—gentle, kind, incapable of cruelty—twisted into something unrecognizable under LeSeur's control. "Experiment? You tried to ruin her! Damn you, and damn your twisted work! I thought Mina was living with her mother by the time she was a teenager."

LeSeur scoffed. "No, remember? She has no mother. That was merely a planted memory, an illusion of a past she never had. I let Mina leave home two years ago. Until then," he glanced around the room fondly, "this was Mina's home."

Something inside Derrek snapped. He lunged at LeSeur like a madman, all control fracturing under the weight of his horror. He twisted LeSeur's arm behind his back, sending the syringe skidding across the floor. His elbow cracked into LeSeur's nose, blood spurting everywhere, his glasses shattering against the concert floor. Derrek's hand shot forward, jabbing hard into LeSeur's throat. The older man staggered back, clutching his neck, his eyes bulging.

Gasping for breath, LeSeur fumbled in his pocket and pulled out a small plastic device—a remote of some kind. He held it to his mouth and whispered into it.

Before Derrek could knock it away, Mina charged him.

Her leg swung around, landing a brutal kick to his chest.

"Mina!" Derrek exclaimed, barely blocking the foot she drove into his face. "It's me." He panted, dodging to the right when she spun around, her fist arching toward his nose.

From the corner of his eye, Derrek saw LeSeur still holding the remote to his mouth. He grabbed a tray and hurled it at him. It struck LeSeur's hand, sending the remote clattering to the floor, where it skidded under a cabinet.

As Derrek turned, Mina had the discarded syringe in her hand.

She struck fast—relentless. He blocked each jab, but his defenses were slipping. His inherent nature prevented him from remaining submissive for much longer. Every blow pushed him closer to the edge. He couldn't hurt her, but he couldn't let her kill him either. His only choice twisted his gut—he had to take her down.

With a swift, calculated move, he struck.

Mina crumbled. His heart clenched, a wave of suffocating guilt washing over him. He brushed the hair from her face, his lips pressing a fleeting kiss to her brow. His thumb lingered at her bottom lip, a silent plea for forgiveness.

Then, he rose, honing in on LeSeur.

He took one step toward the man—

And a voice from behind stopped him cold.

"I didn't realize we were having company, Dad."

Derrek spun to find Clint and Mitch standing in the doorway, their presence sealing off the only exit. His heart plummeted. A thick weight of despair lodged in his throat as his gaze dropped to Mina. He had to fight for her. But he was outnumbered, outgunned—and running out of time.

LeSeur straightened, blood dripping from his nose. "What are you doing here?"

Clint sauntered into the room, his eyes hard as he looked around. "I've got a job to do." A smirk played on his lips as he met his father's gaze. "Just like you taught me."

Chapter Thirty-Six

Derrek's mind scrambled. His gun was gone, somewhere on the floor. He had nothing to protect himself or Mina with. His heart pounded as adrenaline surged through his veins. He eyed Clint, calculating. If he attacked now, he might have a chance. With Clint blocking Mitch, they were bottlenecked. He might not get another opportunity.

He tensed to move when LeSeur's voice cut through his focus, stopping him short.

"You were always a bit of a disappointment," LeSeur said, his tone dripping with the conviction of a disappointed parent. "I gave you everything. I made you who you are today. Without me, you would have been nothing."

Clint snorted, his lip curling into a sneer. "Right. Because a normal childhood would have been such a terrible thing."

"Yes. How could you want something as small as a 'normal family' when you were a part of something so much greater? Look around you. We built this together. And we can build up even more. Together, we could change the course of the world."

"Nah. I've got my partner, and I will be taken care of."

Partner? Derrek's gaze flicked to Mitch. Were they going rogue? The thought unsettled him. A loose cannon like Clint running free wasn't exactly reassuring. But something didn't add up. Neither Mitch nor Clint had the mental capacity to put together a well-thought-out meal—let alone a scheme of this scale.

LeSeur arched his eyebrow. "Oh, really? And who is this partner you speak so fondly of?"

"Enough talking," Mitch cut in, his face sour. "Let's finish this." He shoved Clint aside, gun raised.

Derrek moved, knowing it didn't matter what he did. He stood no chance against the bullet. What happened next still rattled him. Before he could even form a plan, Clint sprang into action. His body twisted in one fluid motion as he spun left. A glint of steel flashed, and then, in a heartbeat, Clint drove the knife upward, burying it beneath Mitch's chin and into his skull.

Clint pulled his knife free. Mitch crumbled to the floor. After wiping the blood from the blade, Clint shoved it into his scabbard and entered the room. His focus remained intent on LeSeur.

LeSeur held a paper towel to his nose, a gleam of triumph in his eyes. "I see you know where your allegiance lies."

Derrek watched Clint move across the room with lethal intent. He saw the clear signs of trouble, though LeSeur seemed oblivious. Desperation clawed at him—he needed to get Mina out of there. Clint was simmering, and it was only a matter of time before he exploded.

Behind him, Clint snarled at LeSeur, demanding the files. Just as Derrek had suspected, someone else was pulling the strings, someone else in the background, whispering in Clint's ear, making all the plays. Maybe it was the woman LeSeur had mentioned. If it was who he feared, dark days lay ahead.

Derrek clasped Mina's shoulders, ready to shake her, but hesitated. The image of her flying at him with that blank, detached expression haunted him. What if she woke up and attacked him again? He couldn't risk fighting both her and Clint. This place, this entire situation—it was a nightmare.

If anything happened to Mina, especially by his hand, he didn't know if he could ever recover. He couldn't imagine a world without her.

A sharp strain in LeSeur's voice snapped him back to the present. The confrontation between father and son was spiraling fast. Pushing aside his hesitation, Derrek gave Mina a firm shake.

"Mina? Come on, baby, you've gotta wake up," he coaxed, glancing over his shoulder. Clint had LeSeur pressed against the wall. Derrek winced and turned back to Mina. She groaned, her head tossing. He brushed her hair from her face. "Mina? Open your eyes."

She didn't respond. Frustration surged through him. He quit asking and started demanding. "Dammit, Mina. Wake up!"

Finally, her eyes fluttered open. Relief washed over him as she gazed up, her eyes filled with a warmth that chased away the shadows of his doubt. He pulled her into his arms, pressing her against his chest. His hand cradled her skull, his fingers sinking into her silky hair. He just held her for a moment, overwhelmed to have her back with him.

"What's going on?" she whispered, her voice muffled against him.

He let her sit back, studying her face for any sign that she remembered. That she knew what LeSeur had forced her to do. Her expression, however, remained completely innocent. She had no idea. And if she ever found out, it would shatter her. He clenched his jaw, hating LeSeur for what he had done to her.

A scuffle broke out behind them, dragging Derrek's attention back to the room. His mouth set into a grim line. "Clint showed up."

Mina gave him a blank stare, tilting her head slightly. Her eyes were still hazy.

"Braxton," he clarified.

Then, as if a light switch had flipped, Mina's expression crumbled. She looked around frantically.

"Where am I? Why am I sitting here?" she choked out, a sob catching in her throat. She shoved at the table, struggling to get up. In her panic, she pushed against Derrek, her fear overriding everything else.

"Easy, Mina. It's all right." Derrek struggled to steady her. She fought him, pulling away.

"I can't be here. Let me off. I don't like it up here!" she cried, tears rolling down her cheeks.

"Shh." Derrek wiped away her tears. "It'll be all right. Let me help you."

He lifted her, guiding her to her feet. The minute she touched the ground, she bolted for the sink, dry heaving as she gasped for breath. Derrek followed, holding her hair back and rubbing slow circles over her back. LeSeur's taunting words rang in his ears. *She would have made a fine operative if not for her unfortunate habit of throwing up when I released her.*

Mina hovered over the sink, her mind tumbling over itself. She couldn't remember. The gaps in her memory terrified her. The last thing she remembered was standing next to Derrek. How had she gotten on the table? A shudder ran through her at the thought of the cold surface pressing against her back. She couldn't recall ever sitting there, yet something about it felt disturbingly familiar. A strange sense of déjà vu left her teetering on the edge of reality.

She barely had time to process the sensation before Braxton had tossed their father. His body hit the wall with a sickening thud. There was a sudden explosion of sound as the lab equipment crashed to the ground.

Her father lay seemingly broken on the floor. She hated calling him that—but he was all she had. If she didn't claim him, she would be alone in this world, and that thought terrified her to her core.

"Braxton!" she screamed, intent on intervening. But before she could move, Derrek grabbed her arm, holding her back. She whirled on him, eyes blazing.

"Let me go."

"No," he said with an edge of steel in his tone. "You're not going near Clint."

"Braxton," she stressed, "won't hurt me. He's my brother."

"No, he isn't. All he is is a lab rat."

Mina's eyes narrowed. "Same as me."

"No, not the same as you. You have nothing in common with him."

"Except our childhood," she retorted.

She couldn't explain it. Derrek would probably never understand, but Braxton could. They have a past—fragments of it, at least. Maybe she didn't know which memories were real, but she refused to believe they were all lies. Some of the good ones had to have happened.

She pulled free of Derrek's grip and charged at her brother. She rushed toward Braxton. "Braxton, put Dad down."

Braxton turned to her, his lip curling into a sneer that made her stomach tighten. But she refused to cower. He wouldn't hurt her—not intentionally. She didn't know how she knew that. She just did.

"Listen to your sister," LeSeur gasped, clawing at Braxton's hands. "She always had more sense than you ever did."

Braxton growled and slammed LeSeur against the wall. "Where are the files?"

"Gone. Destroyed. Along with all my notes. No one will be able to reproduce my work."

Braxton struck the wall in frustration.

Mina flinched, her eyes widening as LeSeur crumpled to the floor near a tall cabinet. Fear twisted his expression as he reached beneath it. Braxton moved to grab him, but Mina stepped in his path.

"Braxton, please don't do this."

He barely spared her a glance. "You've, of all people, should be thanking me."

"Why?" Her voice shook. She couldn't imagine what made him think she would condone violence of any kind.

"Don't," Derrek warned from behind.

She hadn't realized how close he was. His warmth, the strength pulsing beneath his skin, was oddly grounding.

Braxton turned his sneer on Derrek. "Why not? She has a right to know."

"And some things are better left alone," Derrek shot back.

Mina hadn't noticed the body on the floor before. She wasn't sure what caught her eye now, but her breath caught as her gaze drifted down. Then she screamed, the sound slicing through the air.

She spun to face Derrek, her voice shaking. "Who is that?"

"Mitch," Braxton answered without hesitation.

"Who is Mitch?" she demanded.

"He was an operative," Derrek explained.

She turned on him, eyes wide with accusation. "Did you kill him?"

"No." Derrek's lips twisted into a wry grin. "That would be your brother."

Mina's stomach churned. "What were you thinking? I don't know if Dad will be able to get you out of this one."

Her breath caught as she realized Braxton had a gun. She raised her hands, taking a step back. "What are you doing, Braxton?"

Before he could answer, Derrek moved—faster than she had ever seen him. In a blur, he shoved the muzzle of the gun upward. The two men grappled, fighting for control.

"Get out of here, Mina! Run!" Derrek's voice was sharp, but she ignored him.

Driven by a desperate need she couldn't explain, she turned to her father. "Dad, get up." She pulled at his arm.

He fought her off. "I need this. I'm not leaving without it."

"We can come back for it," Mina argued.

"No! It has to be now. It won't be safe if I leave it." His eyes glazed with a manic urgency.

"What? What is it?"

"Everything. It's everything I cherish."

The words struck her heart. She recoiled as pain sprang from the devastating blow. *It's not what he meant,* she repeated in her head, but the ache in her chest said otherwise.

"Dammit, Mina," Derrek grunted, still struggling with Braxton. "Get the hell out of here!"

He swung at Clint. Mina flinched. The gun hit the floor.

Renewed in her efforts, Mina tried to get her father off the floor, but he refused. Heart hammering, she dropped to her knees and reached under the cabinet, fingers brushing against something cold. When she pulled it out, it looked like a remote—small, black, insignificant. *This?*

Her father's face lit up. He snatched it from her hands, kissing it as he scrambled to his feet.

A guttural cry tore through the room.

Mina spun in time to see Braxton lifting the gun again—this time, aimed at their father.

"No!" She lunged, shoving LeSeur out of the way. They tumbled together. Her father seemed resistant to her efforts to save him. He twisted her out of the way a scant second before the sharp crack of a gunshot split the air. She fell, the deafening sound echoing in her ears.

Mina gasped. A hot, heavy weight collapsed against her. The breath rushed from her lungs as her father's body knocked her to the ground.

It took every ounce of strength to roll him off her. She heaved, her muscles shaking. When she finally freed herself, she saw him lying on his back, his face twisted in pain.

No. No, no, no.

Her hands flew to his side. Warm blood slicked her fingers. She gasped, holding pressure to the injury.

"It'll be okay," she chanted over and over, rocking back and forth. *It has to be okay.* Tears stung her eyes as she fought them back.

"That is enough of that," LeSeur groaned. "Listen to me." His voice was weak, his breath shallow. He pressed the black plastic device into her palm. "This is yours to protect. Don't show it to anyone. Do you understand?"

Mina barely heard him. She clutched his hand, waiting—desperate—for the words she had always wanted to hear. *Tell me you love me. Tell me I matter.*

"Dad," she cried, shaking his shoulders. "Don't leave me."

His voice grew faint, a shadow of its former authority. "You are my greatest invention. You are my legacy."

His chest rose once more—then fell, still.

Silence.

Mina stared at him, tears spilling down her cheeks.

Even in death, she was nothing more than an experiment.

Chapter Thirty-Seven

Derrek wretched the gun from Clint, his heart pounding a furious beat as desperation frayed his focus. The gun had gone off. Mina had fallen.

He heard her whimpering. Was she hurt? Dying? A primal, angry beast roared inside him. He turned on Clint, his attack brutal, unrelenting. He stuck him over and over, rage urging him on.

Blood splattered, bright, and red. He wanted more, bloodlust fueling his actions. Clint grunted and collapsed, his body no more than a foot from Mitch.

Derrek panted over him. When Clint didn't move, he went to Mina, his knuckles raw and stinging. He welcomed the pain—it was the only thing tethering him to this world that no longer made sense.

He stumbled, falling to his knees. Mina lay draped over LeSeur. His breath hitched as he reached out, his hand hovering uncertainly over her shoulder before he turned her over.

Mina flinched at his touch and lifted her head, her amber eyes dulling. He ran an unsteady hand over her hair.

"Are you hurt?"

She shook her head, but as she looked down at LeSeur, a raw sob tore from her chest. It was deep and painful, and Derrek felt every agonizing second. He pulled her into his arms, holding her close. Pressing a kiss to her brow, he rubbed slow circles on her back, whispering reassurances until she quieted.

"We need to get out of here," he murmured into her hair.

"I know."

Derrek stood, pulling Mina up with him. As he turned to leave, she hesitated. He glanced back at her, silently questioning.

"It's nothing. We can go."

When they reached the hallway, Derrek froze. His eyes snapped to where Clint had fallen. The spot was empty. His muscles coiled, tension rippling through him as he scanned the shadows. Clint was gone.

"Is something wrong?" Mina asked softly.

He forced a bitter smile. "No. Let's get out of here."

Keeping Mina close, his grip firm, he led her through the house. He stopped long enough in the kitchen to switch on the gas burners.

He rummaged through the cabinets until he found a box of matches. At the front door, he stopped again, lighting one of the decorative candles near the entryway. His pulse was steady as he prepared everything.

"Do you want anything from here?" he asked; the offer came as an afterthought. She might not realize this was her only chance.

Mina shook her head. "I don't ever want to come back to this place."

Derrek kissed her forehead and nodded. "Come on then."

Then he paused, his gaze catching on the journal in the living room. "Wait just a minute." He left Mina by the front door and returned seconds later, the journal tucked inside his shirt. She might not want it now, but someday, it could help her.

He gave her hand an encouraging squeeze. "Let's go."

They stepped outside together. The sky was on fire with the setting sun.

In the car, they watched the house for a minute. Derrek started the engine, and it purred to life. As he shifted into gear, the house exploded, a violent bloom of fire and smoke swallowing the structure whole. The car's windows rattled with the force.

Mina stared at the blaze, her grim expression flickering in the orange glow. "Now what?" she asked, her voice catching.

"Now," he said, voice rough, "you go home."

He pulled away from the curb, the fire shrinking in the rearview mirror. With every mile, his heart shriveled until only a scar remained.

"Derrek!" His mother squealed, pulling him into a hug.

"Hi, Mom," he said, trying to smile, but his mouth seemed to have forgotten how. "When's dinner?"

Tami clucked, wiping her hands on her apron. "In thirty minutes. Your sisters will be here soon."

He grunted and dipped a finger into the batter she had in a mixing bowl. She swatted at his hand. "Stay out of the brownies."

Derrek grinned, wrapping an arm around her waist and tucking her into his side. "Come on, Mom. It was only a little taste."

She laughed, pinching his side. "I know what you consider a little taste. Mark my words, I turn my back, and half the batter will be gone. Then what would we have for dessert?'

He shrugged. "Wouldn't matter to me. I'd already had mine."

"Oh, you," she huffed, waving the spatula at him.

He settled onto the counter stool, just as he had countless times before, watching his mother work. She moved around the kitchen with the ease of someone who had spent years there, humming softly as she stirred a large pot of mashed potatoes.

"I forgot to tell you," she said, glancing at him. "I talked to Mina the other day."

His stomach clenched with a yearning so deep it hurt. He forced a casual shrug, shifting in his seat. "Oh," he said, his voice betraying none of the inner turmoil her name had unleashed.

His mother shot him a knowing smile but didn't push. "Yep, she said she's doing well enough, but I could hear the sadness in her voice. Poor lamb, all alone now." She shook her head.

"She isn't all alone," he muttered, guilting tightening his throat.

"You think not?" Tami arched a brow. "With her father and brother both gone in that tragic house fire and her mother long out of the picture. It's a miracle she hasn't sunken into a deep depression."

He didn't want to hear this. Scowling at the scuffed counter. He spent every ounce of willpower avoiding thoughts of Mina, yet here was his mother, cracking him open like it was nothing. It had been two weeks since he last saw her. Two weeks since he left her standing at the front door of her building, hope shimmering in her eyes.

He could have kissed her. Could have promised to call once he figured things out. But he hadn't.

Instead, he kissed her cheek—because if he kissed her the way he wanted to, he wouldn't have been able to leave.

And leaving had been the right thing to do.

Hadn't it?

He had seen every emotion flicker across her face—confusion, heartbreak—but he refused to be swayed. This was best for her. One day, she would understand. One day, she would thank him.

"Why did Mina call?" he asked, his voice sharper than he intended. "I didn't realize you two kept in touch."

His mother gave him a patient look. "She wanted to let me know she mailed back the things she borrowed. Wasn't that sweet of her?"

Derrek grunted, picking at a stray piece of lettuce on the cutting board. "Did she say anything else?"

"Oh? Like what?"

He shrugged. "I don't know. Anything?"

His mother smirked. "Do you mean, did she ask about you?"

He scowled, pushing off the stool to pace the kitchen. "Well, did she?"

Tami turned back to her cooking. "I can't say."

He turned to his mother, frowning. "Why the hell not?" He snapped.

"Language." She shot him a sharp look. "What we talked about is between me and her. If you want to know how Mina is doing, why don't you call her?"

He ran a hand through his hair, resuming his pacing. "I can't."

"You can," she said simply.

"You don't understand—"

"What?" she interrupted, crossing her arms. "What is it that you think I don't understand? What Mina doesn't understand?"

"I'm not the marrying kind." The words spilled out before he could stop them, leaving a strange sort of relief in their wake.

"Says who?" she demanded.

He blinked. "Who?"

"Yes! Who says you aren't the marryin' kind?"

"Look at me, Mom!" His voice rose in frustration. "I can't do this to someone else."

Tami studied him for a long moment, then shook her head. "I am looking at you. Do you want to know what I see? A silly boy with his head too full of his own importance to do what is right for him. I think you are doing yourself and Mina a huge disservice. This isn't a decision just for you. If you love her, you need to tell her. Let her decide what she wants."

"Whoa, who said anything about love?"

Tami let out an exasperated sigh. "You did. It's written all over your face. A blind man could see it." She softened, resting a hand on his arm. "Son, I love you, but you're as dense as your father sometimes. Now get out of my kitchen and let me cook in peace, or dinner won't be ready in thirty minutes like I promised."

Derrek left his mother to her cooking and went in search of his dad.

For the first time since walking away from Mina, he felt a seed of hope stir inside him.

The café sat on the corner of a busy cross street. Derrek leaned back in his seat, stretching his legs in front of him as he watched the steady stream of people walk by. The chair to his right was suddenly taken. He lifted his cup to his lips.

"Brother, took you long enough," Derrek muttered from the corner of his mouth.

Damian set his cup on the table, his lips twitching. "I had things to take care of."

"Seems like you are doing that a lot lately."

Damian's smirk faded into something more serious. "I spoke with Alex."

Derrek showed no outward sign of his interest, but every part of him tuned in. "And?"

"You need to disappear. Not permanently, but stay off the grid for a while. Are you prepared?"

"Aren't we all?"

"Some more than others." Damian slid a set of keys across the table.

Derrek picked them up, frowning. "What are these too?"

"My boat."

Derrek nearly choked on his drink. "Your what?"

Damian grinned, lines crinkling the corner of his eyes, making him appear more human. "You heard me. I think you need to get lost for a few months. Maybe a little longer. What better place to do that than on the sea?"

"I guess it's a good thing you took me out with you a couple of times. I'm surprised you trust me with your baby. Didn't you threaten to kill me when I dropped part of my sandwich on the deck?"

Damian shrugged. "Same rules apply."

Derrek snorted, sliding the keys back to him. "Never mind then. That's too much pressure. You'll have me as tightly strung as you are."

"I'm not tightly strung."

"Sure, whatever you need to tell yourself."

Damian pushed the keys back, all humor gone from his face. "I'm serious. Take them. Disappear. I'll let you know when it's safe to come back."

Derrek studied him for a long moment before nodding. "Yeah, all right."

A manila envelope appeared on the table.

"What's this?" Derrek asked, frowning.

Damian tapped the folder. "Just in case you feel like some company." Then, without another word, he stood and left as quietly as he'd arrived.

Derrek dumped the contents into his hand. A passport. He flipped it open—Mina's smiling face stared back at him.

His chest tightened. The ache simmering inside him flared into something undeniable. He ran a finger over her photo.

No more fighting this. No more second-guessing. He wanted her, and he was done denying it.

Three long, miserable days later, he was back in San Francisco. Damian's boat was docked at the marina, ready to go. He just needed one more thing before they left.

He stood outside the run-down animal shelter. The same man sat at the front desk, the one Derrek had snapped a picture of the last time he was here.

He looked at Derrek, his expression hard and unreadable. "Can I help you?"

"Yeah, I hear you have a pup named Red."

The man lifted a brow, "And?"

"I want to adopt him."

"Sorry, no can do. I'm saving him for a friend."

Derrek smiled. Mina had a way of getting to people, and she didn't even realize it. "For Mina?"

The man's eyes widened. "Maybe."

"What if I told you I was buying the pup for her?"

The man leaned back in his chair, assessing him. Finally, he nodded. "Well, then, why didn't you say so in the first place?"

Derrek grinned. "What do you need from me?"

"Why don't you go on home?" Kat offered gently.

It had been the same routine for the past two and a half weeks since Derrek left. Mina had come to work, apologized profusely for the worry she had caused, and then given a half-hearted explanation. She had left out most of it. She only explained that she had been called home after her date with Chris. Her father and brother had died in a house fire.

Kat had been sympathetic, but the truth was, Mina's heart wasn't in her work, and it showed. Every floral arrangement she attempted was a disaster—off-balance, clashing colors, a total mess.

It was all Derrek's fault. He had spun into her life, wreaking havoc, knocking down all her defenses. Just when she had started to hope for a future with him—he left.

What a fool she had been.

"If you are sure you don't need any help…"

"None. Please, go home and rest. Maybe take a few days off. Losing your family is never easy. Take the week if you need it." Kat's brow creased with worry. "I think it might help if you grieved."

"Maybe I will take you up on that. I'm not doing all that well here, am I?'

"No, it isn't that. You are doing just fine. Brad and I can see how upset you are. That's all. Please take some time. Come back when you're ready."

Mina gave a weak smile. She grabbed her phone, purse, and coat—funny, she never forgot her things anymore. Evidently, it took dying inside to break bad habits.

The walk home was brisk; her coat turned up against the wind. As she neared her building, she was relieved to see a couple entering ahead of her. With any luck, she could slip past Edgar and Abel.

Sure enough, the two self-appointed door guardians were deep in conversation, allowing her to sneak through the lobby and to the elevator unnoticed.

Avoiding people had become her new routine. It was easier that way. She hadn't been to Squeeze since Derrek left. None of her old habits made her happy anymore.

She unlocked her door and dropped her things by the entrance. A soft yap made her freeze. She tilted her head. A dog?

She held her breath, but the sound didn't come again. Maybe it was her neighbors. They were a young couple—getting a pet seemed like their natural next step.

Her chest tightened. *I should have adopted Red.* Maybe then, coming home wouldn't feel so...empty.

Mina stepped into her living room and stopped cold.

Derrek sat on her couch, one arm resting along the back. He looked tired.

Her heart pounded. She took a hesitant step forward. "What are you doing here?"

"I wanted to see you." His eyes searched hers.

She turned away, blinking back tears. "Well, you see me." The words came out sharper than she intended, but she didn't care. She wasn't going to make this easy for him.

"So I have." He was quiet for a moment. "How are you?"

She raised her chin. "Fine. Why? Don't I look fine?"

"You look tired."

She was, and she hated that he could see it. "It's been a long week."

"Work?"

"No."

Derrek let out a hum of acknowledgment and shifted on the couch. Then he lifted something from his lap before standing.

Her pulse quickened as he approached, his movements slow but deliberate. Mina took a step back. She couldn't let him get close. Not again. She wouldn't survive it if he left her a second time.

"I think you should go," she said, voice unsteady.

"Do you?" His eyebrow arched.

"Yes. I have things to do."

"Really? What?"

Her mind went blank. She couldn't think of a single thing. "Laundry?"

His lips twitched. "Is that a question?"

"Yes. I mean... no." Her thoughts scattered. He was too close. Too overwhelming. She held up a hand as if that could stop him.

"Mina, there's something I didn't tell you when I left."

"Oh?" Her stomach clenched, her gaze flickering to the newly repaired windows.

"Yeah." He sighed. "When I left you at your door. I should have told you a few things. I should have let you decide yourself instead of for you."

"What decision?" Fear pricked at her. "Is someone coming after me again?"

"No, nothing like that." He hesitated. "This is personal."

"Personal?"

"Yeah." He reached out, catching her arms, pulling her into his warmth. "*Very* personal."

Mina sucked in a breath. "Oh." Her eyes were wide.

He exhaled, eyes locked onto hers. "I didn't realize until later that you had a right to know something."

She swallowed. "And what's that?"

"That I love you."

The world tilted. Her knees buckled. If he hadn't been holding her, she would have collapsed.

Her fingers gripped his shoulders, searching his face and eyes for deception—but there was none. Only raw, undeniable truth.

"You... love me?" The words barely made it past her lips.

A wry smile played on his lips. "Yeah. I do. I'm crazy about you. I thought if I gave it time, this hole in my chest would heal. But it hasn't. It's only gotten worse."

She started up at him, lost. "It has?"

He nodded. "And the only way to fix it... is if you fill it. So," he continued, "I'm here to ask you two things."

Mina swallowed, her heart racing. "All right."

His lips twisted into that mischievous smirk she adored. "First... You know who I am, what I am. Do you think you could ever love someone like me?"

Doubt flickered in his eyes.

Her heart ached at the sight. She cupped his face in her hands and kissed him. It was soft, slow—filled with certainty.

When she pulled back, she whispered, "Not only do I think I could love you, Derrek... I *already* do."

His countenance cleared, shedding any apprehension he might have harbored.

"Good," he murmured. "That brings me to my second question."

Mina arched a brow. "And what's that?"

His grin turned devilish. "Would you care to sail around the world with *us*?"

"Us?"

At that moment, a tiny golden head popped up over the back of the couch. A little reddish-brown nose twitched in the air.

Mina looked from Derrek to the little puppy and then back again.

She gasped, her eyes filling with tears. "Is that—?"

"Yep," Derrek scooped up the puppy, who licked his face. "So? What do you say?

Want to take a boat ride?"

She laughed, breathless. "On one condition."

His eyes narrowed. "What condition?"

"I get to steer."

Derrek groaned. "Fine. But *I'm* navigating."

Mina beamed. "Deal."

Chapter Thirty-Eight

The boat rocked with the waves. It had taken Mina almost a week to get used to the constant motion, but now she hardly noticed. She sat in the sun, curled on one of the cushions, the heat of the rays making her skin tingle. Red lounged beside her, his head resting against her side. She rubbed his fur as his tongue flicked across her wrist.

She held her diary, her fingers running over the cover. It had taken her days before she could even hold it. The blinding headache that struck whenever she touched it had finally dulled to a mere throb. She had only started reading the entries yesterday, but nothing so far hinted at the damage done by the man she had once called father.

Someday, she might reconcile herself to what she was created to become. But for now, she was on a quest to recover her memories. There were secrets locked inside her, and although Derrek never pushed, she knew he wanted her to remember as much as possible.

She flipped the journal open to where she had left off and took a sip of water. The cool liquid helped counteract the ache pulsing at the base of her skull.

Derrek appeared beside her, his long shadow falling across the page she was reading.

"Interesting stuff?"

Mina shrugged. "I don't know about that. Evidently, I had a friend. I wish I could remember her, though."

He sat next to her, lifting her legs to rest across his lap. He picked up one of her feet and, with his all-too-knowledgeable fingers, began massaging the tension away with the same unwavering attention to detail he applied to everything else.

Mina sighed, her toes curling in delight as his thumb pressed into the sensitive arch of her foot.

"The good doctor let you have a friend?" Derrek asked with obvious skepticism. She couldn't blame him for it.

"It seems so. She would come over and play once a week for almost a year." She flipped through the pages until the name stopped appearing. "Oh, wait." Pausing at one entry, she read it silently before speaking. "This is interesting."

Jessica came over today. We got to play in the water, but only for a little bit. Dad says we have work to do. I don't like Dad's work, but Jessica makes it better. She makes funny faces that make me giggle. Dad doesn't like it when we laugh. He says we can't get things right if we're messing around.

Derrek's brow furrowed. "I wonder what LeSeur was hoping would happen?"

"I don't know," Mina admitted with a frustrated sigh. She rubbed at the dull ache in her skull.

The next page made her pause.

I cried a lot today. Dad says Jessica won't come back. He said she didn't like me anymore because I wouldn't do the work. I told Dad I'd try harder, but he didn't care. He said it was too late. Jessica is my best friend. Now I'm all alone again.

Mina wiped a tear away. Derrek slipped a finger beneath her chin, gently lifting her face toward him.

"What's wrong?" he asked softly.

"I don't know. All of a sudden, I felt sad. Like I remembered what it felt like to lose my best friend."

"It doesn't say what happened to Jessica?" Derrek asked, pulling the journal from her lap.

"No. I haven't found her mentioned again."

Derrek flipped through the pages, then tossed the book aside. Rising to his feet, he pulled Mina up with him. "How about we let the past lie for now?" There was an odd glint in his eyes.

Mina hesitated but nodded. "I guess."

She let him pull her into his arms, her hand resting on his bare chest. It was hard to believe that just a month ago, she had been alone, trapped in a false past with a bleak future. But now, standing in the warmth of his embrace, the past didn't seem so important.

She leaned back, smiling up at the man with more names than she cared to remember. He may have had several names, but he had only one heart—and it was all hers. For now, that was enough.

His eyes shimmered with love as he gazed down at her. "Do you feel like going for a swim?"

Abigail Weaver lifted her gaze from the file on her desk when the door slammed open, shaking the walls. The room shuddered with the sharp crack of wood against plaster. Her cheek twitched—a flicker of irritation—before she smoothed her expression and placed the file aside.

This conversation should have happened later. When her temper had settled. Timing, however, wasn't one of Clint's strengths.

She exhaled slowly. "Clint, I thought we agreed I would reach out to you. *After* things had quieted down."

Clint sank into the chair, staring at her with a grim, tight-lipped expression. The right side of his face was swollen, and his bottom lip was split and oozing.

"He's gone," he ground out.

Abigail didn't blink. "I know."

Clint leaned forward, glaring beneath his swollen eyelid. "You know?"

She sighed. Finding competent help was such a challenge. "Yes." A slow, chilling smile curled her lips. "Don't worry about Mr. Borup. I'll handle him—when it suits me. For now, we have other—"

His palm slammed against the desk. "I *had* him."

She met his glare without flinching. "Evidently not."

A muscle in his jaw twitched. His breath came sharp and uneven.

"This isn't the time to debate what *should* have happened. We'll address that later." Her gaze was sharp, the pointed look conveying her displeasure. "Since you seem eager to begin, let's go over the next step. With the loss of Stuart and Mitch, I'm afraid you'll have more work ahead of you."

Clint straightened. "I'm ready."

"I can see that." She let the compliment linger before tilting her head, studying him. "But I wonder if you can handle phase two alone."

His eyes darkened. "I can. I will."

"Perhaps," she mused, "but wouldn't you prefer a little help? I've been reviewing a special list of potentials."

He looked at her warily. "Where did you get the list?"

"They were the ones your father declined entry." Her smile deepened. "One in particular stands out."

Clint's fingers curled against the armrest. "Who?"

Abigail let the silence stretch, savoring the moment. Then, with quiet satisfaction, she said, "Jessica."

Thank you for reading!

We hoped you enjoyed *Hidden Truths* by Alane Middleton.

If you enjoyed *Hidden Truths* and would like to get updates on new releases and exclusive content sign up now to join Alane Middleton's mailing list. Be the first to hear about ARC reader opportunities and special promotions!

Sign up now!

https://www.alanemiddleton.com/